VIRUS HUNTERS

A MEDICAL THRILLER | PART TWO

BOBBY AKART

PRAISE FOR BOBBY AKART

PRAISE FOR AUTHOR BOBBY AKART and *THE VIRUS HUNTERS*

"Only Akart can weave a story that begins so calm, so normal and before you know it, you are at the end of the book with your pulse pounding in your chest and your mind screaming for more! ~ Amazon Hall of Fame, Top 2 Reviewer

"Under MY version of Wikipedia, under 'Insomnia – Causation', is a picture of Bobby Akart. I have learned not to pick up one of his books near bedtime as I will be unable to set it aside for hours!"

"Akart is a master of suspense, keeping us on the edge of our seats. But, he does it with fact-based fiction that would scare even the most hardened readers."

"Mixing science and suspense is something Bobby Akart is a master of—writing character driven stories that will have you on the edge of your seat."

"I have highly enjoyed Mr. Akart's literary works because his research is comprehensive and he has an eerie prescience of writing fiction and it becoming reality."

"Mr. Akart has become one of my favorite authors joining the ranks of fellas named King, Grisham & Clancy."

"Bobby Akart is one of those very rare authors who makes things so visceral, so real, that you experience what he writes … His research, depth of knowledge, and genuine understanding of people make his works more real than any movie."

"No one, and I mean NO ONE, does it better!

ABOUT THE AUTHOR, BOBBY AKART

Author Bobby Akart has been ranked by Amazon as #25 on the Amazon Charts list of most popular, bestselling authors. He has achieved recognition as the #1 bestselling Horror Author, #1 bestselling Science Fiction Author, #5 bestselling Action & Adventure Author, #7 bestselling Historical Author and #10 bestselling Thriller Author.

He has sold over one million books in all formats, which includes over forty international bestsellers, in nearly fifty fiction and nonfiction genres.

His novel *Yellowstone: Hellfire* reached the Top 25 on the Amazon bestsellers list and earned him multiple Kindle All-Star awards for most pages read in a month and most pages read as an author. The Yellowstone series vaulted him to the #25 bestselling author on Amazon Charts, and the #1 bestselling science fiction author.

Bobby has provided his readers a diverse range of topics that are both informative and entertaining. His attention to detail and impeccable research has allowed him to capture the imagination of his readers through his fictional works and bring them valuable knowledge through his nonfiction books.

SIGN UP for Bobby Akart's mailing list to receive a copy of his monthly newsletter, *The Epigraph*, learn of special offers, view bonus content, and be the first to receive news about new releases in the Virus Hunters series. Visit www.BobbyAkart.com for details.

OTHER WORKS BY AMAZON TOP 25 AUTHOR BOBBY AKART

The Virus Hunters

Virus Hunters I

Virus Hunters II

Virus Hunters III

The Geostorm Series

The Shift

The Pulse

The Collapse

The Flood

The Tempest

The Cataclysm

The Pioneers

The Asteroid Series

Discovery

Diversion

Destruction

The Doomsday Series

Apocalypse

Haven

Anarchy

Minutemen

Civil War

The Yellowstone Series

Hellfire

Inferno

Fallout

Survival

The Lone Star Series

Axis of Evil

Beyond Borders

Lines in the Sand

Texas Strong

Fifth Column

Suicide Six

The Pandemic Series

Beginnings

The Innocents

Level 6

Quietus

The Blackout Series

36 Hours

Zero Hour

Turning Point

Shiloh Ranch

Hornet's Nest

Devil's Homecoming

The Boston Brahmin Series

The Loyal Nine

Cyber Attack

Martial Law

False Flag

The Mechanics

Choose Freedom

Patriot's Farewell

Seeds of Liberty (Companion Guide)

The Prepping for Tomorrow Series

Cyber Warfare

EMP: Electromagnetic Pulse

Economic Collapse

ACKNOWLEDGMENTS

Creating a novel that is both informative and entertaining requires a tremendous team effort. Writing is the easy part.

For their efforts in making the Virus Hunters a reality, I would like to thank Hristo Argirov Kovatliev for his incredible artistic talents in creating my cover art. He and Dani collaborate (and conspire) to create the most incredible cover art in the business. A huge hug of appreciation goes out to Pauline Nolet, the *Professor*, for her editorial prowess and patience in correcting the same writer's tics after forty-plus novels. We have a new member of the team, Drew Avera, who has brought his talented formatting skills from a writer's perspective, creating multiple formats for reading my novels. I was pleased to introduce Stacey Glemboski, another new member of our team of professionals, for her memorable performance in narrating the Virus Hunters. I may have written the dialogue, but Stacey has created the voice of Dr. Harper Randolph.

A special thank you goes out to Christie Garness, a long-time reader, who provided valuable insight into the current state of affairs in Las Vegas as well as its emergency operations. Lastly, there's the Team—Denise, Joe, Jim, Shirley, and Aunt Sissy, whose advice, friendship and attention to detail is priceless.

Characters come and go, but lifelong friendships do not. Everybody needs that set of friends. You know, the ones that you can call on in a time of emergency, that without a doubt, will be there for you. We have Mark and Kathie Becker. The story of how we met can only be attributed to fate. In early 2017, I posted a photo of my vintage Land Rover, affectionately known as Red Rover, in The Epigraph. I received an email shortly thereafter from a reader that recognized Red Rover as belonging to his new neighbors. We may no longer be neighbors, but we will forever be friends with Mark and Kathie Becker. As you come to love the character of Dr. Elizabeth Becker, eighty-eight percent of what you read in the novels, is the real Kathie. Another eleven percent is Lizzie, a mix between Kathie and her three-year-old niece. And one percent is Boom-Boom Becker. I hope you love the character as much as we love the genuine article.

Now, for the serious stuff. The Virus Hunters series required countless hours of never-ending research. Without the background material and direction from those individuals who provided me a portal into their observations and data, I would've been drowning in long Latin words.

Once again, as I immersed myself in the science, source material and research flooded my inbox from scientists, epidemiologists, and geneticists from around the globe. I am so very thankful to everyone who not only took the time to discuss this material with me, but also gave me suggestions for future novels. Without their efforts, this story could not be told. Please allow me to acknowledge a few of those individuals whom, without their tireless efforts, the Virus Hunters series could not have been written.

Many thanks to Laura Edison, a Doctor of Veterinary Medicine and a Lieutenant Commander in the United States Public Health Service, a Career Epidemiology Field Officer, or CEFO, at the CDC in Atlanta. She has stressed the importance of tracking the vast number of travelers during an outbreak. Her creation of an electronic surveillance system called the Ebola Active Monitoring

System helped the Georgia Department of Health keep tabs on travelers arriving at Atlanta's Hartsfield Jackson International Airport during that outbreak.

Colonel Mark G. Kortepeter, MD, has held multiple leadership roles in the Operational Medicine Division at the U.S. Army Medical Research Institute of Infectious Diseases, USAMRIID, the nation's largest containment laboratory dedicated to biological weapons. His expertise in all related fields of infectious disease study from the battlefield to the BSL-4 and to the coroner's office was invaluable.

Eric Pevzner, PhD, MPH, a Captain in the USPHS, who is the Branch Chief of the Epidemiology Workforce Branch and Chief of the EIS program at the CDC Atlanta. Years ago, when I was first introduced to Captain Pevzner, he reiterated that the next pandemic was only a plane ride away. Of course, as we know, he was right. In his capacity as the head of the Epidemiology Workforce Branch, he oversees the Epidemic Intelligence Service, Laboratory Leadership Service, Epidemiology Elective Program, and Science Ambassador Fellowship. He works tireless hours to ensure those within our charge have the tools and knowledge necessary to protect us from infectious disease outbreaks.

The Virus Hunters novels could not have been written without the support of the former director of the Defense Advanced Research Projects Agency, Steven Walker; Janet Waldorf, Deputy Chief of Communications within the DARPA Public Affairs office, and her staff; and the DARPA program managers and contractors who took the time to speak with me by phone or via email.

Finally, as always, a special thank you to the disease detectives, the shoe-leather epidemiologists of the CDC's Epidemic Intelligence Service, who work tirelessly to keep these deadly infectious diseases from killing us all. They are selfless, brave warriors, risking their lives and the loss of their families in order to fight an unseen enemy more powerful than any bomb.

This is why I wrote the Virus Hunters.

Because you never know when the day before is the day before, prepare for tomorrow.

Thank you all!

FOREWORD BY DR. HARPER RANDOLPH

Spring 2020 - The year we discovered the SARS-CoV-2, COVID-19 global pandemic.

In the story of humanity, communicable diseases play a starring role. From the bubonic plague to cholera to HIV, we have been locked in a struggle for supremacy with deadly maladies for millennia. They attack our bodies with impunity and without prejudice. They're a merciless enemy, just one-billionth our size, and they've existed on Earth longer than man.

In 2020, we were a world under siege. In America, with the whole of the nation in the midst of a declared national state of emergency, most communities were ordered to abide by a mandated lockdown. Infections totaled over a million and deaths were recorded in the tens of thousands. The efforts to protect public health from this novel coronavirus was a striking example of this continuing war. As governments and health authorities battled to stop the spread of the new virus, they considered lessons from history.

As epidemiologists, we strive to understand the exact effects and nature of any strain of virus, a relative of the common cold. Our greatest concern is accepting that this information can remain unknown for months as scientists gather evidence as to its origin, spread, and immunology.

Experts are concerned about the speed at which the disease can mutate. Oftentimes, its presumed that animals may have been the original source—as was the case with severe acute respiratory syndrome, SARS, another virus in the same family as coronavirus—reflecting the proximity that millions in China share with livestock and wild animals.

Once an outbreak occurs and is identified, governments must grapple with a response. Today's strategy of containment—one of the key measures deployed against endemic diseases—would be familiar to civil authorities and medical personnel as far back as the ancient world. The concept of a quarantine has its roots in the Venetian Republic's fourteenth-century efforts to keep out the plague by blocking boat travel.

But the maritime power would have been hard-pressed to institute a *cordon sanitaire* on a scale required in China, where many of these infectious diseases originate. Using the early outbreak of COVID-19 by way of example, the ability to lock down the presumed place of origin, Wuhan, a city equal in size and population to the entirety of Los Angeles County, was a reflection of the power of China's Communist-authoritarian rule. To stop the spread of the disease, every citizen of Wuhan was ordered to stay in their homes. No exceptions for essentials. No excuses to visit a friend. No walks in the park. No mowing of grass. It was a severe measure, strictly enforced.

In 2020, mistrust and politics played a role as well. The Centers for Disease Control and Prevention has always been dedicated to identifying, containing, and eradicating diseases of all types. Too often, however, the CDC had become a political football, but not one handed off or passed from one side of the aisle to the other. Rather, the CDC was often punted, kicked, and fumbled as a result of never-ending budget battles or desires to use the agency's efforts to exploit its findings for political gain.

Misinformation and disinformation are also still prevalent, as they have been in the past. During the outbreak of Spanish flu in 1918–19, conspiracy theories of enemy bioweapons circulated. During an 1853 outbreak of yellow fever in New Orleans, immigrants were to blame. On social media during the COVID-19 pandemic, wild claims were circulating that the coronavirus was exacerbated by 5G cell phone towers. Fear and mistrust may be one of the greatest challenges we face in eliminating infectious diseases.

Technological changes have proved to be a double-edged sword. Modern diagnostic techniques have sped up identification, while data science has made it easier to track the spread of a contagion. But some advances, such as improved modes of transportation, have contributed to the rapid proliferation of infectious diseases around the globe.

Even global health cooperation has been less than straightforward. The conversation has far improved from 1851 when European nations sought to standardize maritime quarantines. Yet the World Health Organization, despite its message of worldwide solidarity and cooperation, continues to exclude Taiwan from key meetings and information sharing, under Chinese pressure. China, one of the most secretive nations on Earth, continues to closely guard information and delay announcements concerning outbreaks for economic and geopolitical reasons. Both of these examples are the kinds of unnecessary risks that create windows of opportunity for infectious diseases to proliferate. Frankly, pandemics and politics do not mix well.

However, perspective is needed. SARS, a disease that spread worldwide within a few months in 2002, gripped the nation's headlines, but killed fewer than 800. The perennial scourge of influenza concerns most pandemic watchers. An estimated fifty to one hundred million died from the Spanish flu during a time when commercial air, rail, and auto travel didn't exist. Even with modern medicine, the CDC estimates an average of 34,000 Americans die from influenza each flu season.

Outbreaks of unidentified diseases demand our vigilance and

study. Novelty does not necessarily make them inherently more dangerous than older foes, only more difficult to establish testing, treatment, and vaccination protocols.

I will leave you with this. Deadly outbreaks of infectious diseases make headlines, but not at the start. Every pandemic begins small, subtle, and in faraway places. When it arrives, it spreads across oceans and continents, like the sweep of nightfall, killing millions, or possibly billions.

Know this. Throughout the millennia, extinction has been the norm, and survival, the exception. This is why the Virus Hunters, the disease detectives on the front lines, work tirelessly to keep these deadly infectious diseases from killing us all.

I am Dr. Harper Randolph and this is our story.

REAL WORLD NEWS EXCERPTS

TIMELINE OF A PANDEMIC

December 31, 2019
  MYSTERY PNEUMONIA INFECTS DOZENS IN CHINA'S WUHAN CITY
  ~ South China Morning Post

January 13, 2020
  CHINA REPORTS FIRST DEATH FROM NEWLY IDENTIFIED VIRUS
  ~ KAISER FAMILY FOUNDATION Global Health Policy Report

January 21, 2020
  FIRST TRAVEL-RELATED CASE OF 2019 NOVEL CORONAVIRUS DETECTED IN UNITED STATES *~ CDC Newsroom*

February 26, 2020
  CDC CONFIRMS FIRST POSSIBLE COMMUNITY TRANSMISSION OF CORONAVIRUS IN U.S. *~ CNBC*

February 29, 2020

WASHINGTON STATE REPORTS FIRST CORONAVIRUS DEATH IN U.S.

~ CBS News

March 1, 2020

22 PATIENTS IN U.S. HAVE CORONAVIRUS, PRESIDENT SAYS *~ CNN*

WORLD HEALTH ORGANIZATION DECLARES THE CORONAVIRUS OUTBREAK A GLOBAL PANDEMIC

~ CNBC, March 11, 2020

"In the past two weeks the number of cases outside China has increased thirteenfold and the number of affected countries has tripled," WHO Director-General Dr. Tedros Adhanom Ghebreyesus said at a press conference at the organization's headquarters in Geneva. "In the days and weeks ahead, we expect to see the number of cases, the number of deaths and the number of affected countries to climb even higher."

Declaring a pandemic is charged with major political and economic ramifications, global health experts say. It can further rattle already fragile world markets and lead to more stringent travel and trade restrictions. WHO officials had been reluctant to declare a global pandemic, which is generally defined as an illness that spreads far and wide throughout the world.

WHO officials needed to "make it clear" that the world was in the midst of a pandemic, said Lawrence Gostin, a professor and faculty director of the O'Neill Institute for National and Global Health Law at Georgetown University.

It "is clear" the new coronavirus has been a pandemic and WHO was "behind the curve," Gostin told CNBC on Tuesday.

PRESIDENT TRUMP DECLARES NATIONAL EMERGENCY OVER CORONAVIRUS

~ BBC News, *March 13, 2020*

U.S. President Donald Trump has declared a national emergency to help handle the growing outbreak of coronavirus. The move occurs two days after the outbreak being declared a pandemic by the World Health Organization.

The declaration loosens regulations on the provision of healthcare and could speed up testing. There are 1,701 confirmed cases of COVID-19 in the U.S. and 40 deaths.

Several U.S. states have taken measures to stem the infections rate, including banning large gatherings, sporting events and closing schools.

The virus originated in China last December, but Europe is now the epicentre of the global pandemic.

CORONAVIRUS NOW PRESENT IN ALL 50 STATES
~ *NPR, March 16, 2020*

Since the first coronavirus case was confirmed in the United States, the number of cases has risen rapidly. A large portion of U.S. cases are centered on New York City. New York state, Connecticut and New Jersey have accounted for about 50% of all U.S. cases and nearly 60% of all deaths from COVID-19 have been in these three states.

In some areas, there are signs of hope. The areas with the earliest outbreaks, such as California and Washington state, have claimed success at suppressing the disease. Six counties in the San Francisco area ordered their residents to shelter in place for three weeks.

Other areas, especially rural communities of the Mountain West and the Southeast, have reported little or no cases of the novel coronavirus. For the most part, no self-quarantine orders are being reported in these areas, thus far.

NEW YORK CITY DECLARED UNITED STATES OUTBREAK EPICENTER

~ ABC News, March 20, 2020

Public Health officials with the state of New York report that more than 15,000 people have tested positive for COVID-19 and account for roughly half of the infections in the country.

The vast majority of New Yorkers with the disease are in the New York City regions which Mayor Bill de Blasio calls the epicenter of this crisis warning that the outbreak will get worse as supplies dwindle.

Governor Andrew Cuomo, anticipating that the state's medical care facilities will be hit hard by COVID-19, has ordered nursing homes and other long-term care facilities to accept coronavirus patients. The policy is intended to help clear in-demand hospital beds for sicker patients.

Some facilities have resisted the governor's mandate who angrily defended his position during a news conference earlier today.

"They don't have a right to object. That is the rule and that is the regulation, and they have to comply with that. If they can't do it, we'll put them in a facility that can do it."

"Life is short, the art long, opportunity fleeting, experience treacherous, judgment difficult. The physician must be ready, not only to do his duty himself, but also to secure the cooperation of the patient, of the attendants and of externals."
~ Hippocrates, Greek physician, father of medicine

"That which does not kill us, makes us stronger."
~ Friedrich Nietzsche

And great earthquakes shall be in diverse places, and famines, and pestilences;
and fearful sights and great signs shall there be from Heaven.
~ Luke, Chapter 21, Verse 11

"He that will apply new remedies must expect new evils, for time is the greatest innovator."
~ Sir Francis Bacon, English philosopher and stateman, 1561 - 1626

"But what does it mean, the plague? It's life, that's all."
~ Author Albert Camus in *The Plague*, published 1947

INTRODUCTION

Thank you for downloading *VIRUS HUNTERS: Part Two* of the
Virus Hunters trilogy by Author Bobby Akart.
For a copy of my critically acclaimed monthly newsletter, *The
Epigraph*, updates on new releases, special offers, and bonus content
visit me online at
BobbyAkart.com
or visit my dedicated feature page on Amazon at
Amazon.com/BobbyAkart

VIRUS HUNTERS

A MEDICAL THRILLER | PART TWO

by
Bobby Akart

PART I

IN POLITICS, NOTHING HAPPENS BY ACCIDENT

If it happens, you can bet it was planned that way.
~ President Franklin D. Roosevelt

CHAPTER ONE

Gold Palace Hotel
Fremont Street Experience
Downtown Las Vegas, Nevada

Dr. Harper Randolph shoved her hands into her jeans pockets and approached her number one, Dr. Elizabeth Becker, who'd been taking notes at the back of the room. The epidemiologists had worked around the clock since their departure from the Centers for Disease Control and Prevention. Once they hit the ground in Las Vegas, their investigation of the mysterious illness that had taken several lives over the weekend kept them running nonstop. Harper's briefing in the Augusta Room at the Gold Palace Hotel had been a welcome respite from their disease detective work.

Then all hell broke loose.

They'd just finished up a two-hour assessment of what they knew about this novel disease. Harper had reached a conclusion. The answers to her many questions surrounding the deaths of the Chinese nationals staying at the hotel would be found elsewhere. Namely, China. She was just about to explain her opinions to

Becker before she released the weary group for a break, when the doors to the conference room suddenly flew open.

"You're not going anywhere," a baritone voice bellowed. A captain in the Nevada Army Guard appeared with two armed guardsmen. The trio filled the space and blocked Harper's exit.

"What?" she demanded without a hint of apprehension in her voice. She'd stared down more dangerous adversaries but never her fellow Americans with automatic weapons. "What's this all about?"

"By orders of Nevada governor George Rickey, this facility has been placed under strict quarantine, and everyone is to remain sheltered-in-place until further notice."

Becker couldn't hold back. "Why are we being quarantined? Do you have any idea who we are?"

"Doesn't matter, ma'am. Everyone is to stay in place until we receive further orders. That includes all of you."

Harper searched the man's chest for a name tag or other form of ID. She didn't understand stripes and bars and other forms of military identification indicating rank or time of service. She gave up on protocol and took the blunt approach. The captain picked up on her attempt to identify him.

"I'm Captain Brant."

"Okay, Captain. My name is Dr. Harper Randolph. Everyone in this room works for the CDC. If this quarantine is related to the infectious disease, you don't want us on lockdown. We're here to—"

The captain cut her off, raising his right hand with his palm only a foot from Harper's face. "No exceptions. We have our orders."

Becker became incensed and her protective nature immediately kicked in. She pushed past Harper and stood as tall as her five-foot-three petite frame would allow.

She began pointing toward the much larger man's chest. "Do you have any idea who you are talking to, Mister Captain? You can't hold us here, especially Dr. Randolph."

The two armed guardsmen stepped forward to intervene. "Back off, miss," one of them ordered.

This enraged Becker further. "I am not a miss. I am a doctor.

And you need to back the hell off. You have no right to treat us this way. Our job is outside this room. You need us now more than ever."

She pointed at each of the men who towered over her. As she screamed, the captain gradually backed up and allowed his men to raise their rifles slightly.

"We have our orders, ma'am. If you're to be released, I'm sure my superiors will let us know. For now, I suggest you calm down and get comfortable."

"I am calm!" screamed an increasingly unhinged Becker. Harper stepped forward and gently tugged her assistant by the elbow.

"Let them go," Harper said in a whisper. She hoped her calm voice would have a similar effect on the fiery Becker. "We'll call Atlanta and get this sorted out."

The guardsmen retreated from the fight and slammed the doors closed. Becker, however, wasn't done yet.

"I have to pee, assholes!"

Strangely, Harper found this to be hilarious. Perhaps it was the tension of the moment or watching her attack dog attempt to take a bite out of the backside of the big bad guardsmen. Either way, her laughter became contagious, and rather than joining Becker in outrage, the hostile mood of the epidemiologists who'd gathered around her turned into snickers.

Harper turned to her charges. "Listen, obviously there's been some kind of mistake. There's no way that Atlanta, or Washington, would've ordered a quarantine without discussing it with us first. As we all know, there is insufficient evidence to order a quarantine of the hotel."

One of the epidemiologists spoke up. "He mentioned the governor. Is it possible they've overreacted to what's happened here?"

"That's my guess," replied Harper. "I have another theory, but I need to call Atlanta first. Let's get comfortable, as the man said. I'll place the call."

Harper was impressed with the way the group was handling the abrupt disruption and revelation that the hotel was under the control of the National Guard. She thought she might be able to diffuse the situation by talking to her boss, Dr. Berger Reitherman.

As the group chatted among themselves, Harper asked, "Other than Becker, does anyone else need to use the restroom?"

Becker answered first. "I don't really have to go. I was just pissed off, so it was all I could come up with."

Harper shook her head and chuckled. "Okay, Becker was faking. Does anybody need a break right now?"

All of them seemed content staying put under the circumstances. More than a few had been intimidated by the guardsmen and their slightly raised weapons.

Harper continued. "Y'all give me a moment to call Dr. Reitherman, and maybe we can get out of here."

She turned to walk away, but Becker hustled to catch up to her.

"Do you want me to get in contact with Joe?"

Harper stopped and shook her head vigorously. "No. Definitely not. He can't get involved in this."

"Why not?" asked Becker with a bewildered look on her face. "He could probably make one phone call and this crap would be squashed."

"Maybe," replied Harper hesitantly. She wasn't so sure. "I think, for now, we should let Atlanta handle it. There might be more to—" She cut herself off.

A curious look came over Becker's face. "What?"

"Nothing. Listen, keep the others calm. And yourself, please."

Becker smiled and waved as she began to walk away. "Yeah. Yeah. They'd better let me out, or else!"

Harper wasn't sure what *or else* entailed, but she was certain it would be entertaining. She slipped to a corner of the conference room and pulled up a chair. She pulled her phone from the back pocket of her jeans and was about to call Reitherman when her phone vibrated. His ears must've been ringing. She dispensed with the formalities.

"Have you heard?"

"Yes, I was just informed. Where are you?"

"I was with the entire CDC contingent in a conference room, going over our case notes and findings on this disease, when the three National Guard guys burst into the room. They've got us locked down."

"What do you mean? Locked down as in your movement is restricted?"

Harper laughed. "I suppose you could put it that way. It was really more like nobody's going anywhere until the governor says so. That kinda lockdown."

Dr. Reitherman paused for a moment and then let out a noticeable sigh. "I received a call from their head of the DPBH earlier today. I gave him what we know and advised him we've barely scratched the surface as to what we're dealing with here. He specifically asked whether a quarantine was in order, and my response was no, not at this juncture." The Nevada Department of Public and Behavioral Health was a part of the Department of Health and Human Services in Nevada.

"Yet they did it anyway," interjected Harper. Her mind raced as she recalled the conversation with the president.

"Yes, they did. The entire Fremont Street Experience is cordoned off."

Harper took a deep breath and relayed her encounter with the president. "Dr. Reitherman, there may be another reason for what has happened." After several minutes of explanation, Reitherman issued his orders.

"I still have friends in President Taylor's administration. Let me look for a connection between the governor's knee-jerk reaction and your conversation. On the surface, it appears they didn't get what they wanted from me, so they roped you into Air Force One to try a different angle."

"That's bullshit, sir."

"It is. Sit tight and let me find a way for you to get out of there. For now, you might be safer in that conference room anyway."

"Why's that?" asked Harper as she whipped her head around to the double doors leading to the hallway.

Dr. Reitherman lowered his voice. "In a word, chaos."

CHAPTER TWO

Gold Palace Hotel
Fremont Street Experience
Downtown Las Vegas, Nevada

"Dr. Randolph! You've gotta see this!"

As soon as Harper disconnected the call and paused to gather her thoughts, one of her epidemiologists called for her. They were all hovered around Becker, who sat near the refreshments with her iPad held in front of her.

KSNV News 3 in Las Vegas, the NBC affiliate, was broadcasting live from the Fremont Street Experience. Their reporter, his producer, and a cameraman had been covering the Poker Stars tournament. They braved the melee to provide a live report from just outside the Gold Palace.

"Make room for Dr. Randolph," ordered Becker. The group created an opening, and Harper eased in behind Becker to look over her shoulder.

"Turn it up, please," someone in the back asked. Becker obliged as the reporter responded to the news anchor's questions.

"I've never seen anything like this in my twenty years of covering news

here in the valley. Even the 2017 shooting, as horrific and fear-inducing as it was, paled in comparison to what people are experiencing here on Fremont Street at the moment."

The news anchor interrupted with a question. "How does it differ?"

"Well, Reed, you and I both covered the MGM shooting, and we commented to one another that the outside venue helped reduce loss of life and injuries. There were many places to exit the concert grounds during the panic.

"That is not the case tonight. As word spread, gamblers and hotel guests poured out of the casinos' exits. They tried to escape into the Fremont Street Experience but were prevented from doing so.

"The hotels began to lock their entry doors for security reasons, leaving many thousands of people running throughout Fremont Street, seeking an exit. Then shots were fired. It's unknown whether the gunfire came from the weapons of the National Guard or not, but the 2017 shooting is still fresh in everyone's mind, as you know."

Reed Cowan, award-winning journalist and a highly respected fixture in Las Vegas, asked, "Was there any kind of announcement by the Guard or the Fremont Street management team as to the reason behind the action?"

The reporter couldn't hear the question due to the screaming and shouting. The female producer ran to his side and cupped her hands over his left ear to shout the question to him.

"No, Reed. None it all. In fact, they still haven't. This is purely speculation on my part, but it's as if they were as much in the dark about this decision as the hotels and their guests."

Cowan furrowed his brow as he addressed the reporter. "I can tell you, from our end, there has been no formal statement from the governor's office or local law enforcement. We've reached out to the mayor's office, and they've not responded other than saying the situation is, quote, *fluid.*"

The reporter spun around and the camera panned the crowd in the street. People were pushing and shoving one another. The elderly could be seen being knocked to the ground, and very few bothered to assist them to their feet. Many people exhibited superficial wounds like bruises and cuts, although one person in the camera's view had a bloodied nose.

"Fluid is not the word I'd use to describe the scene here. Mayhem, bedlam, or pandemonium seem more appropriate. Back to you, Reed."

As the reporter outside the hotel handed the broadcast back to the newsroom, Harper patted Becker on the shoulder and stepped away from the group. Seconds later, Becker joined her side.

"What are we gonna do? We can't just sit in here."

"I don't know that we have a choice," replied Harper.

"I think we have an option," said Becker. She pointed to a side exit door that led through a partition wall into another conference room. "When I discussed the room choices with Figueroa, he said these partition walls could be removed to give us more space if we needed it."

Alejandro Figueroa was the Gold Palace's chief of security and had been very cooperative with the CDC personnel during their investigation. His level of professionalism stood in stark contrast to Donald Wallace, the ill-tempered general manager of the hotel and casino, who was more interested in profits than the protection of his guests.

Harper asked, "Have you tried to call him?"

"Yes, but I just get his voicemail box, which is full. I can't even leave a message."

"I don't think we can break through the partition without our friends outside hearing us," said Harper.

"I have another idea," said Becker. She allowed herself a sly grin and then looked directly over her head.

"Divine intervention?" asked Harper.

"No, ductwork."

Harper looked up at the two-foot-by-three-foot air-conditioning vent blowing cool air onto their heads. She rolled her eyes and laughed. "This isn't the movies, Becker. You can't crawl through the air ducts to freedom. You'll get stuck."

"I'm already stuck," Becker countered.

"This is different and you know it," said Harper, pointing to the ceiling. "That's a different kind of stuck."

Becker pulled her shoulders back in an attempt to lock eyes with the much taller Harper. "I've done it before."

"When?"

"In college. The girls' dorm was adjacent to the guys'. We figured out that we could crawl through the air-conditioning duct to bypass the RAs in the common area."

"You snuck through the ductwork to hook up with your boyfriend?" Harper shook her head in amazement.

"No! Of course not. We, um, were studying."

"Aw, shit, Becker. Regardless, I don't think it's a good idea for you to crawl around up there."

Becker insisted, "I can do it. I swear. I just need a table, a chair, and a boost. Leave the rest to me."

"And then what?"

"Well, I'll try to unlock the partition-wall door, and we'll find a way around those goons. If not, I'll go to Figueroa's office or find another friendly face. I'm not going to sit around here and do nothing."

Harper knew she wouldn't be able to stop the strong-willed Becker from the hairbrained idea. She studied the vent opening and then looked at her assistant. She sighed and shrugged. Becker might just be able to pull it off.

Becker rallied the troops and they cleared off one of the banquet tables. Next, they positioned a chair under the vent. With the assistance of the guys, she was hoisted upward to pull the small latches holding the vent grate in place. It swung open, revealing the boxy, sheet-metal HVAC duct.

Less than a minute later, with her cell phone's flashlight feature illuminated, Becker was crawling along the sheet metal using her elbows and feet to propel her forward. Her movements could be tracked by the sounds emanating from the ceiling. With each movement, the sound of a bass drum echoed through the vent and into the conference room.

Suddenly, her movements stopped and the bass drum stopped playing. Everyone in the room looked to one another out of concern for Becker's safety. The group pushed closer to the opening in the ceiling and looked up. And then Becker's voice changed. It was her best Arnold Schwarzenegger impression.

"I'll be back."

CHAPTER THREE

Office of Congressman Joe Mills
Longworth House Office Building
Washington, DC

Joe had exchanged text messages with Harper earlier that day before she boarded the CDC Learjet to return to Las Vegas. This was what their life together was like.

When Congress was in session, he spent every waking hour working on the business of the congressional committees he chaired and every politician's primary job—fundraising. From the moment a congressman was elected, he began working on his re-election. Their term of office was two years, the shortest of any Washington elected official, and therefore required an inordinate amount of time and money to maintain their campaign coffers.

Joe was well-liked in the 6th Congressional District located in the northeastern suburbs of Atlanta. He'd not had a serious challenge since his first campaign, but he wasn't one to rest on his laurels. That evening, following another contentious budget hearing in which he tortuously challenged the Taylor administration's budget director over perceived fuzzy math and political paybacks, he turned in early for the night.

Like a handful of other congressmen before him, Joe opted to live in his office while he was in Washington. Literally. He'd splurged, to put it mildly, on a Restoration Hardware sleeper sofa. The plush Belgian linen was so luxurious that most visitors to his office hesitated to sit on it, opting instead for the two chairs that flanked his desk.

Joe's work could be mentally and emotionally draining. He always had to be on his toes, which required him to be well-informed of events domestically and internationally. There was always a reporter lurking around every corner with a gotcha question meant to embarrass politicians. His hearings often included in-depth research performed by the Taylor administration and his opponents across the aisle. If he was caught unaware about a topic, the media would have a field day at his expense.

He'd instructed his chief of staff, Andy Spangler, to keep him up to speed on current events, as well as Washington rumors. Joe vowed to avoid being blindsided and the embarrassing task of explaining why he was uninformed.

There had been times in the past when Chief of Staff Spangler had phoned him in the middle of the night. Typically, this occurred during significant international events or potential catastrophes like the discovery of a threat posed by an asteroid dubbed IM86 several years ago. Through the great work of NASA and a true American hero, the diversion and destruction methods had been successful in breaking up the potential planet killer. The nation had come together to respond, much like it had tried to do during the COVID-19 pandemic.

The back-to-back natural disasters were a reminder to Joe that you could never let your guard down when it came to catastrophic events. He recalled having a conversation with Harper about the asteroid.

The day before, they'd spent time with her family at Randolph House, visiting local museums and enjoying pork barbecue in the backyard. The next day, after Spangler had notified him of the threat, they were watching the skies, wondering if it would fall upon them, as Chicken Little had warned. He'd quipped, you just never know when the day before is the day before.

So when Spangler gently tapped on his office door and opened it without calling first, Joe's half-awake state of mind assumed the worst. *Now what?*

"Joe, are you awake?" The two longtime friends and associates were on a first-name basis with each other when in private.

"Andy? Um, yeah. What's up?" Joe sat up in bed and reached over the arm of the sofa to turn on a tabletop lamp. The subdued amber glow lit up the room.

"I'm sorry to wake you like this," he began. "I kinda figured Harper wouldn't call you."

"Wait. What? Is Harper okay?"

Joe jumped out of bed and raced to his desk in search of his phone. He was wearing a pair of gym shorts and an Atlanta Braves tee shirt.

"She's fine. Well, she's not hurt or in any kind of danger. It's just, um—" Spangler searched for the words.

Joe illuminated his phone and studied the display. There'd been no phone calls or text messages. He retrieved his emails as he spoke. "Spit it out, Andy. What is it?"

"Harper's in Vegas, as you know. Governor Rickey called out the Nevada Guard to quarantine downtown Las Vegas."

"Quarantine? I'm surprised Harper wouldn't give me a heads-up."

"Joe, she didn't know about it. I got a call from her boss, Reitherman. He said the CDC wasn't consulted. Well, they were, sort of. One of the governor's people called Reitherman, and he said it wasn't necessary yet because they were too early in their investigation."

"Why'd they do it?" asked Joe. He went around his office and turned on more lights. He closed up his sleeper sofa to allow the two men more room to conduct their conversation.

"Apparently, the president summoned Harper to Air Force One when her plane landed late yesterday. Somehow, the conversation got turned around and used by the governor to lock down Fremont Street."

Joe flopped in his chair and scrolled through his phone to find Harper's number. "This reeks!"

Spangler raised his hand to stop Joe from calling his wife. "I know you want to talk to her, but before you do, we need to look at this for a moment."

"I wonder why she hasn't called me," mumbled Joe.

"She's very sharp, Joe. My guess is she put two and two together and figured the governor was acting as President Taylor's do-boy."

"He did all of this to get at me?" asked Joe.

"Think about it. Nevada is always a swing state. If the governor can cause an uproar, lay the blame on the CDC—and Harper in particular—all roads lead right back to this office. They'll use it in the budget battle with you as well as a hammer in our future political plans."

"Cut me off at the knees before I even get started," Joe surmised.

"Exactly."

"Unbelievable!" shouted Joe as he pounded his fist on the desk out of frustration. He was furious that his wife was being used as a pawn in the president's political games. "Taylor's that desperate?"

Spangler, who'd remained standing throughout the conversation, nodded. "He is, and so are his political advisors. That's the way it works, Joe. As soon as the label *rising star* is attached to any DC politician, the opposition goes into high gear to destroy them."

"And all of this is because of Herbert Brittain's support?"

"In part," replied Spangler, who sighed and finally took a seat. "Listen, this is why we started discreetly keeping up with Harper's activities. Unfortunately, the families of politicians, especially the proverbial rising stars, become the target of their opponents and the media."

Joe exhaled and leaned back in his chair to stare at the ceiling. "I never wanted her to become entangled in the dirty world of politics. I should never have opened myself up for other options besides the one I have right here in this office."

Spangler was empathetic. "Joe, it would've happened eventually. Maybe not something of this magnitude. But your involvement in budgetary and oversight matters would naturally bring heat because of Harper's job."

"I can't ask her to quit," said Joe.

"No, nor should you. First, we need to diffuse this situation. Then we'll need to spend some time with her so she understands how vicious DC operatives can be."

Joe shook his head and rolled his eyes. After a deep breath, he phoned his wife.

CHAPTER FOUR

Gold Palace Hotel
Fremont Street Experience
Downtown Las Vegas, Nevada

"I'm so sorry, Joe. I knew it was out of place for him to drag me into Air Force One. It's not my place to have conversations with the President of the United States. But, honestly, I didn't feel like I was in a position to say no."

Joe comforted his wife and reassured her she'd done nothing wrong. Harper had been trapped, and regardless of what she did, the president and the Nevada governor would pin the quarantine decision on her because she was in charge of the CDC team in Las Vegas.

"No worries, darling. Listen. They may have overplayed their hand. Andy is already working on something that might expose them. Leave that to us."

"Okay, I will," said Harper, who was still remorseful for her unintentional contribution to the lockdown. "In the meantime, I have a room full of epidemiologists who were exhausted to begin with. We have a lot of work to do here, and they need some sleep."

"We're working on that as well, but let me mention one other thing to you," said Joe.

"What is it?"

"Andy suspects they're keeping you locked in there for another reason. He thinks they're gathering a media scrum to confront you when the doors are opened."

"Aw, shit, Joe. I don't wanna deal with that after what's happened tonight. I'll probably blast every last one of them."

"You have every right to be incredulous, and Taylor's people know that. You have to keep your cool and try your best to muzzle your attack dog. While I'd enjoy seeing Becker take a bite out of the media's asses, it won't help us this go-around."

Harper glanced at her watch. Becker had been gone for nearly an hour. She'd already become concerned her loyal assistant might be trapped in the HVAC ducts. She wasn't sure how to respond to Joe's suggestion, so she changed the subject.

"Honey, I love you and thanks for calling. I didn't want to bother you with this."

Joe tried to remove any doubts or fears from her mind. "I'm always here for you, no matter what. Those guys play dirty, but we have our own playbook. Revenge is a dish best served cold."

Harper smiled. That was one of her grandmother's favorite phrases. She wondered if Joe used it for that reason. "Okay."

"I've got your back, Harper. Know that."

"I do. I'll sit tight and keep my opinions to myself. I love you!"

"I love you back. I'll be in committee at nine. Text me or call Andy if something comes up. Promise?"

"Promise!"

Harper disconnected the call and turned to observe the group. Several of the epidemiologists had succumbed to their exhaustion and curled up on the floor next to the walls to sleep. She glanced around the room in search of the light switches. Perhaps the group could sleep through this nightmare.

Ding!

Her iPhone notified her of a text. It wasn't Joe, because she'd assigned a musical notification to his incoming messages. It was Becker. The text was succinct and descriptive.

Becker: Bedlam!

CHAPTER FIVE

Underground Great Wall
Urumqi, Xinjiang, China

In land size, China is approximately the same size as the United States, while its population is almost five times greater. Its major cities were extremely overcrowded, while its rural areas were sparse. Scholars have often referred to the tale of two Chinas—the provinces versus the autonomous regions of Xinjiang and Tibet. The provinces were more tightly controlled by the Beijing Communist government, whereas the autonomous regions, which have a disproportionately higher number of minority ethnic groups, have maintained some semblance of control over their local governments.

Human rights violations had come to light against the native Tibetans since the 1950s when the Chinese military sent thousands of troops into the region to enforce its claims. During this period, known as the Chinese Cultural Revolution, most of Tibet's monasteries were destroyed.

A lesser known human rights issue centered around the Uyghurs, a predominantly Muslim ethnic group that populated

Xinjiang. Beginning in 2018, and for years thereafter, the Uyghurs were the victims of genocide. Via leaked Communist Party documents, the world learned of internment camps being built throughout Xinjiang that coincided with China's brutal crackdown against the Uyghur Muslim community. The Beijing government called them *voluntary education centers*, which had a stated purpose of cleansing the Uyghurs' brains.

As whole families disappeared in the middle of the night, university-age Uyghur students took to social media to spread the word of China's genocidal activity. They also went into hiding—in the massive aqueduct system under Xinjiang, nicknamed the Underground Great Wall in defiance of the Communist Party.

Urumqi was the largest city in Western China and was quite famous for its claim of being the most inland major city on the planet because of its distance from any ocean. It was also located in a geographic location that was mostly desert.

For over two thousand years, a system of water harvesting and underground transmission via elaborate aqueducts provided sustainable water supplies throughout the desert regions of Western China. Known as a *karez*, the Uyghur word for well, it was a marvel of ancient engineering. The thirty-three hundred miles of tunnels crisscrossed the region, bringing water to communities and farms in even the most remote parts of Xinjiang.

Many scientists believed the karez was more impressive than its aboveground brother—the Great Wall of China. The aqueducts connecting the wells spanned a distance equal to that between New York City and the Pacific Ocean. It was dug by hand with primitive tools and had to be done with a precise slope so the water would flow in the direction the ancient engineers required.

Over time, China modernized its water systems in the cities, and the karezes were mostly abandoned. They were used, however, by the dissidents during the Uyghur uprising, and now by China's citizen journalists.

Symbolically, the naming of the hidden tunnels by historians as the Underground Great Wall gave inspiration to the Uyghurs during the period of genocide, and now to the dissidents. The Great Wall of China, built to protect the Chinese dynasties from attack, spanned the entire border of the Communist nation for thirteen thousand miles.

The Underground Great Wall was a symbol of Uyghur ingenuity, and during the period of harsh crackdowns, it became a place of safety from those who'd destroy their way of life. The success of the Uyghurs in using the underground tunnels to evade capture frustrated and angered the Communist Party. They were unable to close off the aqueduct system because it was still used as a water source by parts of the community.

Instead, they attempted to marginalize it with a project of their own beneath Beijing. As part of its nuclear weapons program, Chinese military experts conceived a massive underground system built in a series of subterranean silos connected together by tunnels. The steel-reinforced structure could withstand the strikes of the most destructive weapons on Earth, including the massive ordnance penetrators possessed by Russia and the United States.

To divert attention from the Uyghurs' use of the karez system to hide from oppression, the Beijing government prominently referred to their new missile defense project as its Underground Great Wall, co-opting the more accepted use of the phrase from Western China.

Now, the Chinese government officials were facing a larger problem—a small army of citizen journalists were shining the light of transparency on Communist tyranny, and they were hiding underground in the ancient karez aqueducts.

CHAPTER SIX

Underground Great Wall
Urumqi, Xinjiang, China

Dr. Zeng Qi and his wife, Ying, instantly embraced when they saw one another. It was a rare show of affection between the two in a public setting, even if it was in the underground labyrinth of tunnels. Their nephew, Zeng Fangyu, turned to his fellow citizen journalists and encouraged them to turn away in order for the older couple to have a moment of privacy. Their reunification brought tears of joy to their eyes, but soon thereafter, apprehension swept over them both.

Dr. Zeng broke their embrace and motioned for his nephew to join him. He hugged the young college student as well and thanked him for all he'd done to keep his wife safe.

"Uncle, I would like you to meet my friends. Come with us, please."

Fangyu instructed the young people who'd gathered around the newcomers to disperse, reminding them the new entrance they'd constructed through the basement floor of the apartment building could be compromised as a result of its recent activity.

He led his aunt and uncle deeper into the aqueduct system, using a small flashlight to illuminate the way. Periodically, one of his acquaintances would stop to take up a position near a cross tunnel. Fangyu indicated they were part of an elaborate system of human monitors who'd notify the rest of intruders.

They walked for nearly twenty minutes, Fangyu leading the way through the unmarked tunnels. He never hesitated as he made turn after turn, occasionally into broad aqueducts, at which time he'd pick up the pace. Following a route he appeared to know very well, he led them through cramped side tunnels that were full of water, with thick planks of wood used as walkways.

Eventually, they came into a cavernous opening that was well lit. The space was full of tables, chairs, and even a small kitchen complete with a refrigerator and a microwave. Scattered throughout the large karez were dozens of college-age citizen journalists. When Fangyu entered with Dr. Zeng and his wife, they stopped their work on laptops and computer tablets to assess the newcomers.

"Everyone, this is my uncle, Dr. Zeng."

Spontaneous applause erupted throughout the space. Dr. Zeng was taken aback by the odd reaction to his introduction. He didn't know these young people, nor had he done anything to warrant the ovation he'd received. At least, he didn't think so.

"Nephew, I don't understand. Why are they clapping?"

"You are a hero, Uncle."

He was puzzled. "I have done nothing."

"You took a stand and risked everything, including career and life, to warn others. Now we have a purpose—to protect our countrymen from the secrecy of the government and a new disease."

It was a universal principle held by college-age youth. People go through a period in their lives, often following their teenage years and into their late twenties, when they view themselves as idealistic, activist agents of change. Later, they grow up and get jobs, have families, and pay the bills. In other words, they become adults and their priorities change.

In China, campus activism was not allowed to rise to the surface. It was tamped down by parents, teachers, and civic leaders. If that didn't work, the full weight of the People's Liberation Army was used like a twenty-pound sledgehammer against a porcelain doll.

The stories of dissidents being silenced were broadly disseminated as a deterrent against future activity. Unlike the Western world where campus activism was something to cheer, in China, it resulted in people disappearing.

As a result, following the lead of the Uyghurs before them, the young citizen journalists of Xinjiang went underground to spread the word to those above. These enterprising students were so committed to their task that many found a way to live in the karez aqueducts.

After the demonstration of applause subsided, with Dr. Zeng smiling and waving his hand to everyone in thanks, the young people returned to their workstations.

Dr. Zeng took a moment to observe his surroundings. The young people appeared haggard and disheveled, an almost unrecognizable shadow of the energetic young people he'd observed in Fangyu's dormitory.

"Uncle, at this moment, we are directly beneath your First Affiliated Hospital."

The old doctor looked upward and pointed to the fluorescent light fixtures and hundreds of wires strapped to the rock walls of the large karez. "Are those all electrical wires?"

"Yes, and communications lines also. Some of the wires lead to portable antennas in nearby apartment buildings, which allow us to access the internet via satellite."

"Where are you pulling the power from?" asked Dr. Zeng.

"The hospital," he answered with a smile. "As you know, the government has stopped delivery of electricity to all nonessential buildings in Urumqi in the past. During the Uyghur uprisings, this was a regular occurrence. Also, during the threatened solar storm of 2026. However, they did not disconnect the power to the hospitals. Those systems are not only independent of the business and residential power grid, but the wiring is hardened and supplemented by the solar array generators."

"I am aware of that," added Dr. Zeng. "I could see the generators from my office window. The solar panels are on the roof, correct?"

"Yes. When the hospital was built, the access of this karez was sealed off, and the construction superintendents thought this large opening was buried by rubble. The Uyghur opened up the tunnels into it using the plank boards stolen from the construction as a walkway." He took his aunt by the arm and led them around the cavern. He stopped by the refrigerator and provided them both a bottle of water.

While they drank, he continued. "Years ago, university students found a way to access the hospital's electrical system by slowly boring a hole through the fragments of rock that filled the previous aboveground access. Over time, more lines were run to power all of these workstations and other karezes like this one scattered throughout the city. Also, we tapped into the hospital's communication and internet system, which has enabled us to create thousands of social media accounts without being detected by the government."

"Ingenious," commented Dr. Zeng.

"Yes, Uncle. You see, China's brightest young minds no longer wish to serve the oppressive Communist Party. We want freedoms like the West, and to effectuate this change, we have to fight with our keyboards because a gun battle is a losing battle."

Dr. Zeng studied the group of dissidents and nodded his approval. In a way, he considered himself one of them, and now he understood why they'd given him the applause. However, he was still puzzled by something. "How does my investigation into this mysterious virus help the cause of freedom?"

Fangyu led them to a cubicle made up of stacked boxes of toilet paper and canned goods. He offered his aunt a chair while he and his uncle took a seat on overturned milk crates. The furnishings were spartan but appropriate for a group that likened itself to the French Resistance.

"As I said before, we will save our countrymen from a certain death if this disease is similar to the Wuhan outbreak of a decade ago. Uncle, do you recall how our physicians and nurses were ordered not to wear protective gear in order to avoid the appearance of panic?"

"Yes, I do. Many good doctors died because of this poor decision. The government tried to cover up the coronavirus disease, but it was too pervasive in Wuhan."

"This leads me to the second reason for telling the world about this new novel virus, as you called it," said Fangyu. "The Communist Party successfully evaded the worst sanctions proposed by the Americans by putting their boots on the throats of the World Health Organization and the Europeans. They gave in to the government's demands, and the Americans were isolated. They had no choice but to accept a muted condemnation. When our CDC, in concert with the propaganda machine in Beijing, attempt another cover-up, they will look like fools because of people like you and the hundreds like me."

"You are shining the light on their dark dealings," added his aunt in a solemn voice. Her words were profound.

"It is the only way to expose their tyranny," said Fangyu with a sigh. "It is not easy, and it requires economic funding from others, but we are all committed. Even to the point of risking our lives if necessary."

A wave of sadness came over his aunt's face. After the loss of her own son, Fangyu had become like her own. "I do not like to hear words like risking our lives."

Fangyu give her a reassuring smile, and then his face became serious. "What kind of journalists would we be if we did not dare rush to the frontline of a crisis?"

"I worry for you," she replied, her face awash with sadness.

"I know and this is why I love you. But never have so many of our countrymen used technology to relay their experiences and issue warnings to the world. It is why we live like this." He looked around the karez and managed a smile.

Dr. Zeng reached out for his nephew's hand and squeezed it. These young people were committed to being pioneers in a dogged movement to defy the ruling Communist Party's tightly policed monopoly on information. Armed with smartphones and social media accounts, they were telling their stories and the stories of people like Dr. Zeng. In the decade since the COVID-19 pandemic, the activists presented a daunting challenge to the Communist Party, which had been controlling the narrative of China since taking power in 1949.

"You are the hero, Fangyu. All of you, in fact. Now that we are here, what can we do to help you?"

CHAPTER SEVEN

Gold Palace Hotel
Fremont Street Experience
Downtown Las Vegas, Nevada

Harper was propped in a corner of the conference room, sitting with her long legs stretched out in front of her, and her Ray-Ban Aviator sunglasses on. She looked like a movie star who was trying to catch a few winks after pulling an all-nighter. She was jolted out of her slumber by the sound of the double doors being violently flung open until they slammed into the adjoining wall.

She pressed her hands against the wall and propelled herself onto her feet just as Becker was forcibly shoved into the room.

"I'm gonna sue every last one of you!" She was irate, screaming and waving her arms at the men who'd ushered her inside. "Do you hear me? I'll have your jobs. I'll own your car. I'll be living in your houses. You'll all be broke-ass bitches when my lawyers are done with you!"

"Becker!" shouted Harper as she ran to her assistant's side. "Calm down!"

Becker was undeterred. Her face was red and her arms continue to flail as she pointed her finger from one man to another. "You shouldn't have manhandled me! I've got bruises. I've been harmed!"

Harper wrapped her arms around the young epidemiologist and whispered in her ear, "Calm down, please. We've got to stay under control."

"But—" she argued before Harper cut her off.

"I'll handle this."

Harper turned Becker around, and two of their coworkers led her toward the banquet tables. The food and drinks were now picked over. Becker had preferred a Diet Coke earlier, but she readily accepted a bottle of water for starters.

"I want to see Captain Brant. Now!" Harper raised her voice. She wanted her captors to know she'd had enough.

"Ma'am, he's attending to other matters," said one of the guardsmen.

"I don't care." She pointed to the man's radio. "Does that thing work? Call him. He's got five minutes to release us or I'm calling my husband, the congressman."

It was the first time she'd ever invoked Joe's position to gain advantage. She didn't like doing it, but she sensed Becker's outrage was going to cause the anger to escalate with the other CDC personnel. Besides, she was over it, too.

"You can talk to me!" a man shouted from down the hallway. The voice was familiar, so Harper craned her neck to look past the captors to identify the person. She saw Wallace lumbering toward the doorway.

"Okay, I'll talk to you," said Harper assertively. "Tell these men to stand aside and let us out. Do you know what false imprisonment is, Mr. Wallace?"

"We're under quarantine orders," he barked back. "Thanks to you, I might add."

"That's wrong. It wasn't my—"

Wallace was frustrated and livid. "I don't want to hear it, Dr. Randolph. We tried to accommodate your every request. I practically assigned Figueroa to you and your people full time. And what thanks do I get? A heads-up? A text message saying, hey, I'm about to shut down your casino? Nada. Zero. Zip. Not even the slightest courtesy."

Harper tried to argue her point. "This was not my idea. I never suggested—"

The man was sweating profusely. She'd only interacted with him on a couple of occasions and she'd recalled that he was overweight. But this was different. She was about to speak again when Wallace's chest heaved as he started to cough.

Instinctively, Harper jumped back and pulled her tee shirt over her face, exposing her stomach. Wallace had a coughing fit. He doubled over and tried to suppress it, to no avail.

Under the circumstances, Harper became concerned for her team and the two onlooking guardsmen as well.

"Stand away from him and cover your nose and mouth!" She was being intentionally overdramatic.

The guards retreated, leaving Wallace to finish the hacking.

"It's nothing," he insisted. "I take lisinopril. It makes me—"

Cough. More violent this time. Wallace couldn't finish his sentence.

Lisinopril was a commonly prescribed ACE inhibitor used to widen, or dilate, the body's blood vessels. In so doing, the enzyme increased the amount of blood the heart pumped and therefore lowered blood pressure. However, for ten percent of patients, it also generated a common side effect in the form of a somewhat annoying cough.

Through years of experience gained investigating infectious diseases, Harper had learned that a seemingly innocent cough or sneeze, coupled with the body sweating in an effort to break a fever, could portend something much worse.

The two guardsmen began to shut the doors to lock them back in. Harper did something totally out of character for her, and definitely considered unprofessional. She shouted at Wallace to get in the final word.

"Hey! Wallace! Let us out of here and we'll make sure that cough isn't related to the disease."

The doors slammed shut and Harper held her breath. After thirty seconds, they didn't reopen and she knew her ploy didn't work.

Dejected, her shoulders slumped and her chin dropped to her chest. For the first time, Harper felt herself on the verge of tears. She felt helpless and frustrated. Moreover, she took full blame and responsibility for her team being dragged into this fiasco. Yet it was her team who snapped her out of her doldrums.

"You just gave him something to think about!" shouted one.

Another joined in. "I guarantee he just ran to the hospital."

"They won't let the windbag out of the hotel. Talk about having a fit."

"Yeah, a damn hissy fit!"

The group began to laugh uproariously.

Harper joined the group and sought out Becker first. She sheepishly appeared from the back of the group.

"What happened while you were out there?" asked Harper.

"Well, I made it through the ductwork all the way to the front of the conference center. I was above a hallway, and those soldiers were milling about the entrance. Then some kind of emergency call came over their radios, and they all took off toward the casino. I used that as an opportunity to drop out of the ceiling."

"Did you go looking for Figueroa?"

"I never got that far. I waited for a minute to make sure nobody saw me. Then, just as I stepped into the corridor and headed toward the lobby, big boy rounded the corner with two of his security people. I don't know how they knew—"

"Cameras," interjected one of the epidemiologists. "There are probably two thousand or more scattered throughout the property."

"That fast?" she asked.

"For sure," he replied. "My guess is they've really ramped up surveillance because of the chaos."

"Chaos is right," said Becker. "I thought I was at a Falcons game. It was crazy loud as people shouted over one another."

"Did you see anything?" asked Harper.

"Not really. Just people trying to get out."

Ding!

Harper received another text message. It wasn't from one of her regular contacts.

+1 (702) 778 – 4749: The cavalry is coming.

She read the message aloud to the group.

"Who's it from?" asked Becker.

Harper shrugged. "I have no idea."

CHAPTER EIGHT

CDC Headquarters
Atlanta, Georgia

As the director of the Center for Surveillance, Epidemiology, and Laboratory Services, CSELS, Dr. Berger Reitherman was very much aware of the political machinations of Washington, DC. Prior to coming on board with the CDC, he had been a program manager in the infectious disease office at DARPA, the Defense Advanced Research Projects Agency, an agency of the U.S. Department of Defense known for its secrecy and innovative breakthroughs on behalf of the nation's military.

At times, he missed his days at DARPA. The agency wasn't used as a political football like the CDC was. Politicians on both sides of the aisle understood DARPA's importance in maintaining America's status as the world's dominant democratic superpower, ensuring national security through advanced technology. The ability to bring new defense weapons systems online and make them operational ready was invaluable. As was the agency's ability to combat infectious diseases.

When he left DARPA to join the CDC, he was admittedly

interested in taking on a more high-profile job. He'd fought in the trenches during the COVID-19 pandemic of ten years prior, and now he was mentally gearing up for a similar battle against this newly discovered disease in Las Vegas.

As the chief administrator of CSELS, and Harper's superior, he was also responsible for her actions. He'd been awakened in the middle of the night by the overnight communications director at the CDC with the breaking news from Las Vegas. He hurriedly dressed and hustled into the office. His goal was to gather as much information as possible so the CDC could get out in front of the news story.

He'd been summoned by the deputy director for Public Health Science and Surveillance, his immediate superior, to a meeting with the principal deputy director of the CDC and the associate director for Communications, Mitchell Bonds.

He and Bonds had been friends for many years, as they were required to coordinate press releases on new outbreaks. They'd met earlier in the day just prior to Dr. Reitherman receiving the phone call from Carson City.

The early morning meeting was highly unusual, but the suddenness of the Nevada governor's actions warranted it. Dr. Reitherman appeared to be the last to arrive at the meeting. He looked down at his watch to confirm it was seven, and not a moment later. Puzzled, he glanced around the deputy director's conference room and observed empty cups of coffee together with half-eaten pastries. He immediately got the sense he had intentionally been excluded from an earlier part of the conversation.

"Good morning, Dr. Reitherman," the deputy director greeted him solemnly. "Please have a seat."

"Thank you, Madam Director," said Dr. Reitherman. He glanced around at the faces studying him. "Um, my apologies if I got the meeting time incorrect." He reached for his cell phone and scrolled through his text messages. He knew he was on time. He just wanted someone to admit he had been misled.

"You're fine, Doctor," said the deputy director. "We had other matters to discuss. I'll get right to it."

"Okay," he mumbled.

She continued. "In about an hour, we're going to be facing a media shit storm. Communications has already prepared a preliminary statement as to the CDC's role in the governor of Nevada's decision. Your conversation with the state was relayed to us a little while ago."

"Quite frankly, Madam Deputy Director, the CSELS had no role in the decision. If anything, I advised the Nevada's public health people that a quarantine, much less a lockdown, was not warranted at this time."

The deputy director pursed her lips and locked eyes with Dr. Reitherman. Her agenda was coming to light. "What role did Dr. Randolph play in this decision?"

Dr. Reitherman noticeably gulped and immediately chastised himself for doing so. It was an uncontrolled, spontaneous act as his mind debated whether to tell the truth or try to protect Harper. He studied the deputy director's body language, and then he recalled a statement he'd heard on a television program once. *A prosecutor rarely asks a question they don't already know the answer to.*

He scowled. That was what this meeting was shaping up to be. A prosecution. A witch hunt in search of someone to scapegoat for the governor's draconian actions. He'd have to come clean but stick to only what he knew.

"Dr. Randolph had just arrived back in Las Vegas at my direction. The CDC jet was inexplicably rerouted to McCarran from its preplanned destination in North Las Vegas. Based upon my conversation with Dr. Randolph, it's readily apparent to me as to why."

"I'm listening," said the deputy director.

"She was met as she exited the plane by Secret Service personnel, who insisted she come alone with them at the request of President Taylor."

"Was she flying alone?"

"No. She was joined by her assistant, Dr. Elizabeth Becker. Dr. Becker was prevented from accompanying Dr. Randolph."

Dr. Reitherman paused to gather his thoughts, prompting the deputy director to urge him to continue. "Go ahead, please."

"She met with the president in Air Force One. He peppered her with questions regarding the CDC's activities in Las Vegas."

"Why would she remotely consider that to be appropriate? Those types of conversations should be conducted with someone much higher on the organizational chart, such as myself or the director."

"I agree, Madam Deputy Director. That said, with all due respect, the president knows this as well. I don't have the means, nor the time, to look into why the CDC jet was rerouted to McCarran. It's obvious, however, that President Taylor, his chief of staff, and therefore, the Secret Service were aware of it. They may have, in fact, been responsible for the diversion."

The deputy director furrowed her brow and pressed her back into the chair. "What you are suggesting is quite conspiratorial, wouldn't you agree?"

Dr. Reitherman had opened up this door, and he intended to do everything he could to protect Harper from being railroaded. He'd been around long enough to know that before the directors of any agency got their precious résumés soiled, they'd find someone to throw under the bus first.

"I mean no disrespect. I'm simply stating the facts supplemented by my observations. I had a conversation with Dr. Randolph about this, and she assured me that nothing was said by her that would lead to the governor's use of the National Guard to institute a *cordon sanitaire*. If anything, she, like me, specifically advised against it."

The deputy director took a deep breath. She let out a long exhale and leaned forward in her chair. "Ten years ago, COVID-19 changed the lives of everyone in this country. The concepts of social distancing, self-quarantine, and wearing face masks became a part of everyone's vernacular.

"I also recall how the American consciousness shifted from

awareness to concerned to fearful. Simple routines like going to the grocery store or filling up their cars with gasoline potentially put themselves and others at risk of contracting the disease.

"It was the first time in a hundred years we'd faced a global pandemic. Years later, when the vaccines were proven to be successful and the death toll finally subsided, the public breathed easy. The presumption was infectious diseases would take a break for another millennium.

"That was naïve thinking. We learned from studying the events leading up to those first cases in America that COVID-19 was never containable. Why? Frankly, because we never knew what hit us. By the time the first indications of community spread became apparent, it was too late."

She took a deep breath and studied the attendees. "What I'm about to say cannot leave this room. Let's face it. As medical professionals in the field of infectious diseases, we know the challenges the CDC faces as an agency. We're always placed in an untenable position—open to second-guessing and twenty-twenty hindsight.

"Like COVID-19, from Dr. Randolph's initial analysis, it is difficult to distinguish this emerging disease from other viral infections. The symptoms, even if they manifest, which is not always a guarantee, are identical to influenza. To an overworked medical system, even the common cold can be indistinguishable.

"I don't want to address any conspiracy notions that Dr. Randolph was set up by the President of the United States to obtain cover for the quarantine placed over downtown Las Vegas. I'll leave that up to Congress to ascertain.

"At this juncture, I'm not even sure we are in a position to take a stand against the *cordon sanitaire*. The proverbial train has left the station on that one. Do I believe the Nevada governor has overreacted to the information received from Dr. Randolph, or even you, Dr. Reitherman? Yes. Do we have sufficient evidence from our initial investigation to strongly urge him to reconsider? No. For that reason, the first thing I'm going to say is the quarantine can remain in place until we have more facts."

Dr. Reitherman expected as much. At this point, he was more interested in getting his personnel released and back to work. "May I interrupt?"

She gestured with both hands to continue.

"I would like to increase our personnel on the ground in order to conduct contact tracing. Further, I need to pull our internal EIS scientists to focus on this outbreak. People are being held against their will and deserve a speedy response."

The deputy director nodded. "Do it. However, I want all personnel decisions to be run by me first. No exceptions. I promise a quick turnaround with my input."

"Yes." He glanced over at his boss. "We will."

She continued. "I will reach out to the governor's office directly to get our personnel released. The governor has to understand that we can't help his constituents by locking up the CDC team in a hotel."

"Thank you, Madam Deputy Director. I'll let Dr. Randolph know."

"I'm not finished," she barked. "Also, please inform Dr. Randolph that she's to return to Atlanta *post haste* and that under no circumstances is she to have any conversations with the media. Understood?"

"Is she being sidelined?"

"No, not necessarily. But let's face it. She's a lightning rod now. We need her out of the hot zone."

"Is she confined to the campus?"

"No. She can continue to work on this outbreak. I just want her out of Las Vegas."

"Yes, ma'am."

The deputy director wasn't finished. "One more thing, Dr. Reitherman. Keep her on a short leash."

He gulped for the second time during the meeting. Dr. Harper Randolph wouldn't stand for any leash, much less a short one.

CHAPTER NINE

Underground Great Wall
Urumqi, Xinjiang, China

Dr. Zeng and his wife took up residency in a small karez, sleeping among the young people who worked tirelessly to gather information. Within the larger cavern beneath the hospital, a war room of sorts was created for him to work. Information was received from around China, reviewed and cross-checked for accuracy, and then analyzed by Dr. Zeng. Another puzzling message had just come in from Lhasa although this time its encryption was more sophisticated than the first one.

Fangyu stood and retrieved his laptop off a box. He approached his uncle, who had been given his own desk, chair, and laptop computer. An enterprising young woman had even managed to hack into his office computer located on the fifth floor of the hospital above him.

Fangyu opened it and turned it around so his uncle could view the screen. "This is the new message we've received from Lhasa. I want you to see it for yourself and let me explain the encryption."

"Yes, please. It is mixed with gibberish."

"That is true, but their capabilities have improved. So you know, several of us have compared it to the first message to look for similarities, or common markers. We must be careful to disregard the government's own disinformation being spread across the social media platforms."

First, Fangyu showed his uncle a series of photographs from inside the People's Hospital. One video depicted a body left under a blanket outside the emergency ward entrance. Just inside the doors, a dead man was propped up on a wheelchair, head hanging down and face deathly pale.

The physician who took the video had covered his head with a surgeon's cap, a mask and dark sunglasses. He turned the camera to himself and spoke, his voice trembling with emotion and tears dripping below the sunglasses.

"I am scared for myself and my coworkers. We have the virus all around us, and on our backs, we have the legal and administrative power of the government."

He paused for a moment to look around the room where he was hiding, and then he continued. "I vow to continue my efforts to save patients, but I will also continue to provide the truth to anyone who will listen for as long as I am alive. Death doesn't scare me. Do you think I am afraid of the Communist Party?"

"Very powerful," commented Dr. Zeng. "How do you know this is the People's Hospital?"

Fangyu replied, "Our friends in Lhasa recognized the entrance. One of them is a nurse in the hospital. She has studied the portions of the man's face that are showing and cannot make an identification. However, she did say the room in which he was filming was not part of the hospital."

"How does she know this?" asked Dr. Zeng.

"The walls," responded Fangyu. He pointed to the screen. "Do you see the stainless steel? Our contacts say this does not exist in the People's Hospital."

"Where, then?"

"We don't know yet. We are looking for clues."

"Why don't you just ask him?"

"We don't wish to frighten him away, and for now, it is not necessary."

Dr. Zeng stood from his chair and wandered toward the chalkboard that was created by taking three partial sheets of plywood and painting them with chalkboard paint. The furnishings in the Underground Great Wall were almost always scraps and cast asides from above.

He studied the reported cases and pointed toward Lhasa. The numbers were disproportionately higher than Urumqi.

"The answers are here," he said as he circled Lhasa several times with his chalk.

"Then we should plan on going to Tibet," offered Fangyu.

"Not yet, nephew. We must learn more about this doctor who is willing to risk his life to provide us this information. We must determine if there is a connection between him and the helicopter pilot who died."

"Yes, Uncle. I will work on that personally."

Dr. Zeng appeared pensive, prompting his nephew to approach him and place his arm around the much shorter man's shoulders.

"Uncle, there is more to your concern. Am I correct?"

"This is only the beginning. Soon, the CDC will begin the cover-up, and that means doctors and nurses will be put at great risk. I must warn them."

"We are. Through our posts."

"It is not enough. I must explain in great detail what I know, and what my experience has been in the last week. Only then will the medical community understand they are at risk."

"I will help you. With the proper encryption, we can—"

"No!" Dr. Zeng was forceful in his outburst, drawing the attention of the citizen journalists working nearby. "I will not hide any longer. I must tell the truth as I know it, or I will be forever nailed on the pillar of shame."

CHAPTER TEN

Gold Palace Hotel
Fremont Street Experience
Downtown Las Vegas, Nevada

Harper and her team were getting antsy. It was after four o'clock that morning and almost an hour since she'd received the *cavalry is coming* text. She'd tried several times to call the person who'd sent her the message, but the result was always the same—a full voicemail box. Whoever it was, she lamented, needed to get better organized.

"What happens if we just throw open the doors and bum-rush out of here?" asked Becker as she strode toward the exit with her hands balled up in fists.

Harper was deep in thought, so Becker's question caught her off guard. "Bum-rush?"

"Yeah, you know. Plow right through those guys and make a run for the casino exits."

Harper chuckled. Becker had consumed the last of the Diet Cokes, her beverage of choice. They might have been diet, but they were not, however, caffeine-free.

"Are you gonna lead the way?"

Becker bowed up. "I'm not afraid. They're not going to shoot us."

"They might," one of the epidemiologists countered.

Becker stared at the doors separating them from captivity and perceived freedom. "Nah, they won't. Those guys don't wanna be here any more than we do. I say we go for it."

"No, Becker. Let's give the cavalry, whoever that might be, a chance to—"

Harper's statement was cut off by the sound of loud talking in the hallway. A hush came over the room, and everyone slowly walked toward the double doors to listen. Several voices could be heard, and then, after a moment in which they were raised, it became silent in the corridor.

Apprehension filled the group as they waited to see what was next. The knob turned on the doors and slowly opened. The burly National Guardsmen were replaced by an unlikely figure—Dr. Wolfgang Boychuck.

"You're the cavalry?" asked Harper with a smile on her face that stretched from ear to ear.

The Clark County medical examiner returned the smile. He glanced over his shoulder to locate the two guardsmen and then sneakily raised his right index finger to his lips, indicating that Harper should be silent. With a barely discernible whisper, he mouthed the words *trust me*.

Harper nodded her head in agreement and turned to her team. They all seemed to understand. Her eyes grew wide when several uniformed officers of the Las Vegas Metropolitan Police Department entered the room. They immediately fanned out to encircle the CDC personnel.

An LVMPD sergeant entered the room and took the floor. "Who is Dr. Harper Randolph?"

"I am." Harper kept it simple.

"Good. I have orders to bring you and your team into the DTAC for questioning," said the sergeant. DTAC was an acronym for the

LVPMD Downtown Area Command. "Now, you can come with us peacefully and bring your gear, or we can do this the hard way. We've got plenty of zip cuffs for everyone." He glanced at his officers, who held up the zip-tie handcuffs for everyone to see.

"Are we under arrest?" asked Harper.

"Not yet. You're wanted for questioning first. What happens next will be up to the bureau commander and the state attorney. Now, can we expect your cooperation?"

Dr. Boychuck had never averted his eyes from Harper's. He barely nodded his head, signaling for her to agree.

She didn't hesitate. "We'll cooperate. Everyone, please grab your belongings and follow these officers' instructions."

There were a few grumbles among the team, but most seemed content with being released from the stuffy conference room regardless of the method.

The police officers organized the group in a two-wide line and surrounded them as they were escorted out of the conference center into the hotel lobby. The *perp walk* drew the attention of the frantic hotel guests, momentarily distracting them from their own angst.

The police led Harper and Becker, followed by the rest of the team, to the VIP entrance they'd used so many times during their brief time at the Gold Palace. Once outside, a collective deep breath was taken by the epidemiologists. It had been a horrible all-night ordeal. They were also fraught with uncertainty. Harper had a direct relationship with Dr. Boychuck, so she was confident in what he'd instructed her to do. The others were dutifully following her lead.

Harper and Becker were placed in the back of a squad car by themselves while the rest of the team was loaded into white, unmarked vans. They both sat in silence as the caravan of law enforcement vehicles exited the Gold Palace. After a moment, the officer riding in the passenger seat spoke to the driver, a young officer who easily could've been a rookie.

"Take a left on Bridger."

"Why? It'll be easier to go down to—"

"We gotta make it look good. If they're paying attention, they'll wonder why we didn't head straight for LV Boulevard."

Harper and Becker looked at one another. *Why are they arguing about the route to this DTAC place? What has Dr. Boychuck gotten us into?*

Becker was about to ask, but Harper grabbed her left hand and gave it a squeeze. She shook her head vigorously from side to side.

The officer in the passenger seat continued his instructions. "Take a right on Third. The entrance is on Fourth, but it's one-way northbound."

They drove several blocks, and then the officer driving pointed to a wide intersection. "If we go left on Coolidge, the next left should bring us right to it."

Harper and Becker were looking around in all directions in an attempt to determine where the police were taking them. They turned again and passed the parking lot of a Mexican restaurant. The patrol car slowed as the driver checked his side mirror to confirm the rest of the caravan carrying the CDC personnel caught up.

He eased up to a tall concrete building stretching into the sky. An entrance to an underground garage appeared with two steel roll-up gates and several security cameras pointing in all directions.

Becker leaned into Harper. "This is an awfully tall jail."

Harper grimaced. "I don't think it's a jail. With all of the concrete, it looks like one, though."

The driver pulled the patrol car up to the gate and honked his horn twice. Suddenly, the steel gates clanked as they sprang to life, slowly rolling up into a large curl above the entrance. The officers quickly pulled in and to the end of the ramp, followed by the vans. Seconds later, they exited the car and opened the doors for Harper and Becker.

Harper was the first to emerge, and she allowed her eyes to

adjust to the dim fluorescent light. An unmistakable silhouette appeared out of the shadows.

"*Mi casa, su casa*," Dr. Boychuck announced. "Welcome to Soho Lofts."

CHAPTER ELEVEN

Soho Lofts
South Las Vegas Blvd. and East Charleston Blvd.
Las Vegas, Nevada

It took two trips for Dr. Wolfgang Boychuck to lead Harper and the rest of the virus hunters team up the freight elevator to the fifteenth floor of Soho Lofts. Located in the heart of the Arts District of Las Vegas, this sixteen-story solid concrete structure rose two hundred twenty feet above Las Vegas Boulevard and was topped with a rooftop swimming pool. The interior hallways were decorated in elegant and modern art deco finishes befitting the glamour of Sin City.

Dr. Boychuck had admonished everyone to stay quiet as they made their way to his top-floor, two-story penthouse unit. Most of his neighbors were well-known gamblers such as Archie Karas, famously known for *The Run*, a winning streak in which he turned fifty dollars into forty million during the nineties, as well as the usual late-night partiers. Several of the penthouse units were owned by entertainers, including a member of the Blue Man Group, and comedian Terry Fator, who kept guests of the Mirage in stitches.

The weary epidemiologists moved slowly down the dimly lit hallway to the end of the building. They marveled at the minimalist-style décor. Once they entered Dr. Boychuck's loft, their mouths fell open as they took in the view. His space was eye level to the iconic Stratosphere, now known as the Strat. The floor-to-ceiling windows also allowed a never-ending view of the famed Las Vegas Strip. The Strat was the tallest freestanding observation tower in America. It also contained hotel rooms, a restaurant, and perched atop the structure were amusement thrill rides that slung adrenaline junkies out and over the edge at high speeds.

"This is incredible!" exclaimed one of the epidemiologists.

Several others commented on the magnificent view as they dropped their gear and immediately wandered to the windows overlooking the Strip.

Becker stood next to Harper and looked around Dr. Boychuck's loft. "What a mess. Does he really live like this?"

Throughout the open loft, furniture was haphazardly arranged to create seating areas. Multiple dining tables were spread about, all of which contained books, journals, file folders, and the occasional jar full of formaldehyde-soaked critters.

Harper chuckled. "You should see his office. This is just a larger version of it."

"Well, it makes me nervous," mumbled Becker as she walked to the window to take in the view.

Harper looked around for their host. He emerged from the front door, juggling four boxes of donuts just delivered by Real Donuts #1, a Las Vegas favorite, in one arm and a large box of brewed coffee in the other. She rushed to assist.

"Dr. Boychuck, let me help you."

"Yes. Yes. Yes. Please."

He waddled toward the kitchen island and was about to drop the donuts when Harper took the boxes from him. He immediately smiled and nodded his appreciation.

"Young lady, since we are practically living together now, please call me Woolie. All my friends do."

"Wolfie?" Harper thought she misunderstood him. She was exhausted. It had been a long, eventful night.

"No, Woolie," he said with a smile as he spread the donut boxes out and began pulling mismatched coffee mugs out of cupboards, the dishwasher, and from the sink full of dirty dishes. He washed them out and set them next to the box of hot coffee.

Harper glanced toward Becker, who stood in the middle of the loft with her arms folded and a disapproving look. Harper was relieved to notice that the windows were solid-paned glass and not capable of being opened for fear Becker might try to escape Woolie Boychuck's pandemonium penthouse.

Dr. Boychuck continued. "Many people logically presume a nickname associated with Wolfgang would become Wolfie. That's not the case. I was born in Munich, Germany, and emigrated to America when I was a young child. When I was growing up, or at least when I began to sprout facial hair, I rarely shaved. Soon, the beard and the ponytail became a part of my persona. Hence, the name Woolie." He pulled on the gray ponytail as he explained.

Harper took a deep breath and exhaled. "Well, Woolie, since we're dropping the formalities, please call me Harper. I don't know how you did it, but all I can say is thank you. If you'll pardon the pun, you and your friends certainly pulled the wool over those soldiers' eyes."

"Yes! Yes! Yes!" he exclaimed as he roared in laughter. "We most certainly did, didn't we? Well, I did have some help."

"Hey! Is that where they filmed *Pawn Stars?*" asked one of the epidemiologists to no one in particular.

Dr. Boychuck grabbed a custard-filled donut and wandered toward the gathering of epidemiologists by the window.

"Yes. Yes. Yes." He joined the group and he directed their attention to the Gold and Silver Pawn Shop located on Charleston Boulevard just below the Soho Lofts. He took a moment to point out other sights of interest, ranging from the famed hotels of the Las Vegas Strip to Sunrise Mountain, where the sun was, in fact, beginning to rise.

Becker skipped the nickel tour in search of a donut. She perused the options and chose a glazed donut. She liked to keep it simple, in stark contrast to her host. She took an oversized bite and locked eyes with her boss. "Why does he stutter like that?"

Harper appeared bewildered by her statement and then realized she'd never had a chance to tell Becker about Dr. Boychuck's idiosyncrasies. For the moment, there was too much to tell, especially after what the young epidemiologist had been through that night.

Harper snagged a pink-frosted donut with brightly colored sprinkles. "He's not stuttering. He just feels the need, um, you know, to reiterate."

Becker glanced over at the rest of the group. She leaned into Harper to whisper, "Dr. Randolph, he has body parts and animals in here. Is he, like, bat-shit crazy?"

Harper stifled a laugh. She was beginning to get the sense Becker disapproved of the cavalry who'd rescued them from confinement.

"Okay. Listen, he's a little eccentric. But—"

Becker cut her off. With a mouth full of donut, she asked, "Ya think?" A few crumbs dropped on her shirt and hit the smooth, polished concrete floor. She began to reach down to retrieve them, and then she looked around. She stood, shook her head in a why-bother reaction, and cocked her head to stare at her boss.

"Trust me. He's just a little different. That said, he is an accomplished pathologist and has an intuitiveness about him that I can't put my finger on."

Becker rolled her eyes, shoved the remainder of the donut in her mouth, and then adopted a *yogi-namaste* tone of voice. She placed her palms together in front of her chest. "He is one with the dead."

Harper laughed and then said, "Don't laugh. He really is. That guy's forgotten more about dead bodies than most pathologists have experienced."

"If you say so," said Becker.

"Do you want coffee?" asked Harper.

"Duh!" she replied.

Dr. Boychuck returned to the kitchen area with the group, who immediately ravaged the Real Donut offerings. After some small talk between them, Dr. Boychuck directed everyone to where they could get a little sleep. All but Harper had crashed when she pulled out her phone to contact Joe.

Harper: Hi there! We've been rescued.

Joe: I heard.

He did? How does he always know these things? That explains why he hasn't checked up on me. He already knew I was safe.

Harper decided to tease her husband. Joe had enjoyed Las Vegas the few times he'd been out there.

Harper: I'm stuck in horrible conditions. They only feed me donuts and coffee. This is all I can see through my captor's window.

Harper took a picture of the view and sent it to him via text message.

Joe: That's incredible. So, have you seen Elvis?

Harper: LOL. No time for him or his blue suede shoes. I don't think this is over yet.

Joe: You won't be bothered.

Just as that message came through, three loud thumps at the door reverberated through the loft.

Harper: Gotta go. Love you!

CHAPTER TWELVE

Soho Lofts
South Las Vegas Blvd. and East Charleston Blvd.
Las Vegas, Nevada

The group of epidemiologists had barely dozed off. Still on edge from the ordeal at the Gold Palace, most jumped to their feet and stared at the front door, full of apprehension. Dr. Boychuck emerged from his study, a guest bedroom that had been filled with mementos and journals much like his medical examiner's office was. He didn't say a word as he pushed by a couple of the sleepy-eyed CDC personnel. Nodding his head repeatedly, he simply held up his hands, indicating that there was nothing to worry about.

Harper moved quickly from the other side of the loft to join him in the center of the sprawling open space. If there was going to be a problem with either law enforcement or the National Guard, she intended to take the hit for her team.

Dr. Boychuck leaned into the peephole and observed the hallway. He began nodding his head and smiling. He opened the door, and an elderly woman strode through the doorway with confidence. Harper presumed that she was in her mid to late eighties, but didn't look a day over sixty.

"Good morning, all!" she cheerily announced as she squeezed Dr. Boychuck's cheek. "I trust Woolie is treating you with a better dose of Vegas hospitality than you received at the Palace."

"Yes. Yes. Yes," Dr. Boychuck was quick to respond. "They've been fed our finest donuts and coffee. Most were sleeping, Mrs. Mayor."

Mayor Carol Ann Silverman, affectionately known as *Mrs. Mayor*, had become mayor of Las Vegas as part of a political dynasty that dated back decades. Her husband had been the mayor until he turned eighty and, in a landslide, his wife was elected to office to take his place.

The two enjoyed an interesting relationship since she'd become mayor. Her husband liked to refer to himself as part-time queen consort and full-time ambassador for the city. On the day he turned over the reins of the city to his wife, he bragged how he'd redesigned the space with a balcony to enjoy a martini and cigar after a hard workday.

Her response was simple. *You never worked here.*

The daily banter between the two over the last decade was legendary. She often referred to him as a big buffoon, a phony, a narcissist and a snake-charmer in one breath followed by brilliant in another. Despite their gentle ribbing of one another, they'd enjoyed a great working relationship, promoting the City of Las Vegas while shepherding it through some difficult financial times following the 2008 real estate market collapse and the aftermath of the COVID-19 pandemic.

She smiled, and in a grandmotherly way, she brushed the fingers on both of her hands as if to tell the youngsters to go back to what they were doing.

"I'm sorry to interrupt your slumber," she apologized.

Dr. Boychuck reassured her, "Mrs. Mayor, I haven't yet informed our guests that you are the reason they were rescued from the evil clutches of the governor's henchmen. Had you not come up with this brilliant strategy to *arrest* these fine people, they'd still be locked in that stuffy hotel." Dr. Boychuck used his fingers to place the word *arrest* in air quotes.

"Say nothing of it, Woolie. When you called and explained what had happened, I was glad to help."

She was impeccably dressed in a pricey blue Ann Taylor suit. She tugged at the jacket as she surveyed the team. "Who is Dr. Randolph?"

"I am, um, Mrs. Mayor. Is it okay for me to—"

"Yes, dear. Everyone does. Even my enemies. Well, they're not really enemies. There are those around here who think they can run this city better than our family has over the last thirty years. They just refer to me with a little more snark than my friends."

"I understand," added Harper without disclosing her husband's job.

"One thing they all understand, however, is this. If our fair city is threatened by a serial killer, or a sharknado, or the Yellowstone volcano, my first concern is for our visitors and those who rely upon tourism dollars. And make no mistake, that stupid antic pulled by our so-called governor last night was not helpful to anyone. It was purely a political stunt orchestrated by the governor's puppeteer."

Harper looked around to determine if the group was listening to the exchange. Only Becker was remotely aware of her encounter with the president on Air Force One.

"Mrs. Mayor, I have my theories as well."

She provided Harper a knowing wink and a smile. "Well, don't you worry your little head about it, young lady. Things are about to change, but I need to have a conversation with you about what's happening on Fremont Street. Are you up for a chat?"

Harper looked around for Becker.

"You need Starbucks, don't you?" She was standing behind Harper and startled her with her question.

Harper swung around. "There you are."

"I'll get it for you."

Dr. Boychuck glanced at his watch and approached Becker. The two were standing toe-to-toe for the first time.

"It's seven o'clock, young lady."

"Okay. Starbucks is open, right? Isn't this the city that never sleeps?"

"Yes. Yes. Yes. Very good. It is not New York City. However, there is no need for you to go. I will have the concierge make the arrangements."

Becker scowled. "Well, la-di-da."

The two faced off for several awkward seconds before Dr. Boychuck responded, "If you would like to make a list of everyone's drinks, I will have them brought up to us. It appears everyone is awake again." In fact, the entire team was milling about the loft, viewing Dr. Boychuck's artifacts, all of which had a story behind them.

"Okay, Dr. Boychuck. You've got a deal."

"Woolie, please."

"Woolie what?"

"Please call me Woolie."

Becker studied the medical examiner's face in an effort to ascertain his intentions. She'd need more time to render an opinion of Dr. Wolfgang Boychuck. She retrieved her phone and began gathering everyone's order.

While she did, Dr. Boychuck escorted Harper and Mrs. Mayor into his study and pulled shut the frosted glass doors that hung on a door track system above the opening. He tried to excuse himself from the room, but the mayor insisted he remain. The three of them were now alone and free to talk.

Harper immediately noticed a change in her demeanor, and it was completely opposite her jovial mood in front of the others. Harper sat in a chair offered by Dr. Boychuck. She gripped the arms until her knuckles were white as if she were bracing for an interrogation. Mrs. Mayor paced the floor and looked out the window toward Las Vegas Boulevard.

The mayor began first. Without turning, she said, "We're about to have a very candid conversation."

CHAPTER THIRTEEN

Soho Lofts
South Las Vegas Blvd. and East Charleston Blvd.
Las Vegas, Nevada

Mrs. Mayor had the floor. She was no longer the baby-kissing, one-line-joking jovial mayor pandering for votes. She'd turned into a battle-tested politician who was ready to vent about what had happened at the Fremont Street Experience without her knowledge or consent.

"Before we get to your conversation with the president and the truth about this supposed outbreak, let me tell you where we are on this thing," she began while she paced the floor. To be sure, she would've preferred to be in the living area, where she had more space to place her feet. Dr. Boychuck's study resembled one of the mini-warehouse units where the contents about to be auctioned off on a reality television show.

He seemed to take the hint, so he scampered about, shoving stacks of books and piles of journals under his desk. She waved her hand, indicating he should stop.

"I'm sorry, Mrs. Mayor. I really should get better organized."

She laughed. "Then you wouldn't be quite so charming, Woolie." It was obvious to Harper the two admired one another.

Mrs. Mayor sighed. It seemed to relieve some tension. "My husband, the pompous windbag of a former lawyer, used to rely upon Woolie heavily. Back in the day, as they say."

"Yes. Yes. Yes."

Mrs. Mayor laughed and looked to Harper. "Agreeable, isn't he?"

"Yes, ma'am." Harper was beginning to like Las Vegas. The city was full of interesting characters, it seemed.

"Dr. Randolph, I'm aware your jet was rerouted to McCarran. I'm also aware you were waylaid by the Secret Service."

"How did you—?"

She waved her arm. "This is my town. I know everything. Almost."

"Mrs. Mayor, I didn't say anything to the president that would warrant this. In fact, it was just the opposite. Even my boss had a—"

The elderly woman waved her arm and dismissed Harper's statement. "I know. I had a conversation with our governor last night as soon as I received word of what was happening. He was my first call. I swear, he was in his cups."

Harper laughed. It was a phrase Ma and Mimi used often when referring to one of their acquaintances who'd had consumed too much alcohol.

The mayor continued. "Plus, he was swearing repeatedly in an attempt to intimidate me. Woolie knows that doesn't work. It's another sign of his stupidity."

Harper asked, "Did he say that his decision to quarantine downtown was because of me?"

"Not specifically. Frankly, the more he talked, the more he drank. I could hear him on the phone. Plus, he's overweight. He was breathing heavily as if a half-gallon of scotch was resting on his belly. His lips got loose, eventually."

"So, he admitted there was no immediate cause to call in the National Guard," said Harper.

"Yes and no, not that it matters at this point. The bottom line is he knows he might have to pull back. The local media is losing its mind over this. The *Sun* and the *Review Journal* had camped out at my house before I hung up the phone with the governor. News networks have been staking out my office all night. It's kind of funny, actually. Nobody knows I'm here, and in a way, it's a comforting feeling."

A light tapping at the glass doors interrupted the conversation, and Becker poked her head in. "I've got your drinks and cake pops for everyone, if you'd like."

Dr. Boychuck's tired eyes lit up like a child's. "Yes. Yes. Yes. The cake pops are to die for." The lollipop-style cake on a stick was a Starbucks staple on their menu.

Becker distributed the drinks and provided Dr. Boychuck his chocolate cake pop with baby blue icing. He sat down and enjoyed it while the two women talked.

Mrs. Mayor sipped on her skinny vanilla latte as she leaned forward on his desk and asked, "I need to know. Am I making a mistake lifting this quarantine? Am I at risk of unleashing a disease like that coronavirus on my city? That almost destroyed our economy."

Harper reached out to retrieve a dirt-scuffed baseball bearing the old Las Vegas 51s logo. The minor league team had changed its name to the Aviators when they became a major league franchise a few years prior after the Miami Marlins fled their tepid fan base.

"Mrs. Mayor, we're barely through the first inning of a nine-inning baseball game. We have so many unanswered questions about this unknown virus. I mean, will a self-quarantine or lockdown order be appropriate at some point? Yes. But last night's action only served to make our job more difficult. Now anyone who happened to be on Fremont Street, not just the Gold Palace, will get a tickle in their throat. Or perhaps they'll get flushed. Or even feel sleepy from normal fatigue. They'll be flooding your emergency rooms out of fear."

"It's already happening," the mayor added. "Just before I arrived here, I received a call from our Emergency Operations Center.

Ambulances can't keep up with the false alarm calls. The hospitals have asked for police security to prevent overcrowding at their emergency rooms and admissions desks."

Dr. Boychuck interrupted. "Yes. Yes. Yes. They will never forget 2020."

"Right," added the mayor. "I can't blame them, which is why I'm asking you these questions. Do I need to put protective measures in place to avoid a repeat of COVID-19?"

Harper thought for a moment. This was not her call to make without speaking to Dr. Reitherman, especially at this early juncture. "I think you should have your first responders and medical facilities prepared to take on new cases. I don't believe last night's actions were necessary. And, as I said, it will make our jobs more difficult now. The CDC's resources don't allow for chasing down thousands of leads. Besides that, it was counterproductive. People have scattered all around Clark County and the country at this point."

The mayor continued her questioning. "These first cases. The four gentlemen from China. Did they bring the disease over here with them? I mean, this is a China virus like COVID, right?"

"I won't know for sure until I identify patient zero. If I can identify the source, the first patient, then we can establish control and prevention protocols."

"Well, is somebody in the process of doing that?"

Harper hesitated. The mayor, like other political leaders, wouldn't accept *not yet* as an answer for much longer. Impatience would soon turn into demands.

"It requires meticulous and arduous detective work. We have to go from case to case to establish where the disease made its first appearance. I believe the answer lies in China. Not just because so many diseases begin there, but because these four men, our first known victims to the disease, traveled from there together."

Mrs. Mayor leaned back in the chair. "What do the Chinese say?"

"Nothing. The CDC has reached out to the World Health

Organization and also the Chinese version of the CDC. They deny any knowledge of the disease."

The mayor furrowed her brow and leaned with both elbows on the desk. She pointed a wrinkled, bony finger toward Harper. "You don't believe them, do you?"

"No, ma'am, I don't. For one thing, Asia and China, in particular, are hotspots for novel diseases. It's not a big mystery as to why. They have large, concentrated population centers. Their citizens are used to being in close contact with a wide variety of animal species, and let's face it, at least in some areas, their hygiene is not on par with Western nations."

"They've blocked your inquiries?" she asked.

"Yes, thus far. China is notorious for its misinformation, secrecy, and, of course, censorship. Dissidents are dealt with swiftly and harshly. It's a communist state in which secrecy is assured through government threats. Information is manipulated by state-run media."

"If they won't cooperate, how will you determine the origin of this disease?" she asked.

Harper closed her eyes and provided the response she'd given others. "All I can say is the answers are in China."

CHAPTER FOURTEEN

Soho Lofts
South Las Vegas Blvd. and East Charleston Blvd.
Las Vegas, Nevada

Harper was prepared to answer as many questions as the mayor asked, but she'd already received two phone calls, a voicemail, and half a dozen text messages from Dr. Reitherman. Her cell phone kept buzzing in the rear pocket of her jeans; however neither the eightyish mayor nor Dr. Boychuck, whom she presumed to be in his late sixties, seemed to notice.

Finally, after yet another text message, this time from Becker, Harper stood and excused herself under the pretense she needed to use the restroom. She slowly shut the doors behind her and sought out Becker, who was huddled around the television with the rest of the CDC team.

"What's happening?" asked Harper.

"Come here," replied Becker. "This is a news feed from LA."

A local Las Vegas station was simulcasting breaking news from KTLA, Channel 5, in Los Angeles. The chyron indicated they were interviewing LA County Department of Public Health director Dr. Barbara Chandler.

"*Dr. Chandler, what can you tell us about this patient?*" asked the reporter, who was out of the camera's view.

"*The person who died was a woman, aged sixty-seven, who had recently traveled extensively throughout Asia. Passport records indicate she'd visited Kathmandu, Nepal; Hong Kong; and Taipei before returning to Los Angeles.*"

The reporter interrupted her. "*Are you able to release her name? Is she an American?*"

"*Her identity is being withheld pending notification of family. I can confirm she is an American.*"

"*Do you believe this case is related to the mysterious disease outbreak in Las Vegas in recent days?*"

Dr. Chandler shook her head and then shrugged. "*It's way too early to make that determination. For one thing, unless she left LAX directly for Las Vegas and then immediately returned within hours, that's highly unlikely. From our interviews with her family, she'd felt ill on the twelve-hour flight.*"

"*Which airline?*"

"*EVA Air, I believe.*"

"*Dr. Chandler, what is it about this woman's death that causes you concern? I mean, if there is no connection to the Las Vegas patients, why would you—?*"

The public health official cut her off. "*Her symptoms are very similar to those reported by the Clark County medical examiner. Therefore, I can't rule it out.*"

The reporter persisted. "*Is there any indication that the family members, or anyone she came in contact with during her travels back to the U.S., have become ill?*"

"*We're conducting our own interviews and contact tracing, but the regional office of the CDC in Los Angeles County has been notified as well. Thank you very much.*"

Dr. Chandler walked away from the interview and immediately

approached a representative of the Los Angeles mayor's office. The reporter turned to the camera.

"Well, there you have it. LA may have its first case of this mysterious infectious disease that appeared in Las Vegas initially and somehow, inexplicably, infected this traveler who spent the last month or so in Asia. Back to you."

Harper shook her head and addressed the group. "This was my concern. The local cases have everyone spooked. There is no way to confirm that this woman died of the same virus as our four men from China. Despite the lack of information, the media will start to tie every mysterious death to the disease."

"Do we need to send part of our people to LA?" asked Becker.

"No, that's Reitherman's call," replied Harper. Then she scowled. "Aw, shit. I forgot to call him."

She walked away from the group and called him without checking her text messages or voicemails first.

When he answered, he was salty. "Harper, where have you been?"

"I'm so sorry, sir. I was cornered by the mayor, and she was demanding answers and advice."

"Okay, fine. But you have to keep your phone on. We have a situation. Well, multiple situations, actually."

"I know. I just caught a glimpse of a news report from LA."

He exhaled into the phone. "Add Seattle and Dallas to your list. Seoul and Tokyo, too."

"Gee, are they sure? How can they possibly connect the dots to these patients already?"

"All of a sudden the director-general of the WHO is driving the frenzy. He's afraid to catch the kind of heat his predecessor did during the COVID pandemic."

"Can't blame him there. However, a knee-jerk reaction can be just as problematic."

"There's more," said Dr. Reitherman. "China has clammed up, and they've expelled our personnel from their CDC complex in Beijing."

"They can't do that!" exclaimed Harper. "That was part of the deal for their malfeasance during COVID. It was the least they could do since we couldn't wrangle any reparations out of them."

"I can't disagree, but remember, they're a communist country. They do anything they damn well please."

Harper looked for Becker and got her attention. As soon as she was finished talking with Dr. Reitherman, she wanted to get the troops to work.

"We'll step it up on our end." She began to explain her plans for the day. "Our team's tired, but they're motivated."

There was a brief silence on the other side of the call. Finally, Dr. Reitherman spoke up. "About that. You're not gonna like this."

"Come on, Dr. Reitherman," Harper immediately began to protest what she anticipated was coming. "I just got back here. I'm not a yo-yo."

"Harper, you know how these things are. In the early stages, the entire situation is very fluid."

"Yes." Her dejection was obvious.

"Just trust me on this. Bring Dr. Becker with you. The jet's ready for you."

PART II

WHO IS PATIENT ZERO?

No one wants to be the Patient Zero of their village. Just because you are the first to be diagnosed doesn't mean you started the epidemic.
~ Professor Robert M. Grant, MD

CHAPTER FIFTEEN

CDC Headquarters
Atlanta, Georgia

Within hours of her arrival at her home late last night, several vehicles full of the press managed to follow a news van through her community's gated entry. Soon, others followed suit, resulting in camera trucks and reporters stalking her house, looking for comment. After calling the police, they were removed from the neighborhood and camped outside the gated entry. Much to her chagrin, their backups were waiting for her at the CDC.

Harper shoved her way through the media scrum that blocked her access to the entrance of the main building at the CDC's Roybal campus.

"Dr. Harper! Dr. Harper!"

"Are you denying that you suggested the quarantine of Las Vegas?"

"Did you speak with the governor directly?"

"Are you being reassigned?"

"How is this affecting your husband on Capitol Hill?"

Damn! That last question stung the most. Harper considered herself levelheaded with nerves of steel. Some considered her to be cold. Aloof. Unapproachable. Even too perfect. She'd heard the whispers before. She always sloughed off those criticisms and refused to carry a chip on her shoulder for who she was. They didn't know what she'd been through as a child.

What was important to her, above all else, was her relationship with her husband. She thought she could handle the political games played by Joe's adversaries. She just had no idea how dirty they could be.

Harper took a deep breath and set her jaw. With a determined look on her face, she soldiered through the crowd, ignoring the questions and comments laced with innuendo. She refused to make eye contact with the vultures wishing to pick at her damaged body.

Haters are gonna hate, she reminded herself.

Once she reached the entry doors, armed security personnel stepped forward to stop the rush of bodies attempting to follow her inside. She made a mental note to use a different entrance the next day. Unbeknownst to her, that wouldn't be an issue.

She'd enjoyed the few hours at home that morning. Sleeping in her own bed rather than the CDC Learjet did wonders for her energy levels. Plus, Dr. Dog needed her mommy, and Miss Sally missed fixing a meal for her adopted family. Most of all, she enjoyed lying in bed that night, talking with Joe about everything. He was always a voice of reason and sanity. The only thing that was missing from their conversation was the insane course of action she was intent upon pursuing. That conversation would come, but first she needed to determine if it would be approved by her boss.

Her first stop was Becker's office. In the morning, Dr. Elizabeth Becker became Lizzie Becker—the human dynamo. Harper could never put her finger on what made the young epidemiologist tick. When the two first began working together, she'd noticed the piles of empty Diet Coke cans that accumulated in Becker's wastebasket. Harper surmised it was the caffeine.

Then she noticed there were days when Becker laid off the Diet Cokes, yet her enthusiasm for the day remained high. Harper seriously contemplated a scientific study to determine if Becker's zest for her job, and life in general, could be bottled and sold on Amazon. Perhaps in an atomizer as a perfume or cologne.

"Good morning, Dr. Randolph! Did you see the reporters outside? You're famous!"

Harper didn't share in her exuberance. "Happy, happy. Joy, joy."

"Oh, come on. Any press is good press. When this is all over and you save the day, America will forever remember the name—Dr. Harper Randolph." Becker motioned with her hands to design an imaginary sign in midair.

Harper smiled. Becker had lifted her spirits once again. "Well, hopefully Reitherman doesn't fire me before *Good Morning America* calls for an interview."

Becker scowled and cocked her head. "How did you know?"

Harper became genuinely concerned. "What have you heard? Is he gonna fire me? Aw, shit, Becker. I had no idea—"

"No. Not that. A producer from *Good Morning America* called the communications director this morning. They want you to appear on camera during their last segment."

Harper shook her head. "Not gonna happen. I've done enough damage already."

"Suit yourself. Any pub is good pub. I'll pass it on." She held up two hands and presented stacks of phone messages to Harper.

"What are these?"

Becker gestured as she spoke. "Right hand is from the LA public health officials, Seattle DPH, our counterparts in Austria, and several WHO epis."

Harper spread them apart with her thumb to look at the names. Then, holding up her left hand, she asked, "And these?"

"Media."

Harper smiled and walked around Becker's desk. She tossed the media inquiries in the wastebasket on top of the pile of empty Diet Coke cans.

"Thanks, Becker. I need to see Dr. Reitherman first thing. Have you seen him?"

"The Bergermeister has already been looking for you," she replied, using her nickname for the director.

"What's his mood like?" asked Harper.

Becker thought for a moment, searching her expansive, although somewhat unusual, mental thesaurus. "Engrossed."

Harper chuckled and waved as she headed out the door. "Well, alrighty then."

She made a beeline for her office to avoid idle chitchat with any of the CDC personnel. She had a busy day and didn't need any distractions. She had to stay focused, although not *engrossed*, as Becker had suggested Dr. Reitherman was. Her proposal required one heckuva convincing argument, and she was ready to start the discussion.

However, there was one phone call she wanted to make first. Once in her office, she shut the door and dropped her bag in a chair. She spread the phone messages out on her desk and retrieved the one from an official with the Department of Health within the Austrian Ministry of Labor, Social Affairs, Health, and Consumer Protection. Somehow, the Austrians felt lumping all of these diverse agencies under one made sense.

Harper didn't speak German other than a few phrases. Hopefully, she could find her way through to the proper party. She dialed the international number and waited.

The receptionist answered the phone. "*Guten Tag. Gesundheitamt. Wie kann ich dir helfen?*"

Harper thought fast. She understood good afternoon and the word for help. *Gesundheit* was universally known as a word for health.

"Um, yes. *Ja, Herr Spahn, bitte. Ich bin Dr. Harper Randolph auf CDC America.*"

She cringed as she crossed her fingers and hoped that came out right.

The receptionist, obviously bilingual, switched languages to accommodate Harper. "Good afternoon, Dr. Randolph."

Oh, thank God! Harper smiled as she looked upward. "Good, thank you. I am returning his phone call."

"Yes. *Doktor Spahn* was hoping to receive your call today. *Einen moment, bitte.*"

Harper searched her desk drawers for a notepad and pen. As much as she enjoyed working in the field, it took her a few hours to become reacquainted with her office when she returned.

"Dr. Randolph, thank you for your prompt call. I am Herman Spahn, associate director of Health. I am told by Dr. Reitherman that you are the lead epidemiologist on the Las Vegas outbreak."

I hope so, but that's subject to change.

"Yes, I am. How may I help you?"

"After reading the news reports and the alerts issued by World Health, I revisited a mysterious death brought to my attention a week ago. Officially, the cause of death was ruled as pneumonia, but the pathology is odd."

"How so?" asked Harper.

"The patient was male and in his mid-thirties. He was in excellent health. In fact, he was a member of the Austrian Olympic ski team."

Harper was intrigued. "Did he have any other medical diseases, such as asthma, diabetes, or undiagnosed chronic obstructive pulmonary disease?" Many knew this respiratory illness by its acronym—COPD.

"No. I have reviewed the notes from his initial autopsy and even ordered a second one to confirm. He was a nonsmoker, nondrinker and had no indications of a weakened immune system."

Harper cradled the phone between her cheek and shoulder. She was furiously making notes and then asked the doctor to share the results of the autopsy with the CDC.

While she was thinking, Dr. Spahn continued. "This is a heartbreaking case for other reasons. His wife recently died in a tragic accident while climbing Mount Everest. Their story is surreal. This gentleman was left behind at the base camp when his wife made the climb. He'd become ill with flu-like symptoms, and the medical team in Nepal refused to allow him access to the mountain. Fate took his life a week later."

Harper leaned back in her chair. She stared at her notes and then asked, "Have you investigated their contacts since his return to Austria?"

"Yes, it was quite simple, actually. He and his wife live together with her parents in a small village north of Vienna."

"Did the parents get sick? How old are they?"

Dr. Spahn paused. Harper could hear him thumbing through notes or a file folder. "*Ja*. They did become sick with flu-like symptoms and were admitted to *Wilhelminenspital* for treatment. They recovered without further complications."

"Their ages?" asked Harper.

He paused again and then replied, "Both are seventy-four years old."

After gaining his permission to have the entire family's medical records sent to the CDC and asking about the wife's body who died on Mount Everest, Harper thanked Dr. Spahn. After disconnecting the call, she immediately sent a text message to summon Becker.

This is how these things go, Harper thought to herself. *Seemingly unrelated deaths around the world suddenly get connected by a common element—a virus.*

CHAPTER SIXTEEN

CDC Headquarters
Atlanta, Georgia

Dr. Reitherman had immediately placed Harper at ease once they dispensed with the *welcome home* pleasantries. He'd successfully planted the seed with his superiors, the top echelon of the CDC, that the governor of Nevada was simply a useful pawn in some larger political scheme orchestrated by the president. There was no love lost between the CDC and the current administration, which had sought to drastically cut their budget, making Dr. Reitherman's job somewhat easier.

"With that said, we need you to lie low for a little while unless you enjoy battling the media every day," he suggested.

"You heard about that?" asked Harper.

"Security informed me. I can get you a detail until this blows over, if you'd like."

Harper shook her head and declined. "I'll be fine."

"We're moving toward a whole new phase of our investigation with more possible cases revealing themselves. We both remember the early days of the COVID pandemic. Once it took hold, there were massive disruptions to our social fabric in terms of day-to-day activities. Nobody wants a repeat of those two years."

Harper agreed. "It was the most daunting virus that the world had contended with since the Spanish flu. HIV, SARS, and Ebola were nothing in comparison to COVID. The problem, sir, is that we're just starting our investigation. We don't have near enough facts to identify the disease much less talk about treatment protocols or vaccines. Unlike our experience a decade ago, nobody at the CDC is prepared to jump out there with predictions or conclusions, having only part of the picture."

"What's your gut tell you?"

Harper took a deep breath. "In many respects, the virus behaves like influenza or other respiratory viruses. Over time, humans were exposed to influenza and built up an immunity. Oddly, this virus seems to result in the death of some, but not necessarily all it comes in contact with."

"Are we talking about the usual patient types? Those with preexisting conditions?"

"I don't think I can say that definitively. The four Chinese men in Las Vegas were the picture of health. The young woman who came in contact with them was as well. I've received notification of a similar, unconfirmed case in Austria. The deceased was an Olympian, for Pete's sake." She grimaced and then continued. "Yet, both in Vegas and Austria, the infected patients came in contact with elderly persons who became ill but didn't succumb to the disease."

"That's odd," interjected Dr. Reitherman.

"Yes, sir, but it drives home my point. We've only just begun to gather data."

Dr. Reitherman studied Harper and then leaned forward. "I get the sense you are holding back something or you're going somewhere with your comments. Spit it out, Harper."

"Have you noticed who has been noticeably quiet about all of this?" she asked rhetorically.

"Yeah, the same people who just kicked our personnel out of

their CDC in violation of the UN-negotiated agreement following COVID-19."

"Sir, as is often the case, all of our leads point to China. We've got to either force their cooperation or conduct our own investigation there."

Dr. Reitherman laughed. "Well, as we all know, nobody forces the Chinese to do anything. It's very much a one-way street with them. We have our epidemiologists holed up in the American embassy in Beijing, awaiting my instructions. However, I don't think they're capable of wandering around the country in search of patient zero. They don't have field experience."

"I do."

Harper's response was blunt and to the point. It wasn't necessary for her to ask the question. Two simple words succinctly delivered her proposal.

"I know what you're thinking and the answer is no. First off, I need you here. Second, we need you to lie low. Third, um, I'm sure, given time, I can think of third through seventy-seventh."

Harper smiled. "See, you know I am right. You don't need me here. You have an entire building of capable epidemiologists plus Becker, who's privy to everything I know. Second, how much lower can I lie than in the middle of Communist China."

"Joe won't allow it."

Aw, shit! He pulled the husband card.

"Joe and I have an agreement. I don't tell him how to do his job, and he doesn't interfere with mine. It's worked well."

"Have you suggested this idea to him?" he asked.

"Um, no." Harper was defensive. "But it wasn't necessary until I spoke with you first. Come on, Dr. Reitherman. We need answers to avoid falling behind in controlling this sucker. I'm very good at this."

"The best, but China is different from Africa or even Syria. Do I need to remind you how dangerous those two places were?"

"True, they're different from China. Those places are lawless.

You know, people driving in Jeeps through jungles and sand dunes while firing machine guns at me."

Dr. Reitherman laughed. "Thanks for reminding me. You're never going back to either one of those places, either."

"What? Never mind that. China is different. They don't gun people down in the street."

"Do you remember Tiananmen Square? The tank?"

"Yes, and that was decades ago. Plus, they didn't blast the guy, now did they?"

Dr. Reitherman was losing the argument. He thought for a moment, and Harper sat back in her chair, hoping to gain his approval. For an awkward minute, nothing was said between them. Then Dr. Reitherman pressed on his telephone and buzzed his secretary.

"Yes, sir?"

"Try to get me Congressman Joe Mills on the phone."

"Wait! You can't call Joe. He'll blow a gasket."

"No, he won't. He'll be reasonable, logical, and—"

"On your side." Harper cut off his sentence. She slouched in the chair, dejected.

CHAPTER SEVENTEEN

CDC Headquarters
Atlanta, Georgia

"Harper, I'm gonna have to agree with Berger on this one." Joe began to relay his decision after hearing Harper plead her case. The three had been on the speakerphone for fifteen minutes. "As you said, in China, they don't shoot you. They do, however, make you disappear. Poof! Gone. Knowledge of your existence would have to be totally disavowed by our government."

Harper was undeterred. In a way, she was glad she hadn't brought the topic up to Joe on the phone the night before. She was saving her closing arguments for last.

"I wouldn't just disappear, Joe. Why couldn't I get the CIA to help me? I'm sure the American embassy is full of those guys." She paused and then turned her attention to her boss. "I have a note on my schedule that the same two, I assume, secret agent guys are meeting with us this afternoon. Am I right?"

"Yes, but it's because they want to discuss the files sent over—" responded Dr. Reitherman before Harper interrupted.

"I know, sir. Can I bring this up to them? Maybe they have some suggestions?"

He shrugged and then thought for a moment. "Joe?"

"Yes?"

"I need an honest answer, okay?"

"Sure."

"If certain controls could be put in place, would you reconsider your decision?"

Joe hesitated on the line and then replied, "You know I worry about the safety of my wife. I could never live without her. However, I am not an overprotective husband, and I certainly don't dictate what she can and cannot do."

Harper waved her right arm at Dr. Reitherman. "Hello? Guys? I'm sitting right here."

Dr. Reitherman laughed and ignored her. "Joe, I think the reason I admire your wife so much is because she reminds me of mine."

"I feel for you, my friend."

Harper protested. "Hey! I heard that!"

The three shared a laugh, which helped to ease the tension. Dr. Reitherman explained what he meant by the word *controls*, although he continued to address Joe as he discussed Harper's fate.

"Joe, what if we chip her?"

Joe responded quickly, "Microchip implants have been used in our dark ops people for years. They frequently have to go into deep cover without comms. Oftentimes, it's the only way we can recover them, whether dead or alive."

"That's comforting," quipped Harper.

Dr. Reitherman continued, turning his attention to Harper. "Consider this. Microchip technology has become a method of integrating biology and technology in many ways. It started years ago with pets as a means to locate a lost dog or cat. Then, as Joe said, it was utilized by our Defense Department in special operations missions. If we chip you, we can track your whereabouts and, if the CIA can give us some assurances, send in an extraction team if necessary."

Harper chimed in. "I think you guys have implanted a chip in me already. Why do I get the sense you two track me? You both seem to know where I am and what I am up to."

"That's my job," said Dr. Reitherman.

"Mine too, love," added Joe. "I can go along with chipping as a way to keep abreast of her whereabouts. However, there is something else. I cannot sign off on you going in there alone."

"Nobody here is qualified to do what I need to do. Plus, I wouldn't want them to take that risk."

"But it's okay for you to?" asked Joe.

He has a point.

Harper challenged the two men. "I'm a seasoned veteran. Does anyone disagree?"

"No," replied her boss. "Joe, we do have a meeting with the CIA this afternoon. Maybe they can provide her a security escort?"

"That won't help, sir," countered Harper. "If I'm gonna take a companion, it needs to be an epidemiologist or at least someone familiar with biosciences. I might be seeing patients, both alive and dead, who can provide me lab samples."

Harper paused as she heard Joe cupping the handset and speaking to someone in his office. She and Dr. Reitherman both waited for him to return to the call.

Finally, Harper tried to get his attention. "Joe?"

"Sorry, I'm here. I have a subcommittee work session to attend, and I've got to deal with another issue first."

Harper understood and she was amazed that she was able to have her husband's ear for this length of time during *morning rush hour,* as he referred to the start of any day when Congress was in session.

"I know, honey. I was just saying that if we can make this work, I can't just take someone along who's a hired gun."

"Yeah, sorry. I heard that. Listen, I've got a guy. Text me after you've met with the agency. Love you. You too, Berger."

Joe disconnected the call and Harper smiled at Dr. Reitherman.

"He always has a *guy*. Do you wanna know how many times I've heard *I've gotta guy* since the day we met?"

Dr. Reitherman exuded a sense of calm. "I'm anxious to see what he comes up with, okay?"

CHAPTER EIGHTEEN

House Subcommittee on National Security
2154 Rayburn Office Building
Washington, DC

Joe was the last to arrive at the subcommittee working session. It was not a formally held gathering, but certain House of Representatives' parliamentary procedures needed to be followed. In recent years, House rules were changed to allow spectators in the room subject to the usual decorum requirements. Typically, for working sessions like this one, a junior beat reporter might be in attendance and perhaps a group from a high school civics class.

When Joe entered the room from the rear entrance, he was astonished to find a packed house. There was nothing on the agenda that he was aware of that might warrant this much attention. Cameras were set up by the networks and cable news outlets. He even recognized some of the more prominent television reporters who covered Congress.

He could feel the energy lift as the attendees scrambled to take a seat. All eyes were upon him as he slid into the chairman's seat and reached for the gavel. He spun around for a moment and searched for his chief of staff, Andy Spangler. He wasn't seated behind him, and then he realized Spangler was handling an errand for him. Joe was on his own and in the dark.

He smacked the gavel down three times and made his normal introduction. "This is the Subcommittee on National Security, which falls under the House Committee on Oversight and Reform. I am Chairman Joe Mills.

"Generally, this subcommittee has oversight jurisdiction over matters of national security, homeland security, foreign operations, immigration, defense, veterans' affairs, and jurisdiction over federal acquisition policy related to national security.

"For the media and the general public, no matters of national security are discussed during these working sessions. We do not take questions from the media or the gallery. We do take witness testimony. However, it is not under oath. A working session is exactly what it sounds like. It is an opportunity for the members of this subcommittee to get together to discuss proposed and pending legislation regarding the matters I've outlined at the start of my statement."

Joe paused. He'd made this statement many times over the years, so he didn't need the benefit of notes or a script. There was an agenda, which covered ordinarily mundane things plus several funding issues since Congress was still locking horns with the administration over the budget in an effort to avoid a shutdown.

He flipped through the three-ring binder of the agenda prepared by his staff. He was about to begin when one of his aides tapped him on the shoulder and handed him a handwritten note. It was a message from Spangler. He concealed it from the prying eyes of the ranking member on the committee. He was one of the president's most vocal supporters on the Hill.

Ambush. Vegas blindside. Watch your ass.

Joe took a deep breath and allowed himself a smile. They were coming at him from all sides now. Fine. He was ready.

"We'll be rearranging today's agenda slightly to accommodate a member's schedule. The first topic we'll be addressing is the funding request for the Centers for Disease Control and Prevention. Allow me to defer to the ranking member for two minutes."

Joe smiled inwardly. Everything about his announcement was out of sorts and designed to throw the ranking member of the president's party off-kilter. The only item on today's agenda remotely related to Harper and the outbreak in Las Vegas was the WHO funding. Joe would allow the congressman an opportunity to fire first, leaving him the ability to rebut and make a closing argument. It would be the last words the jury in the court of public opinion would hear.

After stumbling and stammering through the first thirty seconds of his allotted time for opening remarks, the congressman began to repeat the same political talking points given to the Nevada governor and the president's surrogates, who'd flooded the airwaves in the last forty-eight hours. Joe allowed him to speak as he made several references to the falsehood that Harper had suggested the Las Vegas quarantine.

Joe remained stoic throughout, occasionally taking notes, which amounted to nothing more than a doodle on a legal pad. He didn't care what the congressman had to say about Harper or the political spin being disseminated through the media about the quarantine. He was prepared for his response.

The timer hit two minutes. Joe interrupted the long-winded congressman from California. He had to be careful, as he didn't want to be perceived as defending his wife. That was the trap being set for him. Instead, he made a powerful statement on behalf of the CDC.

"Today, we are here to discuss the funding request for the CDC, an agency whose mission is to keep America safe from deadly infectious diseases and other threats. These threats can take many forms. Deadly pathogens are one. Biological weapons and bioterror are another. Zoonotic transmission of zika and yellow fever, for example, are also a threat to the safety of all Americans.

"To be sure, one might argue that nuclear missiles and electromagnetic pulse attacks can bring our country to its knees. Our Department of Defense is well prepared to repel those threats. Our military might, despite prior attempts to slash the DOD's budget, is second to none. I firmly believe the CDC—which is charged with the responsibility of preventing, detecting, and responding to disease threats, both in America and around the world—deserves the same tools other national security departments receive.

"We learned with Ebola that in just thirty-six hours, an outbreak in a remote village can reach major cities on any continent, spurring a global crisis. Even outbreaks that don't cross national borders can have an adverse economic impact on the United States.

"The CDC has put together a means to reduce the impact of global health threats on our nation in many ways. The Global Disease Detection Operations Center monitors threats from nearly two hundred nations daily. The Rapid Response Team of more than four hundred epidemiologists and scientists can deploy in as little as forty-eight hours.

"Infectious diseases will never go away, and the hardworking individuals within the Epidemic Intelligence Service know this and risk their lives to protect us from this real and ancient threat. In fact, nobody—I mean nobody in this room, or in Washington, DC, or around this nation—cares more about protecting American citizens from infectious diseases than the virus hunters of the EIS.

"Let me explain something else. They are keenly aware that the decisions they make and the suggestions they give our government officials have a profound effect on people's lives. They recognize the human toll goes well beyond the illness of infected patients. The impacts of global outbreaks tear into the souls of families, healthcare systems, communities and economies, which can become destabilized by their advice.

"The CDC doesn't get the benefit of second guesses. Monday-morning quarterbacks or bigmouth pundits—who, if they're wrong, simply slough it off and wait for their next media appearance—

don't impact lives like the disease detectives. That's why they're meticulous, detailed, and methodical about their work. That's why they move quickly when a possible outbreak occurs to gather all the facts *before* they make suggestions to our government on how to act.

"You see, they understand that while global health security is good for the United States, instilling panic in its citizens is not. Just as disease outbreaks can cost lives, responding to a perceived threat out of fear can destroy communities, economies, and families."

Joe paused and glanced down at the timer. He was well beyond his five-minute time allotment, but he held the gavel, and nobody could stop him. He took a deep breath and concluded his statement.

"Call me cynical, but the use of the CDC, an agency critical to the protection of our country, as a political pawn in any manner is outrageous even by Washington standards. If this subcommittee wants to debate the necessity of the dollars requested in the current budget, let's have that debate. But to use an isolated event, which is disputed, as a form of leverage is unconscionable.

"I yield the floor to the ranking member for two minutes."

When he was done, he realized that Harper's reputation was on the line. As much as he wanted her to stay home and discard this notion of an undercover investigation on Mainland China, he realized that if she was successful, her reputation would be repaired. He didn't care what the California congressman said; he'd heard it all before.

Joe swung around in his chair to ask his aide to check in with Spangler. Instead, he was greeted with a smile and a thumbs-up from his chief of staff. Harper was one step closer to a long flight to Beijing.

CHAPTER NINETEEN

CDC Headquarters
Atlanta, Georgia

"Dr. Randolph, even if we were to sign off on this ridiculously risky suggestion of yours, there are people way above our pay grade who'd need to review this from all angles. That takes time."

"We don't have time!" Harper shot back.

The scheduled meeting with the two CIA agents was contentious from the start. Harper didn't make matters any easier by calling the men out for changing their names.

Apparently, you've forgotten you're from East St. Louis, she'd said. She issued a reminder. *Belleville and O'Fallon, if I recall.*

The two agents had introduced themselves to Dr. Reitherman's secretary as Agents Aiken and Williston. Harper immediately recognized the names as towns just east of Augusta, Georgia, where she and her grandmother used to shop for clothes when she was growing up.

That started the meeting off on an awkward footing. Ignoring the purpose of the agents' visit, Harper set the agenda with her request of assistance to investigate the disease in China. The blindside resulted in the somewhat hostile atmosphere.

The shorter agent, who'd been a twinge more friendly on their first encounter, tried to strike a conciliatory tone.

"Dr. Randolph, we want to cooperate with you, just as you have with us," he began, holding up a thick file folder of data on the four Chinese men who were the first to succumb to the mysterious virus. "You have to understand something. China is second only to North Korea in their determination to control every living human being on their soil. Certainly, there are more brutal regimes, but none are as technologically sophisticated as the Chinese. Establishing a dossier for you takes time. Then it takes even more time for us to plant the data in the Chinese surveillance system."

"How long?" asked Harper.

"For what you're suggesting? Weeks, with a caveat. If you plan on having direct interaction with any Chinese government officials, whether intentionally with their CDC, or unintentionally, with the PLA or PAP, you'll be exposed." PLA was an acronym for People's Liberation Army, while PAP stood for People's Armed Police—both undeniable oxymorons in China. They were anything but *for the people*.

"Excuse me a moment," said Dr. Reitherman abruptly. He darted out of his office, leaving Harper alone with the two CIA gentlemen. The change in dynamic gave Harper an opportunity to restart their conversation.

"Guys, listen. I have the utmost respect for what you're saying, and I apologize for my attitude earlier. There are no excuses, but we're under a lot of pressure here. Everyone in this building and throughout the CDC is hell-bent on defining this disease to avoid another pandemic like in 2020."

The taller agent, who was the more senior of the two, softened his tone as well. "We understand, Dr. Randolph. I'm not saying that's not important to us, because it is."

"We all have a job to do," added his partner.

The senior agent continued. "Doctor, we are very much aware of who your husband is, and off the record, let me say everyone I work with knows Congressman Mills to be a friend of the agency. We want to lend an assist, but we can't compromise national security and our own investigation."

Harper went for it. "Just tell me what concerns you, and maybe I can help."

"Classified," said the senior agent.

"It always is," Harper countered. "Talk around the edges and let me fill in the blanks."

The two men whispered to one another, and the younger agent took the lead. "We'll deny everything I'm about to say and make your life miserable if it's disclosed. That's a promise, Doctor, regardless of who you are. Understood?"

Harper was taken aback by the man's demeanor, as he'd been the less forceful of the two agents during their encounters.

"Roger that," she replied with a smile. *Where did that come from? That was so military sounding.*

He gave his partner a look and then he explained, "China has one of the most advanced chemical warfare programs in the world. Our intelligence indicates in the decade since the COVID-19 pandemic, they've expanded their R&D, production and weaponization capabilities. Their current inventory is believed to include the full range of traditional chemical agents, which can be dispersed through a wide variety of delivery systems."

The other agent interrupted. "Naturally, there are the conventional methods, including artillery rockets, aerial bombs, spray devices, and even short-range ballistic missiles. Our satellite recon has picked up the PLA conducting defensive CW training. Without question, they've integrated the biological weapons program into their overall military doctrine." CW was a reference to chemical warfare.

Harper asked, "Do you think these men were part of that training and something went wrong? Exposure in an accident?"

"Possibly, or worse," replied the senior agent. "We have reliable information that the Chinese have taken a page out of the ISIS terrorist playbook."

It didn't take much for Harper to read between the lines. In 2017, the CDC had engaged in bioterror simulations with the Department of Defense in which terrorists had weaponized the pneumonic plague. In the war-game scenario, the terrorist group had purposefully infected immigrants crossing the U.S. southern border with Mexico in an effort to spread the disease throughout the country. The results of the exercise were not pretty.

"Weaponized humans," she interjected.

"Yes. Exactly. Our theory, unproven, of course, which is why we're here, is that these four PLA soldiers were infected during an exercise, accidentally or intentionally. They were allowed to enter the United States as a test of China's bioweapons capability and a possible human delivery system."

Harper perked up. This information could lead her closer to patient zero. The men could, in fact, be what she was looking for. There was just one problem. Other cases were springing up around the world wholly unrelated to the travel itinerary of the four soldiers.

"Have you been able to trace their whereabouts prior to their arrival in America?" she asked.

"We're still working on that."

"Will you share it with me?"

Before they could answer, Dr. Reitherman returned to the room with three file folders. Harper glanced at the front of one and saw it was marked *personnel*.

He stood there in silence and opened the first folder. His eyes darted from the contents to Harper's face and back again several times. Finally, he addressed the group.

"I may have a solution." He made eye contact with the CIA agents and showed them the contents of the file. The senior agent shrugged and his partner nodded.

"What?" asked Harper, impatient with the intrigue.

Dr. Reitherman handed her the file, and Harper stared at the contents.

"Hello, doppelgänger."

CHAPTER TWENTY

CDC Headquarters
Atlanta, Georgia

"Meet Dr. Eloise Blasingame," began Dr. Reitherman. He explained for the benefit of the CIA agents. "She was one of a trio of our personnel embedded within the Chinese CDC by agreement with World Health and the American government. They were there in a consulting and training role, but make no mistake, their primary purpose was to report anything unusual back to us."

"The resemblance is uncanny," commented the senior agent. "I can see where you're headed with this. But I have to ask. With all due respect to Dr. Randolph, can't this person do the investigative work since she's already there?"

Dr. Reitherman replied, "For one, she and her team were expelled from the Chinese CDC building without explanation. They are currently at the American embassy in Beijing."

"Kicked out of the country?" asked the other agent.

"No. They're free to leave the embassy compound without restriction. Well, other than the usual requirements of foreign citizens on Chinese soil."

The CIA agent was looking for reasons not to take these extraordinary measures. "Sooo she could do the investigation. Am I right?"

Harper was about to speak up, but Dr. Reitherman raised his hand to stop her. "No. Frankly, Dr. Blasingame is more lab rat than disease detective. Because her role required strict confinement to the Beijing facility, we needed somebody of her expertise who enjoyed being tethered to a microscope and a desk."

"That's not me," quipped Harper.

"No kidding," added Dr. Reitherman with a scowl. "Anyway, my question is whether you guys can expedite this dossier, as you called it, for Harper to assume Dr. Blasingame's identity."

He pulled her photograph out of the personnel file and handed it to the senior agent. He held it up to compare the woman's face to Harper's.

"Is their build the same?" he asked.

"Close enough, from my recollection. I believe Dr. Randolph might be a little heavier."

"Hey!" Harper stood a little taller. She'd been eating like crap since her return from Africa. Plus, all the plane travel made her body retain water.

"Relax, Harper. These gentlemen need all the facts."

The other agent took a turn at studying their faces. "With a ball cap on to shield her face from their never-ending supply of facial-recognition cams, she might be able to pull it off."

"We could have the docs printed at the embassy where they'd make the switch," added the senior agent. "The doppelganger, as Dr. Randolph called her, would have to stay confined to the embassy throughout the operation."

"She'll understand. Also, we've already discussed microchipping Dr. Randolph so your people can track her."

The senior agent furrowed his brow. "If they're onto her, their jamming devices will render it useless. This whole operation depends upon her not being exposed. Not easy."

"Do you have a better option to determine if this is a biological weapon in the most literal sense of the term?"

The senior agent sighed. "No. Not really."

"Good, let's get started," Harper said with a hint of excitement. "What's the first step?"

"We have to sell our higher-ups on all this. With a little luck, we won't be reassigned to a desk job in Argentina hunting down wayward Nazis."

Harper found the statement odd. "Um, wouldn't they all be dead at this point?"

"Yes, ma'am," the younger agent replied. "However, their descendants still carry the flag of the *Schutzstaffel* in their hearts." The *Schutzstaffel* was the enforcement arm of the Nazi Party under Chancellor Adolf Hitler. Known as the SS, they were responsible for more war crimes than any other organization in modern history.

Dr. Reitherman made a suggestion. "I'm going to provide you access to the personnel files of these three employees after I gain the proper permissions, of course. Harper, may they have yours as well?"

"Absolutely."

Dr. Reitherman continued. "Let me mention something else. We've discussed this entire scenario with Dr. Randolph's husband. I believe he might be working on something that would help her during the investigation. May I message him to advise him of your involvement?"

"Yes," replied the senior agent. "But, respectfully, we're going to take you out of the loop at this point."

"Fine by me," said Dr. Reitherman. "You guys call it *plausible deniability*. Am I right?"

The senior agent laughed. "Sorry, Doctor. We're beyond that level of CYA. Actually, it'll just make things move quicker. Dr. Randolph has convinced me we have a hell-fire emergency on our hands, and we need to act accordingly."

Harper smiled. "And to think I really disliked you guys a little while ago."

"The feeling was mutual," said the senior agent.

Harper continued. "Since we're now kumbaya and all that, will you tell us your real names now?"

"Nope."

With that, the CIA set the wheels in motion for Harper's investigative journey into the People's Republic of China.

CHAPTER TWENTY-ONE

Chinese Center for Disease Control and Prevention
Changping District
Beijing, China

Hua Chunying, the spokesperson from the Chinese Foreign Ministry, stood before the cameras with representatives of the Chinese CDC standing lined up behind her in lab coats. None of the trio had seen a laboratory in many years. They were, in fact, the buffer between the actual scientists at the CDC and the Communist Party leadership.

"Just as before, the brave workers of the Center for Disease Control and Prevention have made a valiant effort to identify the disease in Tibet and other isolated parts of our country. The source has been determined to be a diseased yak.

"Once again, through the heroic actions of our scientists, we have bought precious time for stemming the regional spread of this virus. In fact, only a small number of individuals have been infected. Those who've died had serious underlying conditions that resulted in their death.

"During the process of caring for these patients, a treatment protocol has been established, and a vaccine has been identified. Further, we have contained the disease at its source, effectively protecting the people who live in these remote and isolated areas."

She took a deep breath and looked at her notes before staring at the camera.

"Already, as was the case in the past, Western media and politicians have engaged in a shameless and immoral attack on China. Slandering, smearing and blaming cannot help the fight of infectious diseases. This childish behavior only stifles cooperation between our nations. It must stop, and all nations should focus on their own house before they demand to peer into ours."

The camera and artificial lighting were turned off, and she immediately left the room with notes in hand. This was act one of the Chinese cover-up of the outbreak. As news broke of the deaths of the four men in Las Vegas, all the attention immediately became directed at China because of their nationality. The world feared a repeat of the COVID-19 pandemic. In America, the media, following the lead of President Taylor, immediately sought scapegoats for the disease. Hua's statement was part of the Beijing government's global offensive to downplay the outbreak. They would work overtime to push the narrative they had the disease under control and the Las Vegas cases were unrelated, even originating in the States.

Deception had always been central to the Chinese Communist Party's conduct of international politics, business, and military dealings. Sun Tzu, the ancient Chinese general who authored the treatise *The Art of War*, once wrote—*all warfare is based on deception.*

China's deception during the COVID-19 pandemic was the basis for the playbook to be consulted in future outbreaks. First, cover up the outbreak by withholding information on the nature and progression of any new infectious disease. Second, suppress the facts, including the number of infected and the death toll. Third, point the finger of blame elsewhere. In this case, the United States.

It made logical sense. In the minds of the Party leadership, the first reported deaths were in America. The fact that the individuals were Chinese was irrelevant. In fact, they used this as an additional tool of deception by blaming the overworked American healthcare system for the deaths and xenophobia for pointing blame at China.

The media manipulation was highly orchestrated and well thought out. It was designed to deflect attention and bide time while their own CDC tried to find answers. Asking for help was out of the question because it would expose them if the disease proliferated.

The trio of representatives retreated to a quiet office and closed the door behind them. Their leader, a longtime member of the Communist Party leadership and highly respected by President Xi Jinping for his handling of the COVID-19 pandemic, addressed his subordinates.

His baritone, gravelly voice sounded sinister and was a true reflection of the man. "We will fight long and hard to maintain this cover story. However, that is the job for others. We, like all of China, must stay prepared for the tricks from the West. The first step was removing the Americans from our CDC. The next will be to isolate or eliminate the Europeans."

"Eliminate, sir?" asked the female subordinate.

He frowned. "Not in the sense that you ask. We will be cooperative and open with the Europeans. But we will take them in a direction far away from Tibet."

"Liaoning?" asked his other subordinate.

"No, fool!" their leader growled. "There are no yaks in Liaoning!"

"Yes, I am sorry, sir," he sheepishly apologized.

Their superior continued. "Our people will claim to have discovered a new outbreak in another part of China. We will assemble a team to escort the Europeans to the Great Khinogan Mountains in the northernmost region of Inner Mongolia. There, they will spend many weeks in search of diseased yaks."

The female subordinate managed a smile. "I know this region.

There is no communications capability in the mountains. And, sir, very few yaks, I might add."

"That is true, but enough to make it believable. We must appear to be cooperative to the Westerners. This is an important step."

The male subordinate had recovered from his stinging rebuke. "Sir, we have made great strides in stifling the citizen journalists. Several dozen dissidents feeding information to Terminus 2049 have been apprehended and charged with many offenses, including treason."

Terminus 2049 was an internationally crowd-sourced project that archived materials published on Chinese media outlets and social media platforms before they have been removed by censors. Terminus 2049 was hosted on GitHub, the world's largest open-source code-sharing and publishing site.

Chinese citizens preserved the dissident posts from social media sites within China and immediately uploaded the information to GitHub, one of the few websites not blocked by China's Great Firewall, as its closed internet system was called. The Communist government had attempted to block GitHub in 2013, and the site suffered a barrage of cyber attacks in 2015 that were later traced back to the Chinese state telecommunications company, China Unicom. After a worldwide outcry for transparency, access to GitHub was resumed.

"Where were these criminals located?" asked their gravelly-voiced leader.

"Beijing and Xinjiang," the subordinate replied. "Some of the publishers are professors at two universities here."

"Any papers that published this information must be severely managed," the superior snarled. By managed, he meant punished. "I will have the Ministry of Education issue a directive that prohibits these entries and requires additional layers of approval for even unrelated posts. The State Council will be asked to form a task force to ensure compliance."

"Sir," the female subordinate began, "should we consider a lockdown of Lhasa, where the most cases are being reported?"

"It draws too much attention. I will request an increased military presence there. I will also request a much larger contingent of the People's Armed Police to be deployed to Urumqi. We will flush the dissident vermin out of every hiding place!"

CHAPTER TWENTY-TWO

CDC Headquarters
Atlanta, Georgia

After a brief meeting with Dr. Reitherman, reality began to set in for Harper. The way had been paved for her to travel to China, assume the identity of Dr. Blasingame, and begin the hunt for patient zero. It would be the greatest challenge she'd ever faced other than coping with the death of her father. This was different. It would be something that would've made her dad proud, if he could've been alive to witness it.

She'd spoken to Joe's chief of staff, who made the arrangements for her air transportation via military jet to Fort Belvoir, Virginia, near the Potomac River. From there, she'd be driven twenty miles to DARPA in Arlington, located halfway between Alexandria and McLean, home of CIA headquarters.

The best news of all was that Joe would be meeting her at DARPA to introduce her to the person who'd be accompanying her to China. Spangler was unable to answer any of Harper's questions about the man other than to say she should trust her husband's judgment on this.

Dr. Reitherman gave Harper some words of advice and then a little background on his days at DARPA. He was certain that anyone Joe picked from the agency would be capable of assisting Harper in her investigation. Most likely, he'd added, the man would have other useful attributes.

Harper didn't question Dr. Reitherman on what said attributes might entail. His cryptic statement coupled with Spangler's reminder to have trust in Joe's guy was too much to think about for the moment. She needed to prepare Becker to take over her duties while she was gone.

She'd been tied up preparing for her trip to China. Harper had an opportunity to speak with Dr. Blasingame, who had no knowledge of the operation. They couldn't take the risk that the Chinese intelligence apparatus was listening in. Harper kept the conversation casual as if it were part of a follow-up report on the CDC trio's expulsion. Mainly, she wanted to know how much of their investigative kits they had been able to remove from the facility. She was pleasantly surprised.

In the final hours of the day before she was to catch a ride to Dobbins Air Force Base, she was able to give Becker her undivided attention.

Several more cases were being reported to the WHO. In addition to Austria, patients with similar symptoms were being reported in France, Germany, and the UK. As was customary, the two disease-fighting organizations exchanged data and information so the brightest minds on the planet could get a handle on this novel virus.

"We've had another situation in Las Vegas," began Becker. "Quite interesting, to use your friend Woolie's words."

"Dr. Boychuck brought this to us?" asked Harper.

"Yes. Yes. Yes. Yes," replied Becker in an attempt to mock the pathologist's peculiar idiosyncrasy.

"Just three," corrected Harper. "You know. Like the jelly beans."

Becker, who was a whiz at numbers, seemed genuinely confused by what Harper said. "Ya lost me."

"Just three times. Dr. Boychuck never says *yes* once or twice, or even four times. It's always three times."

"Oookay. And what about the jelly beans?" asked Becker as she picked through her Bradley University coffee mug to pluck three pink jelly beans. Then it struck her. "Three. Really? Do I take three every time?"

"At least when I've watched you," Harper responded. "It's just a thing."

Becker furrowed her brow and then slowly popped the sugary treats into her mouth, one at a time, as if she were counting them. She chuckled. "Maybe I should've been a bean counter?"

"Huh-huh-huh," Harper jokingly replied three times. "So what's the story?"

Becker finished chewing up her jelly beans and organized her notes. "So, you remember the elderly couple, right? The lady had come in contact with our index patient, Mr. Yao."

"Yes. Yes. Yes." Harper's face broke out in a grin.

Becker scowled. "Shut up! See? It's contagious!"

Harper was gonna miss her sidekick. Naturally, Harper would've preferred Becker to come along, but she'd be in constant fear that her assistant might punch a Chinese soldier in the nose for some reason or another.

"Okay, okay. I'm sorry. I couldn't resist."

Becker raised her right palm in the air and directed it to Harper's forehead. She used her best Luke Skywalker voice. "You must resist, Rey!"

Harper sighed. She'd opened up this can of worms. She tapped the desk and pointed to Becker's notes. "Focus. The old people?"

"Anyway, the two elderly people were taken to Dignity Health, where they were initially treated in the ER and then moved into quarantine."

"Are they still alive?"

"Yup, but there's more. There was a breakdown in quarantine protocols by the hospital staff. It was inadvertent and unfortunate. Despite their training during trial runs, it happened."

"Oh no," lamented Harper. "Please don't tell me they infected someone else."

"They did, but hear me out." Becker gathered her thoughts and continued. "They were all old friends, literally. Every Sunday night, they'd gather at each other's homes to play poker. They'd go on cruises together and visit casinos in the islands. Supposedly, nothing like the high-stakes games. Just hundred-dollar pots or less.

"When they heard their friends were sick, they descended on Dignity Health to see how they were doing. Apparently, one of them was a retired nurse who knew the staff in the emergency room. They got permission to see them, and one thing led to another."

"And they broke quarantine."

Becker sighed. "Yep. It gets better, sort of. After the visitors left the hospital, they all got together for their regular poker game. The usual hugs, banter, exchanging of cards, chips and cash occurred. They even double-dipped in the cheese fondue."

"Jeez Louise," said Harper.

"Whoever didn't get close enough to their hospitalized friends to contract the virus via airborne transmission picked it up at the weekly poker soirée. By the following week, they were beginning to show symptoms of the flu and were soon admitted to hospitals around the city."

"What is their condition?"

"All but two are improving, and their prognosis is good," replied Becker. "Two more, a man and an unrelated woman, are in critical condition on ventilators."

Harper sat forward in her chair. "Were they all in equal proximity to one another?"

"Yes."

"What about health history? How do the two criticals differ from the others?"

"When Dr. Boychuck heard of these cases, he contacted me immediately. I've moved part of our team to conduct interviews, gather documents, and conduct our own investigative tests. I'll do a comparison of their health and genetic characteristics."

"There has to be something that differentiates the more critical patients from those who are improving. And here's what really puzzles me. It's the elderly who seem to have a fighting chance while seemingly healthy adults, whether it's the Olympian from Austria or the five victims of Asian descent in Las Vegas, die."

Becker set her notes aside and leaned back in her chair to finish up another Diet Coke. "It doesn't add up, does it?"

Harper shook her head as she pondered this new information. "Keep digging. Compare all of the known and suspected patients, including the one from Los Angeles. First, confirm the toxicology to determine whether they were infected with the same strain of the virus. Second, compare all of the genetic and health markers. Third, look at everything from a health perspective right down to the medications and vitamins they take. There has to be a pattern."

"I'm on it," said Becker reassuringly.

Harper glanced at her watch and sighed. It was time to go. She stood and stretched out her arms to hug her assistant. It was a rare showing of affection for each other, but if there was ever time the two women needed a hug, it was now.

They held each other for almost a minute, allowed a few tears, and then nervously laughed as they broke their embrace. Harper wiped the tears off her cheeks.

"Becker, basically, you're in charge while I'm gone."

"Great!"

"No, not great. Careful what you wish for."

CHAPTER TWENTY-THREE

People's Liberation Army
85th Air Defense Brigade
Lhasa Gonggar Airport
Lhasa, Tibet, China

Dr. Basnet Dema walked alone down the lengthy hallway connecting the offices at the base infirmary of the 85th Air Defense Brigade located at Lhasa's Gonggar Airport. Dr. Basnet had been born and raised in Tibet. After receiving his medical degree and training, he requested assignment to a hospital located in Lhasa.

For years, he was an esteemed surgeon at the Tibet People's Hospital until he began to notice mild symptoms of Parkinson's disease. The occasional shakes prevented him from continuing his career as a surgeon, so the hospital administrators transferred him to oversee the medical personnel at the PLA's base located at Tibet's largest airport.

It was a position well beneath his knowledge and capabilities, but it paid the same and was far less stressful. In recent weeks, as the mysterious disease began to take its toll on the people of Lhasa, he was called back into service at the People's Hospital. He treated the ill and lent a hand in the emergency ward to triage new patients. After several long days at the hospital, he longed for the relative quiet and serenity of the base infirmary.

It also suited him in another way. The solitude and the lack of a direct supervisor allowed him a lot of free time. Dr. Basnet was a citizen journalist. Over the years, he'd been instrumental in shedding light upon human rights abuses in Tibet.

When China deployed tanks, howitzers, and air assets along the Tibetan border with India in an effort to lay claim to Arunachal Pradesh as a part of South Tibet, the PLA staged their incursion at Lhasa Airport.

Dr. Basnet reported this activity via WeChat and onto GitHub. Word spread to the northeasternmost state of India, and the inhabitants sought refuge away from what appeared to be a potential war zone. The disputed territory, often referred to as the *land of dawn-lit mountains*, had no particular geopolitical benefit to China other than Beijing had adopted an expansionist mindset.

Dr. Basnet was also instrumental in reporting accurate numbers during the COVID-19 pandemic, which eventually made its way into Tibet. He worked with the locals to make the best use of traditional Tibetan medical techniques to treat the infected. During that time, his reputation within the mysterious autonomous region swelled.

He was not on hand when the helicopter arrived from Mount Everest with the body of the Australian, Adam Mooy, one of the first to die during the climbing accident. Through gossip in the local medical community, he'd suspected that there was more to the man's death than simply a climbing accident.

Meanwhile, a second medical emergency caught his attention. The helicopter pilot who'd participated in the rescue mission became inexplicably ill. He was treated at a local hospital first and then brought to the infirmary at the 85th Air Defense Brigade when his condition didn't improve.

Dr. Basnet immediately connected the dots and surmised that the pilot's illness was possibly connected to the Australian man, although he'd heard nothing from Xinjiang about the results of their investigation.

He'd tried to reach out to the First Affiliated Hospital and was ignored at first. When he insisted upon answers, claiming that a man's life was at stake, he was transferred to a hospital administrator, who stonewalled him. Shortly thereafter, while in the quarantine unit, the pilot died.

Dr. Basnet had seen it all before. This was a classic case of Communist Party cover-up. He took to WeChat to express his frustration and soon received a strict admonition from his superiors at the military facility. The words of the base commander were simple.

You will not speak of this again. Dismissed.

Dr. Basnet knew immediately that he would do just the opposite. Only, he'd be far more careful next time. He spent every waking moment scouring the social media groups at both GitHub and WeChat. The levels of encryption were beyond anything he'd ever practiced during his years of whistleblowing, as the Westerners called it.

He studied the combination of symbols, emojis, and written text. He began to fully understand the intentional, incorrect use to create confusion. Once he felt confident, he began to create a few posts about the unexplained illnesses that were occurring in Lhasa. He bravely went into the local hospital to videograph the dead who were being abandoned because the hospital was either overwhelmed or afraid to treat the patients.

When the pilot died, he learned the young man had no family or next of kin. So he stowed him away in the small morgue located at the infirmary. The pathology lab was small, as most autopsies were sent to the regional hospitals. It was rarely used and therefore never inspected by the military's constantly prying eyes. In fact, the pilot's body was the only one kept in refrigeration.

Dr. Basnet was not trained in pathology nor was he capable of identifying infectious diseases. There was an office of the CDC in Tibet, but it was controlled by Beijing, and he didn't trust their personnel. As a result, he undertook the only course of action available to him. He posted the patient's case notes to WeChat.

CHAPTER TWENTY-FOUR

Defense Advanced Research Projects Agency
DARPA
675 North Randolph Street
Arlington, Virginia

The year was 1958, and the new chief scientist of an obscure arm of the defense department known as the Advanced Research Project Agency submitted a proposal to the agency's director. Four months later, nine naval vessels departed for the mostly uninhabited Gough Island in the far reaches of the South Atlantic. The vessels carried forty-five hundred government personnel and contractors. They also carried three nuclear weapons designed to launch into the magnetosphere. This was Project Argus and it cemented the use of advanced technology into America's war arsenal.

The concept had germinated in the panic after the successful launch of the Soviet Union's Sputnik satellite. The Pentagon immediately raised their concerns. How can we defend our nation from an incoming nuclear warhead?

Armed with the physics evidence resulting from the Starfish Prime nuclear tests, the new agency hatched a plan. Explode nuclear weapons in Earth's magnetosphere to create a long-lived radiation belt that would degrade the missiles.

The first detonation set off a spectacular luminous fireball, triggering a staggering blue-green aurora that captivated the thousands of onlookers. However, beyond the vividly colored night sky, the bombs failed to produce sufficient high-energy electrons to keep the shield in place long enough to deter a speeding nuclear missile.

The ill-fated *death belt*, as it was called, did lead to further research into electromagnetic pulse weapons. It also convinced America's military leaders that the new agency was of vital strategic importance to the nation's national defense.

Over the years, DARPA became known as the *Imagineers of War*. It's the agency that conceived the internet, the laser, and the stealth fighter. DARPA became a uniquely nimble governmental agency, unbound by the usual red tape and constraints associated with congressional oversight. It was allowed to conduct the kind of high-risk, high-reward research that went way beyond the purview of other branches of government.

Through the use of very tight public relations control, only exposing what it wanted politicians and the public to know, the agency has succeeded in creating a massive technological research and development arm of the government while establishing a worldwide intelligence apparatus in which its operatives operated without rules.

Like its counterpart at the Defense Threat Reduction Agency, or DTRA, in nearby Fort Belvoir, DARPA scientists and operatives were looked upon as ghosts—individuals who not only created the technological gadgetry deemed necessary to protect America, but who used these advanced weapons to conduct counterinsurgency operations.

The driver picked Harper up at Fort Belvoir and barely spoke a word to her during the twenty-mile trip north to Arlington, Virginia, located across the Potomac River from DC. He navigated the black sedan onto North Randolph Street, where DARPA was located.

Harper glanced up at the sign and smiled. Her family were lineal descendants of the Virginia Randolphs. They were a prominent political family historically considered to be the most powerful in the Virginia colony even after she received statehood.

She was proud of her Randolph ancestry. She was a direct lineal descendant of Thomas Randolph, a close friend of Founding Father Thomas Jefferson. Thomas Randolph had thirteen children, including Dr. John Randolph, the former governor of Virginia, whose daughter moved to Washington, Georgia, and lived to her death. The home where Harper's grandmother and great-grandmother lived, known as Randolph Mansion, was constructed in 1795.

Harper's mind wandered to the two old biddies, as Joe lovingly referred to them. She missed the women who'd raised her when her mother was no longer able to. Then she thought of her mother, who was two hours away just south of Richmond. She closed her eyes to bring up the fondest memories of her mom that she could muster, but was unable to do so. All that resonated with her at the moment was their last visit together almost a year ago. It didn't go well.

Harper's mood had turned from apprehensive to melancholy as the driver pulled into the secured parking area at DARPA. She barely remembered him opening her car door and leading her to the secured entrance of the seven-story all-glass building. The windows contained an odd grid pattern designed to block all types of electronic intrusions. The glass panes might have enticed America's adversaries to sneak a peek, but DARPA technology foiled their access.

"Here we are, ma'am," said the driver as he opened the door for her. "I've been instructed to wait for you. I'll be keeping your luggage in the car."

Harper opened her eyes wide, snapping herself out of the trance that had overtaken her. "Um, yes. What? You're going to take me back?"

"Yes, ma'am. Those are my instructions."

"Okay."

She walked into the building, and a rush of air-conditioned air swept over her. The lobby was quiet and unoccupied except for plainclothes security personnel and two armed guards standing on opposite ends of the open space. Harper paused and glanced around the lobby to get her bearings. Then her heart leapt.

On the other side of the glass partition stood Joe. He was dapperly dressed, as always, in one of his Tom James custom suits. He waved his right arm so that it could be seen over the X-ray machine that sat beside the full-body scanners.

Before she entered, she reported at an administrative desk. The pleasant receptionist checked her credentials, confirmed whom she was there to visit, and then issued a visitor's badge, which she attached to the lapel of her blazer. Harper had dressed up for the occasion. She still wore her usual Levi jeans and white Nike sneakers, but over her white, French-cuffed shirt, she'd put on a black blazer.

She tugged at it. Like life, she didn't want her clothes to feel constraining. Also, she wanted to make a lasting impression on her husband, whom she may not see again for a while. She concentrated to stifle the words *if ever* as she cleared security.

Once she passed the scrutiny of the DARPA security team, she rushed to greet Joe. All of the negative thoughts and emotions associated with her mother were immediately washed away. Her face broke out in a smile, and tears rolled down her cheeks.

She ran into his arms and they held one another without speaking. It was a reunion that seemed different than others. It was more emotional. But then, because it was their nature, it turned playful.

"Oh, Rhett," she cooed, channeling Scarlett O'Hara in *Gone with the Wind*. "Please, kiss me proper."

Joe laughed and then his face turned serious. He became Captain Rhett Butler. "No, I don't think I will kiss you, although you need kissing badly."

"But, Rhett …" Harper's version of Scarlett begged.

"You should be kissed, and often, and by someone who knows how."

"Please, Rhett, do kiss me!" she demanded in a Southern drawl that would make Margaret Mitchell proud.

So he did. The two's public display of affection was not frowned upon by passersby, but admired. They were truly in love with one another and it showed.

Joe pulled away and looked into Harper's eyes. "Better?"

"More better." She smiled and then planted a gentle peck on his cheek. "God, I've missed you."

"More than ever, it seems. Are you all right?"

Harper wiped away the tears and smiled. "Yeah. I just had a moment thinking about Mom."

"Did something happen?" asked Joe.

"Oh, no. You know how my brain works. I noticed this building was located on Randolph Street. I went down the rabbit hole to the family history from the old Randolphs to the new. The stroll down memory lane ended with my last visit with her."

Joe gently wiped the last remnants of her tears from her cheeks and hugged her. They embraced for half a minute until she regained her composure. She pulled back and then noticed his visitor's badge.

"Hey, why is yours a different color than mine?"

"It allows me to do things you can't."

"Like kiss me in the lobby?"

Joe laughed. "Yeah. That and going through doors to check out all the neat shit."

"I wanna see!" Harper jokingly demanded.

Joe grabbed her by the hand. "Welcome to the Department of Mad Scientists."

CHAPTER TWENTY-FIVE

Darpa
Arlington, Virginia

Joe checked his watch. They had ten minutes before they were to meet with the man with whom he would entrust the safety of his wife. He walked Harper through the hallways and shared some of DARPA's long list of technological accomplishments.

"Berger has undoubtedly told you about his role working with infectious diseases in the Biological Technologies Office," he began. "Since his departure for the CDC, I was able to fund a new program for DARPA."

"PREEMPT," interjected Harper.

"Preventing Emerging Pathogenic Threats," added Joe. "While you're hunting viruses, these guys are modeling viral evolutions in animal populations. They focus on quantifying the probability of human pathogen emergence and pursuing interventions to prevent viral spread to humans."

"They place a huge emphasis on zoonotics," said Harper. "Very smart considering most viruses start in animal reservoirs and are later passed on to humans through a variety of vectors, including insects or intermediate reservoirs—small mammals, poultry, and swine."

"Or biological weapons," said Joe solemnly. "As you know, the Department of Defense works around what's known as the *threat timeline*. At the DTRA, the guys at Fort Belvoir refer to it as *right of boom*—a phrase that referred to the timeline of a disaster, in particular the aftermath. In a world at war with terrorists, governments had concentrated their efforts on what happens after a catastrophic event, hence the phrase *right of boom*. The DTRA, like DARPA, has evolved now to address the events *left of boom*."

"Prevention."

"Yes," said Joe. He paused for a moment before continuing. In his position as chairman of the House Oversight Committee, he held a security clearance equal to that of the Speaker of the House. He always had to be cognizant of the potentially classified information he provided Harper. His concern was not that she would intentionally use or disseminate the information for any purpose. Sometimes, those who don't work in a world of secrecy could accidentally slip up.

"Most of what I'm about to tell you is available through FOIA requests. It's public knowledge and anyone could make a request to see it. However, it's safe to say very few people know to ask for it." FOIA was an acronym for the Freedom of Information Act, which allowed private citizens to seek full or partial disclosure of previously unreleased documents and information from the government.

"Sounds mysterious," said Harper.

"It is, but essential to our national security." Joe checked his watch again and pointed toward the elevator. "With PREEMPT, DARPA has followed a model initiated at Fort Belvoir known as Project Artemis."

"She was the Greek goddess of the hunt," said Harper.

Joe wrapped an arm around his wife and gave her a squeeze. "Not unlike yourself, darling."

"Wow, you're certainly buttering me up for something."

"Maybe," he said as the elevator doors opened. The cab was empty, so Joe continued. "Anyway, Project Artemis was designed to liaise with the CIA and the NSA to stop the use of biological weapons by terrorists—before *boom*. Whether it was the use of anthrax by domestic terrorists within the United States or weaponized smallpox throughout Europe, the team at Project Artemis works around the clock to prevent bioterror events from happening."

Harper was somewhat familiar with the secretive project. The Project Artemis team was known for its outside-the-box thinking and employment of covert operatives. They were adept at analyzing data and intelligence and piecing threads of evidence together that might seem far-fetched to some. Sometimes their working theories didn't pan out. When they did, and a bioterror attack was thwarted, it was a rewarding feeling for those who worked tirelessly for the country he loved.

Joe continued. "PREEMPT was created to focus on the zoonotic side. They looked farther left of the timeline, before the bioweapon was created, and began to identify opportunities to contain viruses before they endangered humans."

Harper was about to add a comment when the elevator door opened. A long, sterile corridor appeared before them. A receptionist sat behind a half-wall enclosure. She looked up and immediately recognized Joe.

"Welcome back, Congressman. You and your guest may proceed to conference room A at the end of the hall. It will be just a moment."

"Thanks," said Joe with a smile. He finished his explanation. "Ebola is a high-profile example that you're familiar with. As you know, it's a zoonotic disease that's difficult to spread, requiring direct contact with fluids from an infected animal or person. PREEMPT looks at Ebola as, well, let's call it tame compared to other biothreats. Influenza and other airborne pathogens are more vexing. And then you have the vector-borne transmission of zoonotic diseases that are on the rise courtesy of mosquitoes, ticks, and fleas."

Harper leaned in to her husband as they walked toward the conference room. "I'm impressed, Joe. You've got a tremendous grasp of this stuff. You *have been* paying attention to my rants at the dinner table."

"I have," he said with a chuckle. "Dad's death has always made this a topic of importance to me. That's why I've made so many friends in this field, like Dr. Reitherman and the folks at the DTRA and DARPA, including the gentleman you're about to meet."

"Your guy?" asked Harper.

"One of many, darling."

They entered the conference room and Joe retrieved a bottle of water for each of them. Harper wandered along the wall of windows and took in the view of the surrounding area. Immediately below them was an Enterprise Car Rental location built on a postage-stamp-sized lot. Yet it contained three structures in which cars were stacked three rows high and removed by a massive lift. She was astounded by the technology. As she would soon learn, as the saying goes, *you ain't seen nuthin' yet.*

CHAPTER TWENTY-SIX

Darpa
Arlington, Virginia

Dr. Li Kwon's entrance into the conference room was completely unnoticed by Harper and Joe. She caught a glimpse of him out of the corner of her eye before he announced himself, immediately making her wonder how long he'd been standing there. She gasped slightly as she made eye contact with his dark eyes. Kwon was an imposing, mysterious man who could star in any action and adventure movie.

He locked eyes with Harper and then turned his attention to Joe. His greeting was simple.

"Congressman."

Joe turned abruptly and greeted his guy. "Right on time, as always, Kwon. I'd like you to meet my wife, Harper."

Kwon nodded. "Hello. I don't shake hands. No offense."

"None taken. Nor do I."

Harper studied the man. Either Dr. Li Kwon was a humanoid robot, yet another secretive project of DARPA, or he had little or no personality. One thing was certain, she'd never met someone so intense. His black eyes were almost lifeless. Devoid of emotion. Piercing.

Joe, who knew Kwon well, was used to his demeanor. "Let's take a seat and talk."

Everyone pulled out a chair, with Joe at the head of the table and Kwon seated across from Harper. Harper was beginning to question whether the two of them would be able to work together. She reserved judgment until she learned more about him.

"Dr. Randolph, I'm very familiar with your work."

Harper raised her hand. "Please, call me Harper. May I call you Kwon?"

"Yes, Harper. Absolutely. Even in Beijing. Li Kwon is a common name."

"Is it your real name?" Harper asked with a smile. "I've had contact with some CIA agents lately who can't seem to keep their names straight." Harper was trying her best to add some levity to the conversation. It didn't work.

"Yes, it is."

Harper nodded. There was an awkward silence. It appeared she'd have to pull the words out of Kwon, so she got started. "Well, Kwon, I know absolutely nothing about you. First, may I assume you know what I'd like to accomplish in China?"

"I do," he replied.

Great, Harper thought to herself. *We're up to two-word responses.* If our adversaries ever captured this guy and tried to interrogate him, they'd end up shooting themselves in the face out of frustration.

"Okay, would you mind telling me a little bit about yourself?"

Kwon's eyes averted to Joe, who provided him an imperceptible nod. Harper, however, picked up on the subtle interaction. She turned to her husband.

"Joe, am I missing something here?" She was perturbed and ready to get on a flight by herself despite her husband's protests.

Joe took a deep breath and explained, "Harper, within our government, there are people like Kwon who, for all intents and purposes, don't exist. Certainly, you see him, and he has a life outside of his work for DARPA, but there is no trace of him otherwise. No pay records. No personnel file. No Facebook page. No social security number. It has to be that way for his safety, and yours."

"Okay, I understand," she said, turning her attention back to Kwon. She tried to show some empathy for the man who chose to live his life as a ghost. "Kwon, you've made great sacrifices for our country. Far more than I would ever endure. That said, I need to feel comfortable that you can help me when the time comes. Are you allowed to tell me anything about yourself? I mean, the CliffsNotes résumé at least?"

Again, the eye contact between the two men. Joe nodded and Kwon began.

"I was born in San Diego. My father is Chinese and my mother is South Korean. Following high school, I enlisted in the Navy as a Seaman recruit. I completed Hospital Corpsman training and then reported to BUD/S training at NAB Coronado."

Joe interrupted. "Harper, BUD/S is an acronym for Basic Underwater Demolition SEAL training. It's conducted at the Naval Special Warfare Center in Coronado." He then nodded at Kwon to continue.

"After completing my training at the NSWC, I reported to the JFK Special Warfare Center at Fort Bragg, North Carolina. There, I completed the Special Operations Combat Medic Course. I was assigned as a Special Warfare Operator to SEAL Team 3, Charlie Platoon, in San Diego."

"The Punishers," added Joe.

Kwon nodded and continued. His voice and facial expression remained unemotional. "With SEAL Team 3, I obtained qualifications as a Military Freefall parachutist, Combatant Diver, Naval Special Warfare Recon Scout and Sniper, and was designated as being qualified in Advanced Special Operations Techniques."

Harper raised her hand slightly. She turned to Joe. "Really? All of this is real?"

Joe smiled. "Trust me. Let Kwon continue. He's just getting started."

Harper shrugged and leaned onto the table, resting her arms crossed in front of her as she took in the rest of Kwon's résumé.

"I was commissioned through the Navy's enlisted-to-officer commissioning program following graduation from the University of San Diego. My rank was elevated from Seaman to Admiral – 21." The Admiral – 21 was the U.S. Navy's commissioning program for the twenty-first century designed to enable active-duty sailors to obtain their college degree and become commissioned officers.

"You're an admiral?" asked Harper.

"No. It's not the same. I then went to MIT and obtained my degrees in computational biology and genetic epidemiology. Afterwards, I began my medical internship in the Harvard Affiliated Emergency Medicine Residency program. I held a position as a resident physician in emergency medicine with Partners Healthcare at Mass General until three years ago when I was recruited by DARPA."

Kwon stopped speaking and Harper simply stared at him in amazement. She'd never heard of such a résumé. It couldn't be real. She tried again to catch Kwon off guard.

"You're smarter than I am."

His face remained emotionless although Joe couldn't contain himself as he burst out laughing before addressing her statement. "We all have our strengths and weaknesses."

Harper leaned back and shook her head. "Aw, shit, Joe. This guy is a Navy SEAL, an MIT grad with a dual degree, and an ER doctor. He's gotta be some kind of AI project, right?" She studied Kwon for any type of reaction. He remained stoic.

"He is very real, Harper. And he's a great American patriot. This gentleman has willingly allowed our government to erase all of these accomplishments so he can fight the war against deadly diseases before they hit our soil. He is one of two people on this Earth with whom I'd trust your life, and the other gentleman doesn't have the medical background Kwon has."

Harper looked toward the ceiling and leaned back in her chair with her arms folded. She turned to Kwon. "I have one more question."

He nodded.

"Do you ever smile?"

She got nothing in response.

CHAPTER TWENTY-SEVEN

Darpa
Arlington, Virginia

Harper, Joe and Kwon continued their conversation for another hour as she explained to her new partner what she hoped to accomplish in China. They then left for a medical laboratory, where they were injected with microchips developed by DARPA. They would be tracked by the technology teams located within this facility as well as by the CIA stationed at the American embassy in Beijing.

Over the course of the afternoon, Kwon loosened up somewhat. He was still not open to playful banter and jokes. Harper surmised he never would be. She was interested in breaking through his tough shell to determine if he'd always been this way or if something had occurred in his life that caused him to become so closed off. In the end, it didn't matter to her because he would serve a twofold purpose—bodyguard and well-trained physician.

"Follow me, please," said Kwon as he led them through a door marked Secured Access. Using an eye retina scanner, he unlocked the door, and then once inside, he explained to a guard the purpose of his guests accompanying him. He turned to Harper.

"One of the challenges we'll face throughout China is their extensive, sophisticated facial-recognition technology. Because you'll be assuming the identity of Dr. Blasingame, our AI team has created a few methods to confuse their surveillance. This way."

Joe looked at Harper and smiled. He leaned in to whisper, "Whadya think about Kwon?"

"Very impressive, but his personality is a far cry from Becker's."

"You need this kind of balance in your life."

"I still think he's a robot," said Harper.

Kwon led them into a room full of glass-enclosed cubicles, each of which was occupied by DARPA personnel wearing white lab coats.

"I'm told by the CIA liaison that they'll be manipulating the commonly used Chinese apps like AliPay and WeChat, together with what we call the blue-green app. We'll talk more about that once we arrive at the embassy."

He turned into one of the cubicles, where the technician turned to address him. "Hello, Dr. Li. You're all set." He handed Kwon a ziplock-style plastic bag. He opened it and pulled out several surgical masks. Two were dark blue and two were light blue. He handed one of each to Harper before turning to the technician.

"Are you ready?" he asked.

The technician made several entries on a keyboard, and then the screen changed to reflect the view from a camera that was attached to an extra-long USB cable stretched under his desk. He picked up the camera and pointed at Harper's face.

The software immediately recognized her. A split screen appeared with her face appearing on one side and her biographical details—such as age, height, weight, address, and job—appearing on the other half.

"These are the types of things facial-recognition software feeds into any airport security system, for example," began the technician. "Now, Dr. Randolph, please put on the light blue face mask."

Harper obliged and turned toward the camera. The screen immediately changed, and the face of Dr. Blasingame and her biographical data appeared. Harper's eyes grew wide.

"Wow! It's my doppelganger."

"Excuse me?" said the technician, somewhat confused by the reference.

"Never mind. How does it do that?"

"Within the light blue mask are fine electronic threads that emit a signal to fool the cameras. You will be able to pass through security checkpoints and fly under the radar, if you will, across Mainland China. The cameras will see you as Dr. Blasingame."

"Amazing," said Harper.

"Now, if you will, change to the dark blue mask," the technician requested.

Harper changed masks and the tech took her image again. This time, her actual face appeared on the screen, but her biographical information was completely different.

"Maria Randolph. How did you—?" She began to ask how the technician was aware of her ancestor's name and the pronunciation as *Mariah*. He answered the question for her.

"Miss Maria was the person who renovated your familial home, was she not?"

"Yes, but you even pronounced her name as Mariah. How did you know that?"

"It's our job, Dr. Randolph. When we work with the agency to create covert dossiers, we ascertain everything we can about the individual. Then we mix in mostly fact with just enough fiction so they can avoid their true identity from being discovered while giving them some truth about their lives to divulge and still not get confused."

"I'm impressed. So this mask enables me to be me, sort of. How do I know when to use them?"

"Light blue when you're concerned with eyes in the sky, dark blue when you're face-to-face with the darkness of your adversary."

Kwon explained, "During our travels, we will be asked to provide identification by actual human beings who will compare them to the database. The dark blue mask will be consistent with our reason for traveling to China."

"Which is?"

The tech responded, "English language instructors contracted by boarding schools spread across the country. ESLs are in high demand, and the boarding schools are the perfect cover. Their agreements with ESLs are typically informal. Further, they're scattered throughout the countryside, giving you a reason to travel by car almost anywhere you choose."

"Brilliant," said Joe.

Kwon thanked the technician and then escorted Harper and Joe outside the room. "One thing I forgot to mention is that the CIA contacts at the embassy will provide us with HyperFace. It's an extension of the agency's earlier work with CV Dazzle."

"Please explain," said Harper.

"CV Dazzle is makeup, for lack of a better term, that targets the facial area to alter the image seen by the cameras. In essence, it distracts the computer algorithms long enough for you to avoid detection.

"HyperFace is different. It targets the surrounding area as well as the face. Like camouflage where the objective is to reduce the confidence score of the true face by redirecting more attention to regions near the face. It generates a false-face detection that is rejected by the algos."

"Good grief, Kwon. Is this the kind of stuff they taught you at MIT?"

"Yes."

Harper looked at Joe. "I see why you picked him."

Kwon added, "HyperFace also serves to disrupt the detection of suspicious body language. Today, through the use of AI technology, a surveillance system can identify a shoplifter, a liquor store robber, or an untrained individual engaging in espionage."

"Like me," added Harper.

"Newton's Third Law of Motion is very much in play as it relates to today's technology," said Kwon. "For every action, there is an equal and opposite reaction. For every advancement in surveillance, there are countermeasures to take advantage of weaknesses in the program."

After another hour in which Kwon introduced them to imaginary, inventive gear that at first glance seemed ordinary, but which possessed extraordinary personal defense capabilities, he left the two of them alone in the conference room where they began their day.

Joe closed the door and reached his hands out to take Harper's. He drew her close to him and hugged her. "How do you feel?"

"Like I'll be in very good hands. This was way more complicated than I imagined. I thought I was going to run around chasing down leads like I did during the MERS outbreak in Greece and Syria. I really didn't think about the fact they track every movement of every human being."

"That's okay," Joe reassured her. "We have specialists for that. Brilliant people like Kwon, who is also a very capable operative. Nobody should cross him to try to get to you. Ya can take that to the bank."

"I believe you. Truthfully, I wasn't sure this would work. He's pretty scary, but it wasn't just that. I need somebody to bounce ideas off of. You know, a second set of eyes. I believe Kwon is more than capable. Heck, with his background, I may be able to learn a few things from him."

Joe sighed and kissed his wife. They embraced without saying a word for nearly a minute. Then he asked the question that was on both of their minds. "Is this absolutely necessary?"

Harper grimaced and nodded her head. "It is. Joe, we're absolutely nowhere, and thanks to your friend the president, we're on the clock. A normal, methodical investigation has turned into a race against time by the actions of the governor working on behalf of President Taylor. Plus, the Chinese are less cooperative now than they were during the COVID-19 pandemic. They learned how to avoid scrutiny during that time."

Joe was angry over the president's actions, and it served no purpose to bring it up to Harper. She felt responsible for what had happened in Las Vegas. He wanted his last few moments with his wife to be positive, and he'd deal with the politics of the matter later.

"I love you and I trust that you'll be safe and not take any risks. I'll worry, of course, but I'm not gonna wring my hands while you're gone."

Harper smiled and hugged him again. "I have to put my game face on while I'm in China. If I'm emotional or scared, I'll make a mistake. Of all places, that could be dangerous. I think you've done all you can by picking Kwon to escort me. In fact, I think he's perfect under the circumstances. Thank you."

The two kissed again, and less than two hours later, Harper and Kwon were wheels up on a military transport to Joint Base Pearl Harbor, where they would catch a commercial flight aboard Hawaiian Air to Beijing in the heart of the Red Dragon.

CHAPTER TWENTY-EIGHT

Office of Congressman Joe Mills
Longworth House Office Building
Washington, DC

It was after dark by the time Joe parked his car in the secured parking lot at the Longworth House Office Building and made his way to his darkened office that doubled as his residence while he was in town. He was tired, but not from physical exhaustion.

He'd made the mistake of listening to satellite radio on his drive from DARPA. DC pundits, talking heads, and commentators of all sorts were weighing in on the quarantine of Las Vegas and the perceived inaction of the CDC. The negative news surrounding the Nevada governor's actions weren't focused on his decision, or even the connection to the president. It was almost uniformly directed at Harper and the CDC. And now toward him by extension.

The president's political machine was cruel, calculating, and extensive. His operatives used every method in the dirty politics playbook, from ridiculing their opponents to misinformation campaigns and their use of the media to push negative narrative so often that it eventually became accepted fact.

Both he and Harper were targets. The administration seemed laser focused on taking him down before he even got started. While he listened to the barrage of attacks on the radio, he considered speaking with Andy Spangler or his campaign manager about distancing himself from Herbert Brittain and his wealthy circle of donors. He tried to consider what was best for Harper. He thought the best course of action was to make it known throughout Washington that he didn't have any aspirations for higher office. He was just fine being the congressman from Georgia's sixth. Leave me be and I'll be content chairing committees.

Then his blood began to boil. Joe was a fighter, just like his dad. Being conciliatory was one thing. Allowing his family to be bullied was another. If he backed down, he'd never forgive himself for not defending Harper's honor.

"Dammit!" he shouted to his empty office as he poured himself a drink. "She's gonna risk her life to save other people's lives!"

The least he could do, he surmised, was fight back against his political enemies. Joe had resources, too. They might not be into doxing or willing to throw Molotov cocktails through campaign office windows, but they were rich and powerful.

He would not fight his adversaries through fear. That wasn't his nature. He'd do it through messaging. It was the honorable way to govern a country. It required taking the high road, something that seemed to have been lost in politics of late, but it was necessary to stop the rancor.

Joe set his jaw and finished off his straight whiskey. He picked up the phone and placed a call to Ken McCarthy, his campaign manager. McCarthy answered the phone on the first ring.

"Hey, Joe." The two men had been friends since law school. Ken and his girlfriend used to tailgate at Washington Redskins games with Joe and Harper.

"Ken, get 'em on the phone. Tell them I'm all in."

"Wait. Are you sure?"

"Damn straight. A hundred percent."

After a moment in which McCarthy soaked in Joe's directive, he said, "Okay, here we go."

Yeah. Here we go.

PART III

FIND THE TRUTH

Laud China's actions. Admire China's responsibility. Thank China's assistance.
~ Publicity Department of the Central Committee of the Communist Party of China
March 25, 2020

CHAPTER TWENTY-NINE

U.S. Embassy Complex
Chaoyang District
Beijing, China

Harper and Kwon were picked up at Beijing Capital International Airport after a fourteen-hour flight from Honolulu. The city was beset by a heavy rain, which suited the travelers just fine. The normal security scrutiny that followed American passengers all the way to the time they left the airport was lax due to the distraction.

A foreign service officer working in the public diplomacy sector of the U.S. Embassy in Beijing was their escort. She provided them some basic information about the city and directed their attention to some points of historical interest.

Neither Harper nor Kwon were interested in idle conversation. The long trip from the East Coast to the Hawaiian Islands and on to Beijing was tiring. It had been a great opportunity for the two to establish a rapport with one another. By the time the jet touched down on the runway, they had their game faces on and were prepared for the arduous task at hand.

They approached the embassy complex. The main buildings

were barely noticeable in the center of the perimeter security wall and fencing. At one entrance, despite the inclement conditions, a long line stretched down the block and around the corner of the wall.

The driver noticed Harper's interest in the long line. "Visas are in high demand right now. Reports are beginning to surface of another viral outbreak in the western part of the country. The Chinese people are used to the threats of disease, but since the Wuhan outbreak, they tend to want to leave the country at the first sign of trouble."

"Are there signs of trouble?" asked Harper. "In the media, I mean."

The young woman laughed. "It's impossible to know what is real and what isn't, here. Some of the career embassy personnel recall the days when the Wuhan outbreak occurred. There were a few reports here and there. The next thing we know, we were absorbing all of the staff from the U.S. Consulate General in Wuhan. Chengdu and Guangzhou, also."

"Was that our decision or Beijing's?" asked Harper.

"From what I've heard, they didn't say anything to us. Our people in the consulate building noticed one morning that the streets were empty. They said it was surreal. A city of ten million people became a ghost town overnight. Our people evacuated, and the next thing you know, the pandemic was on the move."

She parked the car and led the two of them through a covered entrance into the security area. There was a short line, as everyone entering the building was heavily scrutinized with the latest technology. It was far beyond what was required to enter the CDC and more invasive than used at U.S. airports.

After they cleared security, their escort led them to a conference room adjacent to a library that contained both fiction and nonfiction books, together with treatises on international law. One section contained all the current issues of American magazines and even some comic books.

"This way, please," she said politely, gesturing for them to enter the room. "This kitchenette contains snacks and drinks. Nonalcoholic, of course. May I get you something?"

Harper and Kwon both declined. They wandered around the windowless room, opting to stretch their legs after the long flight. Their escort took a seat at the end of the conference table and sat with a smile on her face. Harper glanced at Kwon and furrowed her brow. She expected to be greeted by someone, she just didn't know who.

"Um, is someone coming to meet with us?"

"Yes, they're aware of your arrival."

"Okay," said Harper hesitantly. She was anxious to get started and was slightly aggravated at the delay. She sat in one of the chairs and studied her escort. "Are you CIA?"

The woman laughed and replied, "Oh, my heavens. No. There is no one from the CIA here, Dr. Randolph. We're all career foreign service workers in the diplomacy sector. Mostly, we deal with visa applications."

Harper smirked. "All of you?"

"That's correct. It's a very meaningful job, you know. Once, I helped an elderly man whose wife had passed away on a plane to procure her ashes while still in Beijing. It was a touching moment. Don't get me wrong, living and working in a foreign nation like China takes a fairly big toll on one's personal life. There are days that are long and grueling. Often, you hope for a change of pace. Thankfully, I was chosen to escort you to the embassy."

"Will you be assisting us as we travel?" asked Harper.

"Oh, no. Your travel arrangements have been made by others with an expertise in that area. My job is to escort you this far and wait until your point of contact arrives."

Kwon, who'd stood with his back against a wall, had said practically nothing since their arrival at the embassy. He added, "And observe us."

"Pardon me?" the woman asked, feigning misunderstanding of his statement.

"Your role is to observe our mannerisms and attitudes," he

replied. He studied her body language. "My guess is you have a psychology degree. Further, you're well trained in martial arts. You've become adept at making casual conversation while your eyes dart from one mark to the other. Even while you portend to sit casually in this chair, your body is somewhat tensed and you're capable of springing into both a defensive and offensive attack posture."

The woman smiled. "Dr. Li, you have quite the imagination."

Before Kwon could respond, not that he planned to, a light tap at the door interrupted his conversation with the covert operative. The woman had been an agency employee for more than a decade since finishing her doctoral studies in psychology at UCLA.

As two men in dark suits entered the conference room, she rose and excused herself. She locked eyes with Kwon one more time before exiting. The two shared a look of mutual respect.

"Dr. Randolph, Dr. Li, I am Charles Downs, deputy assistant secretary for Transnational Affairs and Public Diplomacy. This is station chief of the Central Intelligence Service, Brad Levy."

The four of them exchanged greetings and then settled in around the conference table. Levy took the floor.

"First, I want you both to know that I was against this operation, at least initially. Let's make no mistake, I've read your personnel files and have nothing but respect for your capabilities. Especially you, Dr. Li. However, the Chinese military and police forces are operating in a heightened state of awareness. This disease is spreading and they're working every angle, as is customary for them, to cover it up from global scrutiny."

Harper interrupted. She didn't like being marginalized. "If I do my job properly, then there will be nothing to scrutinize. Dr. Li and I are looking to the CIA to pave the way for us to enter China with at least a head start on their advanced technological tracking system."

"You will have that, Dr. Randolph. I can assure you that we have nothing but professional respect for what you are trying to accomplish. Your mission arises out of China's penchant for secrecy. We understand that. Everyone here is committed to serving our country, and that means we have every intention of helping you succeed."

"Thank you," said Harper. She leaned forward to rest her arms on the table. She directed her remarks to the CIA's head spy in Beijing. "Mr. Levy, I appreciate your concern for our safety, but we're ready to get started. Infectious diseases don't call a time-out in the middle of a race."

"Understood," he said. Then he turned to Kwon. "You'll leave the embassy without a weapon. Upon arrival, if you deem it necessary, you can obtain one from our CIA safe houses. However, I must caution you, they are near impossible to conceal from the extensive surveillance system utilized in Urumqi. After the Uyghur uprising, the city was swept of weapons—and the Uyghurs, I might add. Urumqi is one of the most-watched major cities in China."

Kwon simply nodded his acknowledgment.

"Okay, then," interjected Deputy Assistant Secretary Downs. "Let me take you upstairs to meet Dr. Eloise Blasingame and the other two members of her CDC team. After that, we'll talk about your travel documents and dossiers."

CHAPTER THIRTY

U.S. Embassy Complex
Chaoyang District
Beijing, China

Harper was the first to enter the much larger conference room on the top floor of the main embassy building. Several temporary workstations had been created around the room in the form of cubicles. Whiteboards were scattered about with notes concerning regions of China and entries marked *presumed positive, confirmed,* and *dead.*

"Dr. Blasingame, may we interrupt?" asked Downs. "Your counterparts from the States have arrived."

Harper didn't wait for the career CDC epidemiologist to say hello. "It's even more true in person."

"What's that?" asked Dr. Blasingame, and then a look of recognition washed over her face. "Hey! You're a younger, prettier version of me."

"Hush, doppelganger," she said with a chuckle. "That's what I called you when they showed me your photo. Are you aware we're trading places for a little while?"

"I am, but I'm also very envious. I'd give anything to be out there with you, but I'd only be an extra set of hands. You're hunting down a killer. I'm more like the CSI people back in the lab."

Harper smiled. She was glad that the senior epidemiologist wasn't upset at being excluded. "We all have our roles, and quite frankly, chasing patient zero is one I relish. Naturally, I'd prefer a different venue."

Kwon and Dr. Blasingame were introduced, and then he was asked to join Levy to meet with the agency personnel who'd prepared their dossiers. This allowed Harper to discuss the outbreak with the epidemiologists who'd been expelled from China's CDC.

"Tell me what you know," she requested.

Dr. Blasingame approached the whiteboard centered in the room and Harper followed. "All we have is from CIA intercepts of social media posts and chat room conversations. The media clampdown is unprecedented."

"Worse than Wuhan?"

"Absolutely. The Chinese CDC and their propaganda machine learned a lot from the pandemic. One, there are no consequences for their subterfuge. Two, they can gain economically from the world's suffering as a result of their secrecy."

Harper studied the whiteboard and pointed toward the word *Urumqi*, which was located at the center of the whiteboard. "This is where we plan to start."

"That's a logical place because the physician we've deemed the *whistleblower*, Dr. Zeng, is … um, I mean, was employed at the First Affiliated Hospital in Urumqi."

"Was he fired?" asked Harper. "He's the first person I want to talk to."

"We don't know. Our friends in the CIA tell us that he disappeared several days ago after posting a series of enigmatic messages on social media. The chat rooms where they were contained exploded with conversation about the possibility of another major outbreak leading to a pandemic. The Chinese police clamped down on the posts about the time we were tossed out of their CDC complex."

Harper had a concerned look on her face. Her primary lead had disappeared. "Do you think he was arrested? Or even killed?"

"Nobody knows. It hasn't stopped the conversation, however. Based upon what the CIA has relayed to us, the epicenter of this outbreak may actually be in Tibet. Possibly Lhasa, the capital."

"Are these chat rooms and social media posts reliable?" asked Harper.

"The CIA analysts seem to have insight into how they work and especially into the person behind the post. Chinese government hackers infiltrate the group and try to spread disinformation. The CIA seems to know how to differentiate them from the rest."

Harper was frustrated. She'd already hit her first brick wall. "Do you think we should bypass Urumqi and go directly to Tibet?"

Dr. Blasingame walked over to her cubicle and handed Harper a large envelope. "This is a detailed summary of what we know as well as a list of people affiliated with, or known associates of, Dr. Zeng. It's a much better start than going to Lhasa, where you might end up wandering around aimlessly. We have absolutely nothing on who is reporting on those cases."

"Thanks," said Harper.

"Oh, one more thing," began Dr. Blasingame. "The only news reporting on the illnesses in the Chinese state media acknowledged that an outbreak has occurred, but that it was limited to those who may have come in contact with yaks. A team of European epidemiologists have accompanied the Chinese CDC personnel to the northeastern part of the country to investigate. I believe that to be a waste of time and misdirection. The hot zone is in the western parts of China."

Harper nodded and began to thumb through the reports, when the door to the conference room opened.

Levy and Kwon returned with two CIA analysts in tow. Harper was handed another plain manila envelope. Then Kwon gave her a dinosaur, figuratively speaking.

She chuckled before speaking. "Does this thing even work?" She held up the battered and scratched Blackberry phone. She turned the iconic cell phone over and over in her hands while she studied it. Harper hadn't seen one since high school.

"Yes," Levy replied. "It's Android powered, but it still has the guts of the original Blackberry devices from twenty-plus years ago."

"What are we supposed to do with it?" she asked.

"It will perform basic functions such as text messaging and phone calls. Plus, it's designed to include all of the social media apps and other applications, which will make your travel through China somewhat easier."

Harper turned it over and studied the back. It appeared to have been dragged along the concrete by a car. "Why is it beat up so badly?"

"Any Chinese officials you encounter will presume this device to be inferior and not worthy of inspection. Unlike Americans, the Chinese people don't have the wherewithal to trade phones every year or two."

Kwon asked, "SIM cards?"

"Very good, Dr. Li," replied Levy. "The Chinese surveillance state relies heavily upon the integrated circuits that identify mobile devices to track anyone in the country. The use of subscriber identity modules, or SIM cards, was largely abandoned with the advanced technology developed by Apple. May I?"

He reached his hand out to take the Blackberry from Harper. He slid the back of the phone open and popped out the SIM card. He explained, "We have given each of you three SIM cards to be removed and discarded throughout your investigation. Based upon our understanding of your travel plans, you'll use this one until you clear the security checkpoint in Urumqi. Then you'll replace it with another. This will effectively eliminate your being tracked through possession of the phone. After that, you'll find two more SIM cards that have been assigned a five-digit code and a phone number. SIM card three can be changed in the event you leave the country. This will notify us of your departure and cut off any further tracking by the Chinese government."

"What about the fourth one?" asked Harper.

The CIA station chief paused. "If you are in danger of being apprehended, then insert the fourth SIM card and discard your phone. It will begin to melt the internal circuitry within thirty seconds."

"Well, that's very *Mission Impossible*," quipped Harper.

"It is," said Levy. "Dr. Randolph, you have to understand. You're on your own out there. We have to treat you no differently than any other deep-cover operative of the U.S. government. Dr. Li understands this. If you are captured, you will be disavowed. I need you to confirm your understanding of this."

Harper took a deep breath. It was gettin' real, as they say. "I understand."

Levy glanced down at his watch. "I want to place you on the last flight to Urumqi. The airport is fairly quiet at the end of the day, and the security personnel are watching the clock, awaiting the end of their shift. Please get something to eat, study the materials you've been provided, and consult with the analysts who've accompanied me."

CHAPTER THIRTY-ONE

Underground Great Wall
Urumqi, Xinjiang, China

The citizen journalists were all abuzz in the main karez beneath the hospital. Dr. Zeng and his wife had settled in, and each had adopted a role within the underground community. His wife relished the opportunity to act as a mother figure to the students in exile. Dr. Zeng was an icon in their eyes although he maintained they were the true heroes. He'd given them a cause and an opportunity to flummox the Communist Party.

There was another person who'd been instrumental in giving the citizen journalists a voice. Despite living in the functional equivalent of a giant water tunnel, the group needed computer technology and other supplies to keep their undercover journalism operation going. This required money, and they relied heavily upon a financial benefactor who was supportive of their activity. They had just learned that their money source might soon dry up.

Ren Zhang was a multimillionaire. A retired real estate tycoon who'd never been shy about sharing his feelings toward the

Communist Party leadership or any other persons in power, right down to the administrators of hospitals.

Ren was angered by a recent decision of the Beijing government to enact a hugely controversial security directive in Hong Kong. Using the rubber-stamp parliament under the thumb of the Communist Party, a law was enacted to bypass Hong Kong's legislature. The law declared a ban on sedition, secession and subversion of the central government in Beijing. The move would allow the Chinese government to crack down on any form of anti-government protest but was largely seen as an erosion of Hong Kong's autonomy.

Hong Kong lawmakers retaliated in kind by adopting a national anthem in spite of the Communist Party's explicit threats not to do so. As a result, widespread unrest broke out in Hong Kong that became increasingly violent and disruptive throughout the night.

Ren, who was politically astute, saw the parliament's activity as a distraction from the news reports related to the mysterious illness that was emerging in the western part of the country. As he had often done in the past, he took to social media to go on a rant.

He referred to President Xi Jinping, easily the most powerful leader in modern Chinese history, as a clown. He commented on the president's address to parliament when the Hong Kong Sedition Bill was voted upon.

He said in his social media post that President Xi was not an emperor standing before the parliament in his new clothes, a veiled reference to the Hans Christian Andersen fairy tale from the early nineteenth century. He said the president was nothing more than a clown stripped naked for all to see, yet insisting he was an emperor.

He went on to say the Communist Party control over the parliament and the country's lack of a free press and free speech had led to the burial by China's state-run news media of another burgeoning viral outbreak.

To be sure, Ren Zhang had a megaphone and millions of Chinese listened to his every word. He'd had a busy night making the rounds on Chinese social media. And then he vanished.

At first, the citizen journalists were convinced he'd gone into hiding, as he had several times before. Many times, he'd traveled from Beijing to Urumqi to seek refuge in the Underground Great Wall. They'd waited throughout the day, not only for him to post something to prove to his loyal followers that he was safe, but also to rejoice in his sudden appearance in the karez.

Neither occurred.

As day turned to night, the group became increasingly concerned. There were rumored sightings of him on the high-speed bullet train from Beijing to Urumqi. Despite his wealth, he was a frequent traveler aboard the hard sleeper, the name assigned to the less expensive, bunk-style train operated by China Railway High-speed. The other type of CRH train car, known as a soft sleeper, was similar to what you might find on an Amtrak passenger train in the U.S. or train travel across Europe.

The concerned journalists immediately left the relative safety of the aqueduct tunnels and made their way above ground to assist in the search for Ren. They staked out all of the depots for public travel between the two cities as well as some of the hotels Ren was known to stay in. Soon, a discreet army of two hundred citizen journalists were canvassing the city, hoping to assist their beloved benefactor.

Dr. Zeng, seeing the disappearance as an attack on free speech by the Communist Party, didn't share the hopeful mindset of the young ideologues. He saw Ren's disappearance as the government's way of stifling dissent by making the problem disappear. It caused him to look for a quiet place alone while he reflected on his plight. After he thought it over, he sought his wife and nephew. The three of them, while wholly supporting the cause of the dissidents, needed to make an unemotional decision without getting caught up in the excitement surrounding Ren.

"Wife, nephew, I am seeing a repeat of the events of a decade ago. The Party continues to disavow its inherent system failures in dealing with viral outbreaks. They punish those, like me, who try to deviate from official orthodoxy or even reality. They continue to commit the same mistakes while expecting a different outcome."

"It is the same, husband. They will never disclose information regardless of the consequences. We agree there should be more openness and transparency. However, we cannot demand it."

Fangyu agreed. "It must be forced. Ren knows this. His mistake was getting personal in his criticism. It is a common mistake that serves no purpose."

Dr. Zeng wasn't so sure. "Perhaps he wanted to be arrested. He believed China needed a martyr. Until now, he was but a gnat in the president's ear. With the direct insults, he could no longer be ignored."

His wife squeezed his hand. "Husband, what is troubling you? Are you concerned for Ren? Or for yourself?"

He nodded and allowed a slight smile to come across his face. "I tried to warn my colleagues. Fangyu circulated the posts and the information on WeChat. Some have shared their information with us while others have not."

"We are doing our best, Uncle."

Dr. Zeng squeezed his nephew's shoulder. "You are a hero to me. You are making your best efforts, but my refusal to speak out, in my own voice, is delaying the ability to learn about this disease from others. I must speak in my own voice. I must be brave like Ren."

Ying became distraught. "And go to jail? Or disappear? I cannot live without you, husband!"

Fangyu stepped in to calm her fears. "Aunt, I can help him speak his truth without putting him at risk. He will not speak ill of the president or even the Party. Am I right, Uncle?"

"That is correct. I simply cannot be silent any longer. As you say, I must speak my truth."

CHAPTER THIRTY-TWO

Beijing Capital Airport
Security Checkpoint
China Southern Flight 6912
Beijing, China

Their foreign-services agent turned CIA escort drove them to Beijing Capital Airport. Neither Harper nor Kwon were interested in making idle conversation with the CIA agent. It had just turned dark as she wheeled the sedan onto the 3rd Ring Road, which led them to terminal 2. Their China Southern flight, the last nonstop departure of the day to Urumqi, departed in two hours.

Harper's mind wandered to Joe as they approached the passenger drop-off zone at terminal 2. It was eight in the morning in DC. He'd likely showered and was hanging out in his office. She wanted so badly to speak with him. Even a text message would have calmed her nerves. Harper was not doubting her decision. She convinced herself it was natural to be nervous considering the position she'd put herself in.

"Just to confirm, you are on CZ 6912 to Urumqi. Departure time is 10:08. I'm sorry, but it's agency protocol to book passengers in economy class. The China Southern Boeing 737s are part of an older fleet, so they are a little roomier."

"That's good," said Kwon. "We both need it." It was a rare commentary and hint at humor by the intense DARPA operative. Kwon was six feet three inches tall and Harper was close to five feet ten. The tall Americans would stand out in a crowd of Chinese nationals, who, on average, stood five feet five inches for men and five feet one for women.

They exited the car and grabbed the duffle bags provided by the CIA. Each of them had hidden pockets sewn in to hide the Blackberry SIM cards from prying X-ray machines. They also had external Velcro enclosures for Harper to switch face masks quickly depending on the situation. While traveling, she would be using her dark blue mask, which would reflect her CIA-generated cover as an American English teacher.

As for Kwon, there was no record of his existence in any spy agency worldwide, or Interpol-type database. For each of his missions, he could become whomever DARPA or the CIA needed him to become.

They held ticketed boarding passes printed through a local travel agent frequented by the American embassy. To avoid undue scrutiny by security, they traveled with just carry-ons, enabling them to avoid the ticket counter line. With some time to spare before they made their way to the gate, they followed the instructions of the CIA personnel to approach security as late in the evening as possible.

Harper and Kwon decided to wander the airport before they made their way through the final security checkpoint. Something caught Harper's eye and she tugged at Kwon's arm. She made an immediate beeline for a corridor that led away from security.

She passed by the airport lounge, which was full of a variety of travelers of all nationalities. They were chatting and drinking, pulling down their masks in between sips. The aromatic scents of food filled their nostrils as they walked past the bar.

While the food options included a variety of Chinese cuisines and teahouses, a quick way to gain an appreciation of the local culture, there were also Western standbys like McDonald's, Kentucky Fried Chicken, and Harper's favorite—Starbucks.

Kwon checked his watch. He was not as impulsive as Harper and believed in a structured approach. Harper noticed his hesitancy.

"Come on, it'll make us look like normal travelers. Spies don't walk around with caramel lattes in their hands, do they?"

Kwon furrowed his brow and then tilted his head. He saw her point. While Harper ordered her beloved latte with extra caramel and extra foam, Kwon downed a bottle of water and searched their surroundings. He resisted the urge to glance at the multiple security cameras that were affixed to the walls at just above eye level. A passenger's searching eyes obsessed with security cameras was an immediate mark for those monitoring them.

"Heaven on Earth," said Harper as she took a drink and sighed. She glanced around and spied the duty-free shop. "Hey, let's see what they have."

Once again, she darted off from Kwon, who found himself slicing through a group of people approaching the Starbucks counter to catch up. Harper was perusing the souvenir shop when he joined her.

He leaned in to whisper to her, "When we're on the ground in Urumqi, please don't run off from me like that."

"I looked before I leapt. Besides, I'm just trying to see if you can keep up."

"You don't need to test me."

Harper was smiling as she spoke. "I'm not. But you can trust me. I'm not a twit and I can play the game. Besides, to be honest, I'm a little nervous, and acting normal helps me bury all of that deep inside."

Kwon nodded and dutifully followed her around the shops as if they were a couple. After half an hour of browsing, she purchased a *netizen* tee shirt. In Chinese pop culture, the term *netizen* appeared often. It's a blending of the words *internet* and *citizen*. Netizen described someone who was actively involved in online communities. Harper was on the hunt for a man who was relying heavily upon an underground network of citizen journalists. She would use any advantage she could to get people to open up to her about his whereabouts.

With Harper having undertaken a little retail therapy, and with the soothing familiarity of the Starbucks caramel latte nestled in her belly, she was ready to approach the security checkpoint, which was far more stringent than U.S. airports.

The Transportation Safety Administration, or TSA, was looking for travelers who might try to commandeer or destroy an aircraft. Basically, terrorists. The security personnel of the China Civil Aviation Administration were not only looking for dangerous substances or domestic terrorist activity, but they were also searching for dissidents, foreign spies, and anyone else who seemed to be pursuing a nefarious purpose.

The line was still fairly long considering the late hour, but Harper immediately noticed the demeanor of the security personnel. They appeared tired and somewhat lethargic. In her mind, the group of four handling her lane was simply going through the motions until their shift ended.

Just as was the case in American airports, passengers were quizzed about electronic products, lighters or matches, and liquid articles. Signs indicating that weapons and explosives were prohibited were scattered about. Harper chuckled to herself and thought, *Who in their right mind would try to smuggle a gun through airport security in Communist China?*

The two of them were half a dozen passengers away from entering the scanning equipment when suddenly four new, fresh security agents arrived to replace the existing crew. Unlike the heavyset, uninspiring bunch who had worked this checkpoint moments earlier, the new group appeared hardened and intense. Well, like a quartet of Kwons.

Harper immediately became nervous. Her anxiety levels shot up and her palms became sweaty. She tried to remain calm, controlling her breathing the best she could. Kwon noticed her change in posture. She was no longer relaxed and confident. She slouched somewhat in an effort to crawl into her shell.

This was not good.

"Breathe," Kwon whispered in her ear. "I will answer all questions unless they direct them specifically to you in English."

Harper kept her eyes forward and whispered back, "They're spending more time with each passenger. They're scrutinizing their documents, too. Before, they were just walking through the screening machine."

They were almost to the front of the line. Two of the screeners began to assess Harper and Kwon. They leaned into one another and nodded toward her. Harper took a deep breath and exhaled, forcing the front of her mask away from her face like a balloon expanding. She reached up and adjusted it to let in some fresh air, as she suddenly felt claustrophobic.

Kwon uncharacteristically made physical contact with her. He reached for her hand and squeezed it. She made eye contact with him. His piercing dark eyes looked deep into her soul, imploring her to relax. Harper didn't want to disappoint him. She was trying not to derail their mission before it even started.

First Kwon and then Harper passed through the scanner. There were no alarms sounded, as they had packed all of their belongings in their luggage. The person manning the luggage scanner took an inordinate amount of time studying their duffle bags. Then Harper's heart jumped in her throat.

"You, step aside for special screening," ordered one of the security agents in Chinese.

Kwon gently took Harper by the arm and pulled her aside. She nervously followed his lead and then, out of the corner of her eye, she saw their bags pushed forward along the conveyer belt. However, the security personnel held up the rest of the passengers while they focused on Harper and Kwon.

Two of them now stood face-to-face with the Americans. They were giving orders to Kwon in Chinese, and as he received them, he told Harper to do as he instructed. Another security guard appeared and took their bags off the conveyer belt and set them on a stainless-steel table. He began to rifle through their belongings.

"Papers! Papers!" the security agent demanded.

Kwon responded politely and pointed toward their duffle bags.

They waved the electromagnetic wands in search of any metal hidden in their clothing. The Chinese had also developed the ability to identify traces of gases emitted by explosives residue.

Harper began to sweat. Her palms were sweaty. Her breathing had become more rapid. Keep it together, she told herself. All eyes of the three security personnel were on her now. One of them had her documents in his hand. He handed them to the other guard, who held them up to compare Harper's face with the passport.

The lead guard reached for a portable radio nestled in his utility belt. Harper closed her eyes for a moment, as she presumed their true identities had been discovered. And then alarms began to sound.

From the far end of the security checkpoint, the high shrill beeping and flashing lights indicating a breach in the secured area was causing the passengers standing in line to cover their ears. Other security guards began shouting and waving their arms as the alarms screamed throughout the concourse.

The guards scrutinizing Harper's documents shoved them into her bag. The trio ran toward the alarms and lights, as did several other security personnel.

Kwon forcefully grabbed Harper by the arm. "Let's go. They can only help us so long."

"Who?" she asked, turning around to look for an answer on her own.

"Probably the agency. The timing was too perfect. Hurry!"

They walked quickly toward their bags, stuffed everything spread out on the table inside, and slung the straps over their shoulders. They separated, with Kwon hanging back while Harper walked briskly up the concourse until she reached the long moving walkway.

I can do this.

Harper kicked herself in the pants. After there were a dozen people between her and anyone who might have been trailing her, she rested her bag on the moving handrail to retrieve a light jacket from her luggage. She quickly slipped it on. Then she whipped her hair into a ponytail, pulled out a solid white Ralph Lauren Polo cap, and placed it on her head with the ponytail pushed through the back clasp. Finally, she changed her mask from dark blue to light blue.

This was a risk, but a calculated one. At this point, she presumed all security personnel were concerned with the breach at the checkpoint, but the eyes in the sky, as she called them, were still monitoring passenger movement. Until she reached the gate, she'd change identities. Then, at boarding time, she'd switch back.

All of these crafty maneuvers might have been unnecessary, but to Harper, she felt the need to do something. In the moment, it changed her level of confidence. She was no longer an out-of-place epidemiologist. She was playing the part of an undercover detective in search of a killer. Most importantly, she believed in herself.

CHAPTER THIRTY-THREE

Underground Great Wall
Urumqi, Xinjiang, China

Fangyu had just created the final post to social media. He'd already sent a detailed email to several news media outlets that were at least receptive to publishing dissenting opinions that ran against the official statements of state-run media. He also blasted it to hospitals and doctors' offices throughout the two westernmost autonomous regions of China.

After a day of searching for their financial benefactor, many of the students and citizen journalists had returned to the karez disheartened. Most were hungry and needed rest. Fangyu thought they needed a reason to lift their spirits.

They were in an intense information war with the Communist Party. The battle would not be won with bullets or bombs. It would be won by the dissemination of ideas and suppressed information. He approached his uncle and asked him to read his open letter aloud.

After gathering everyone around the center of the karez, Dr.

Zeng picked up the paper with his handwritten statement. He began by reading the title aloud.

"Why I must disturb the sound of silence.

"My name is Dr. Zeng Qi. I was formerly a physician and professor at First Affiliated Hospital in Urumqi. With this post, I am suppressing my apprehension and fearfulness. I am speaking because others must remain silent. My words are whispered, but they will be shouted by many. And when they are, I fully expect that I, and even my family, will face harsh punishments from those who stifle dissent. Yet I may no longer stay silent.

"For many decades, China has been the origin of viral disease outbreaks that, when not contained, can be transmitted around the globe. A decade ago, a novel virus, labeled COVID-19, began as an outbreak in Wuhan and soon spread to nearly every nation.

"Physicians like myself knew it was highly likely a disease of its kind would arise. We warned our government of this fact, and we were ignored. When it happened, the Party instinctively organized a cover-up, ordering the police to crack down on physicians who were accused of improperly trying to alert others of the risks. Party news programs repeatedly denounced us as rumormongers and condemned us for hating our country. This, of course, was not true.

"Now we face a similar catastrophe. There is a new disease. It's one that is so unique, so novel, that it is nearly impossible to define it. Until now, it is a virus that has outsmarted me and others who've tried to identify it. Let me explain.

"It cripples the body's immune system in a manner similar to HIV/AIDs, attaching to white blood cells. This, in turn, triggers a cytokine storm just as we witnessed during the avian influenza outbreak. Like H5N1, this new disease results in uncontrolled inflammatory cytokines, which target the human respiratory system and then other internal organs, leading to sudden failure.

"Then comes death. I have never seen nor studied any infectious disease like this one. It is, quite simply, the perfect killer. Without further study, I cannot name a test kit used in our medical community that would be deemed accurate. I cannot propose a single treatment protocol that would be more effective than educated guesswork. I cannot even point to a specific manner of death to guard against.

"As the disease engulfs the patient, severe lung infection results in inflammation, which causes systemic sepsis. In other patients, the cytokine storms result in severe infections of the gastrointestinal tract, the urinary tract, and the central nervous system. Heart failure is likely if other vital organs don't fail first.

"We are in the early stages of an outbreak that rivals that of COVID-19. I am issuing a call to all physicians and health care professionals to make preparations. But, most of all, protect yourselves.

"I implore you, please do not disregard this warning or you will lose your lives. Stand up to the pressure that will come to bear when my words break the silence. I will stand with you for as long as I am allowed to stand."

When Dr. Zeng finished reading, he dropped his chin to his chest. He was emotionally drained. He could hear the young people around the karez openly crying. They comforted one another and whispered words of praise for his statement.

Then a single clap came from the group. Followed by another. And another. Soon, amidst the tears and sniffles, everyone in the Underground Great Wall was standing, cheering and applauding their inspirational leader.

CHAPTER THIRTY-FOUR

Ministry of State Security
Beijing, China

Unlike the CIA or Great Britain's MI6, China's Ministry of State Security didn't have an official website. There was never a spokesman made available to the press. There were no publicly listed contacts or organizational charts. Its building was not open to the public, nor was it accessible by most governmental officials.

Intelligence agencies were secretive by nature, but China's MSS seemed to operate under a heavier veil of secrecy than most. Formed in 1983 as China's main civilian intelligence agency, it was responsible for counterintelligence, foreign intelligence, national security espionage and domestic surveillance as well. Many considered the agency to be a cross between the CIA and FBI.

Like other ministries under the Communist-controlled State Council, the equivalent of China's cabinet, the MSS had a vast network of provincial and municipal branches across the country.

Their powers were broad and unchecked. The MSS was authorized to conduct various types of espionage activities both in China and overseas. Their duties included investigating foreign and domestic individuals, and they frequently engaged in intelligence activities against foreign governments.

Their control over any individual in China was well documented. By the National Intelligence Law, and in the name of national security, they were empowered to administratively detain any person who impeded their intelligence work or who was deemed to be a terroristic threat, for fifteen days.

Unlike America, where due process was clearly defined in the Constitution, in China, the MSS did not have to provide a detainee a phone call. Or a lawyer. Or a visit from a loved one. Targets of their investigations were locked up, and the key was left on the wall until the fifteen days expired. The detainee's calculation of fifteen days was often far different from his jailers at the MSS.

At the MSS regional station in Urumqi, Ren Zhang sat in isolation. His cell had no windows. The door was solid steel and had a small four-inch sliding door to allow his guards to look in on him once in a while. The steel bed had no mattress or pillow. The combination toilet and sink barely provided him enough water to flush.

For the first twenty-four hours of his captivity, he screamed, protested, acted out and generally created mayhem in an effort to get someone's attention. Nothing worked. He was ignored, a technique that had worked in the past for the MSS agents.

Now, however, their attention was turned to another problem— Dr. Zeng.

The Urumqi physician had boldly gone public with his *manifesto*, as social media had labeled it. Naturally, the state-run media made no mention of Dr. Zeng or his statement on the mysterious virus. After Ren's outburst in which he called President Xi a clown, none of the secondary news outlets dared to bring attention to themselves by republishing the manifesto.

Yet it had garnered the attention of the MSS and the Chinese CDC. As a result, a directive was issued.

Find Dr. Zeng and his wife.

Lock them up and the Ministry of Public Security will make

room for them at Qincheng Prison, a maximum-security facility located in the Changping District not far from the CDC. The CDC personnel would have access to him to learn what he knew, and he could then spend the rest of his life separated from his wife in the Soviet-constructed prison known for holding a who's who of political prisoners.

The director of the Urumqi station of the MSS paced the floor of the situation room. Half a dozen analysts worked at their computer stations while several more monitored activities on the streets of the city. They were following up on leads and information concerning the whereabouts of Dr. Zeng. Their agents in the field were directed to stop all other surveillance projects until he was found.

One of the analysts began searching for the whereabouts of Fangyu, the only living relative of Dr. Zeng other than his wife. A team had been sent to the university to raid his dorm room and interrogate the students who might have known him.

Another analyst focused on Dr. Zeng's hospital associates. Everyone from coworkers to staff and students were swarmed by a dozen MSS agents, with the assistance of the Ministry of Public Security.

Finding Ren Zhang had been much easier. The arrogant businessman had an extensive dossier built over the years he'd spoken out against the Communist Party's rule. The MSS had tracked his activities and were able to determine his travel habits. He had been taken into custody on the bullet train before it had pulled into the station at Urumqi.

Dr. Zeng would be more difficult. Urumqi was a medium-sized metropolis, by China's standards, of two and a half million people, roughly the size and population of Chicago. It was replete with high-rise residential buildings and multitudes of retail stores with back room apartments attached.

The MSS would have to rely upon their advanced surveillance capabilities and their ability to instill fear in any possible witnesses in order to trace Dr. Zeng's whereabouts. Thus far, they'd struck out.

The airport, train station, and bus depot had extra security assigned to them. Major arteries leading out of the city were monitored, and roadblocks were established in some cases to prevent Dr. Zeng from escaping.

On the streets, hundreds of Public Security officers supplemented MSS operatives as they combed the streets with the aid of the surveillance cameras. The search for Dr. Zeng had become personal for President Xi as well. He'd had enough of dissidents openly defying his authority and making a mockery of his power. The directive was clear.

Eliminate Ren Zhang and Dr. Zeng. Then frighten their families into submission. Finally, search and destroy the citizen journalists. They were trying to force transparency upon the Communist government, a direct threat to maintaining control over the people.

CHAPTER THIRTY-FIVE

Urumqi, Xinjiang, China

After their arrival in Urumqi, Harper and Kwon made their way through the airport terminal without incident. As instructed, they exited the sliding doors onto the sidewalk outside arrivals at terminal 3. T3, exclusive to China Southern Airlines, was known for its rooftop that protruded above the sidewalk in the shape of eagle's wings.

The night air filled their lungs as they searched for a Chinese-made Volkswagen C-Trek. At two in the morning, the airport had very little activity. Within minutes of their stepping onto the sidewalk, the C-Trek station wagon driven by a CIA operative gathered them up. He escorted them to a safe house, turned over the keys to the vehicle, and then disappeared into the night.

The apartment building was walking distance to First Affiliated Hospital, where Dr. Zeng had been employed. In Beijing, the CIA had confirmed he'd been suspended. The safe house was centrally located and convenient to many possible hiding places. Meanwhile, Harper and Kwon had no idea what had transpired since their flight departed Beijing.

"Home sweet home," quipped Harper as she and Kwon entered the modestly furnished flat. The two-bedroom, one-bath apartment was barely eight hundred square feet. It contained a small efficiency kitchen that was fully stocked with nonperishables and drinks. The living area was furnished with a sofa, two matching chairs, and a dinette table for four. Otherwise, it didn't contain any type of décor.

Kwon excused himself and went to the restroom. When he returned, he showed Harper a key ring with three small plastic keycards attached. They resembled the customer loyalty cards a grocery store might provide its customers to track their purchases or obtain special deals.

"Where did you find those?" she asked.

"The embassy. I was told during my briefing there are a series of hidden compartments within the apartment. These emit electronic signals that trigger the locking mechanisms. I just need to find all of the safes."

Harper put her hands on her hips and looked around. She pointed to the ceiling, where a two-foot-by-three-foot air duct return was located next to a smoke alarm.

"Too obvious," said Kwon. "We're looking for something with a seam. You might not notice it at first glance."

Harper wandered around the living area and then found her way to the kitchen. A gray breaker box was installed flush with the wall separating the kitchen from the guest bathroom. She opened the door, viewed the breakers, and shrugged as she closed the door.

Exhausted, she wanted to consider giving up the hunt until morning. "Can it wait?"

Kwon shook his head. "No, not really. They have a laptop for us with secured wireless capability. We can access the CIA's servers in Beijing as well as communicate directly with our team of handlers monitoring our activity. Remember?" He pointed at the top of his forearm where the microchip had been implanted.

Harper continued her search. She looked inside kitchen cabinets and appliances. She'd given up on the kitchen and had rounded the corner toward the bedrooms when she stopped in her tracks. She held the wall with her hands and looked back into the kitchen. Then, to get a different perspective, she stepped back away from the wall separating the two areas of the apartment.

"Hey, look at this. Does this wall seem a little wide to you?"

Kwon joined her side and eyeballed the wall separating the two rooms. He walked into the kitchen and held up the three keycards, swiping each one slowly around the edges of the breaker box. On the third try, a clicking sound could be heard, and the left side of the breaker box popped open. He carefully pulled the box open on its hinges and peered inside.

"Here we go. Good work, Harper."

He reached in and handed her a hard-plastic case the size of a laptop computer. He also retrieved two Sig Sauer MPX gun cases and several rounds of 9 mm ammunition. Lastly, there were two boxes containing Sig Sauer SRD9 suppressors. He laid out all the weapons and accessories on the kitchen counter and handed Harper the computer.

"Would you mind powering this on? It might need to be charged. But don't navigate anywhere just yet. I have passwords."

"Okay," she replied. "Did you write them down?"

Kwon looked at her and tapped the side of his head. "No paper trails."

"Um, is one of those for me?" she asked, pointing at the fully automatic carbine.

"Maybe. We'll talk about that in a moment."

Kwon opened the cases, pulled out the two identical weapons, and set out six thirty-round magazines. After searching through the void behind the breaker box and finding it to be empty, he closed up the space and joined Harper.

She'd plugged in the power source and powered up the IBM laptop-style computer. It was thick and bulky, unlike her thin silver MacBook. "I haven't seen one of these in a long time."

"Like the Blackberrys we were assigned, it's designed to appear antiquated," began Kwon, who had used similar devices during other operations. "It's not actually an IBM product. It's made by

Lenovo and is exactly what we need in an environment like this. We will have satellite internet and communications via secured message streams from anywhere. If it is taken from us, it will initially appear as junk to the Chinese. If they try to access it, after three incorrect password entries, an acid-like substance will be released, destroying its motherboard and hard drive."

"You guys get all the fun toys," quipped Harper. She nodded toward the guns. "I can shoot, you know."

"I know," said Kwon dryly. "You grew up in a rural community. Your family owned weapons, and your father frequently took you to the range to practice. That's also been nearly thirty years ago."

Harper angrily walked away from the table. "I know how long it's been. You obviously know a helluva lot more about me than I know about you. So was it necessary to remind me when I saw my father last?"

Kwon raised his hands. "Look, I'm sorry. I'm not very ... I'm not subtle, okay. Yes, I learned everything I could about you from your personnel file and during my conversations with Joe. I asked him to be completely honest and up front with me."

"Why?"

"So we don't get our asses killed in China. Harper, this isn't a game. These people don't give a damn about us, our lives, or what we're here for. When I say our lives depend on our abilities to fly under the radar and then get the hell out, I mean it."

Harper turned away toward the kitchen and wiped a few tears that streamed from her eyes. She tried to control her emotions and silently cursed herself for still being sensitive about her parents after all these years. She looked at the ceiling above the oven-range combination. Her eyes followed the wall along the hood vent. She took a deep breath and changed the subject.

"I think I found another secret hidey-hole."

CHAPTER THIRTY-SIX

CIA Safe House
Urumqi, Xinjiang, China

They stayed up for another hour and took the time to get to know one another. Kwon opened up about his family and what had led him to follow the unusual career path. He'd never set out to be a doctor but was encouraged to do so by the military. As a Navy SEAL, he was ideally suited for becoming a covert operative in any branch of the military. However, his extreme intelligence and aptitude to learn resulted in his superiors pushing him toward the medical field. After Harvard, he was too valuable to lose as a doctor, and his SEAL training was too important to cast aside. The logical landing place for Kwon was DARPA.

After a good night's sleep, Harper woke up first and fixed a pot of coffee. She stood at the dirty window overlooking a large park, hoping to catch a glimpse of a Starbucks or the golden arches of a McDonald's sign. She decided not to press it when Kwon urgently called her into the living room.

"Take a look at this," he said. He turned the IBM laptop around and faced it toward the chair across from the sofa. "A lot has happened since we left the embassy."

"How is this Ren guy connected to Dr. Zeng? And why, after effectively getting the word out without disclosing his identity, would he stick his head out of the fox hole?"

Kwon scowled and shrugged. "This has made our job a lot more difficult. According to this briefing, the city is covered with both MSS and Security Police. They're gonna be turning over every rock looking for this guy."

Harper flopped in the chair with her mug of coffee. "Everywhere we go, they're gonna be there already searching for him. I guarantee their investigators have a better idea where to look than we do."

Kwon stood from the sofa and wandered around the small living room. He made his way to the kitchen and poured himself a coffee.

"Here's the good news," he began. "They're still looking, which means we've got a shot. Also, that means we can eliminate the obvious two stops at the top of our list."

"The hospital and his apartment," interjected Harper.

"Exactly. Think about it. This whistleblower was using social media outlets to spread the word about the disease. Last night, using the same types of platforms, plus some friendly, on-the-edge-of-dissidence websites, he publishes this manifesto-style diatribe."

"Diatribe, criticism, whatever you wanna call it. He's obviously kicked the hornet's nest in Beijing."

"Guaranteed," added Kwon. "They're conducting a sweep of anyone who publicly disagrees with them or speaks out about the disease. The financier, Ren, is known for funding these citizen journalists. It appears Dr. Zeng is using these same people to spread his message and gather information. Let's find them, and maybe they'll lead us to our doctor."

"Where do we start?" asked Harper.

"The home of all malcontents. The university."

Harper laughed. "I've got a shirt for that."

"The one you bought last night?"

"Yes, indeed. I am going to woo them with my *Netizen* tee and my charming smile."

Kwon rolled his eyes. "Will you let me do the talking despite the fact that most of these college kids are fluent in English? It's a second language for them."

"At first, maybe. Kwon, I'm not the same person who started to freak out at the airport last night. Give me a chance, okay?"

"I will. Get your shirt and let's get started."

"Are we taking the guns?" she asked with a smile.

"No. Would you forget about those things for now? The last thing we need is a gun battle, especially now. Besides, they've got all kinds of surveillance cameras that can detect them under our clothing. Let's play it smart and avoid contact with any police or MSS."

Harper gave him a thumbs-up and went to change shirts. While she was gone, Kwon studied the map of the area to determine which of the universities was closest to them. He pointed at the screen, identifying Xinjiang University as their first stop. Then he recalled that Dr. Zeng's nephew was a student in the College of Journalism there. He slammed the computer closed and stowed it away with the weapons behind the wall.

"Come on, Harper. You're late for class."

She returned from her bedroom wearing the crimson-colored tee shirt with white letters that read NETIZEN.

"Aha!" she exclaimed jokingly. "You can be funny."

"Maybe."

They exited the apartment building and realized they were in the midst of more than a dozen high-rises in the complex. Kwon directed Harper's attention to a parking garage located on the main road in front of the complex where they'd parked the car the night before. The CIA operative who'd picked them up had disappeared into the night, most likely picked up by a vehicle following them.

They made their way in the direction of Xinjiang University. As they did, they passed a kindergarten-age school, where some of the children were sitting outside at round concrete picnic tables. Each of them had a hat affixed to their heads with multicolored foam sticks protruding in each direction like a propeller.

"Check it out," said Kwon.

Harper noticed they weren't wearing masks. "Social distancing. Very interesting."

"They're teaching safety because they live in a world susceptible to infectious diseases. Hard to imagine, isn't it?"

The two slowed as they passed, taking in the teachers giving the five- and six-year-old children instructions.

"I don't know much about kids," began Harper. "But I can't imagine finding two dozen five-year-olds in Georgia sitting still like these kids are. That's just as amazing as the teaching tool."

"It's discipline, Harper. This culture is entirely different from what we have in America."

"I can't imagine having children growing up in fear of contracting an infectious disease. I mean, have you seen anyone on the street yet who isn't wearing a mask?"

"No, but it could be a signal that the general public knows something that the Communist-run media doesn't want the world to know."

"The disease is spreading," suggested Harper.

"Right. As much as I despise social media, it is obviously a force of good in a Communist country that controls the news. These people remember what happened in Wuhan a decade ago. They're willing to sacrifice their vanity, if they even have any, and endure the inconvenience of the mask. Face it, Urumqi doesn't have the air pollution problem they have in Beijing or even Hong Kong. This city may be the size of Chicago, but it's surrounded by desertlike landscape with lots of breeze. The mask isn't because of the air quality. It's because of disease."

Kwon suddenly wrapped his arm through Harper's and pulled her close.

"What?" she asked, her eyes darting around to look for a threat.

"Up ahead, just inside the entrance to that small store, are two men in suits and dark sunglasses. They are completely out of place for this residential area. We're gonna duck down this side street and then look for another route to take us to the university."

They continued their steady pace, and when the opportunity arose, they dashed down the side street. As they did, the wail of a siren could be heard approaching them.

"Now what?" asked Harper.

"Stay calm. Eyes forward. Shorten your stride. We don't need to look like we're in a hurry."

The security police car slowed as it pulled alongside Harper and Kwon before abruptly speeding away.

"Good call," said Harper.

"Listen, it's easy to be paranoid. I like to call it a heightened state of awareness or even managed paranoia. The key is to act calm and disinterested, but don't overplay it."

"I began to learn that last night," Harper said.

"I've been trained how to appear aloof and detached from my surroundings. It's kept me alive, but it's also kept me single."

Harper glanced over at Kwon's face. For the first time, he showed a hint of emotion. Perhaps he was human after all.

CHAPTER THIRTY-SEVEN

Xinjiang University
Urumqi, Xinjiang, China

Kwon led the way with Harper close on his heels. The two sensed the greater police presence. The Communist Party didn't rule with the same sadistic, iron fist that North Korea used, but every one of its citizens lived with a sense of fear of crossing those in power. The fact that both the security police and the military were sweeping the streets in search of someone who hadn't committed a murder, much less a violent crime, was a testament to how important it was for them to crush dissent.

"This will help," said Kwon, pointing at a three-sided monument sign portraying a map of the campus and a legend of its buildings. He took a moment to get his bearings, and then he pointed at a three-story building on the far edge of the university adjacent to a park. "This is the School of Journalism and here is the closest dorm. It appears there's a dorm in close proximity to each of the major fields of study. It's just a hunch, but with a little luck, the nephew lives here."

Kwon traced his finger from the School of Journalism along the sidewalk adjacent to the park until he rested it on the nearest dormitory.

"This is all we've got to go on," said Harper as the two walked briskly across the open compound. They gave the campus security officers a wide berth and walked on the outskirts of the grassy area where dozens of students had gathered. "Somehow, we've gotta get lucky and convince one of these students to talk to us."

"Luck is predictable," said Kwon as he picked up the pace. Since being noticed by the security police on the streets, his innate sense of urgency had kicked in. "You apply your experiences, street smarts, and preparation to limit your options. This improves your odds of getting lucky."

Harper raised her eyebrows and nodded. "Common sense told you to forget about interviewing hospital contacts or anyone in Dr. Zeng's apartment building because those were logical stops for the police."

"Exactly. Of course, the nephew's dorm is a logical place for the MSS to investigate, too. But these kids despise authority and would absolutely pretend they didn't know Zeng Fangyu even if they were classmates."

"You think they'll treat us differently?" asked Harper.

"Well, yes. With a little luck." Kwon smiled. He'd made an attempt at being funny twice in one day.

Harper chuckled and the two made their way to the sidewalk, entering the School of Journalism. Kwon immediately began stopping students who made eye contact. Many refused to talk with him, but several at least said they didn't understand. Growing frustrated, he considered a different tactic.

"I look too much like a person of authority. I think you should try."

"Me? I don't even know how to say hello in Chinese."

"That's my point. Many of these students can speak conversational English. In fact, they'd love to speak with a genuine American. Let's try the dorm, and instead of me approaching them, you do it."

"Kwon, are you sure about this?"

"We've got nothing to lose. Just speak slowly and enunciate your words clearly. Don't use contractions or slang and definitely don't yell."

Harper tilted her head and a puzzled look came over her face. "Why would I yell?"

"Because that's what Americans do when they speak to someone from another country. They think they have to yell to get the non-English speaking person to understand. They're not deaf."

Harper thought for a moment and realized Kwon was right. On all counts. She might have better luck with the students because they'd be curious about her and she was nonthreatening. And his point about yelling was well taken. She wondered if she'd been guilty of that in the past.

They walked through a tree canopy and found the entrance to the dorm. There was a group of students hovering around the double doors, staring at a glass-enclosed bulletin board. A dorm administrator had just posted something inside it and was locking the door. The students gave him room, and once he entered the building, they crowded around to see what the post was about.

Kwon and Harper inched closer. The excited voices of the students grabbed their attention.

"They have been searching for Fangyu."

"I heard they destroyed his dorm room looking for something."

"He has disappeared."

"Is he in trouble?"

"No, the notice says his uncle is looking for him."

"That cannot be true. He was with his uncle the other night. I saw them in the common area."

They spoke over one another, but Kwon clearly understood what they were saying. He whispered to Harper, "Now's your chance. One of them knows the family. Remember, they'll be helpful to you because—"

"I've got this," said Harper, cutting him off. The students appeared ready to disperse and she wanted to speak to them before they left. She confidently approached the group. The students weren't wearing masks. She didn't want to appear shady, so she removed her mask. She arrived behind them and announced herself.

"Hello. Can somebody help me?"

Their heads whipped around to observe Harper.

She asked again, "Hi. I am looking for someone. Can you help?"

A young woman stepped forward. "Are you an American?"

"Yes, I am. My name is Eloise." Harper winced. She immediately realized she was supposed to be someone else when in public. Hopefully, it wouldn't matter.

"Hello, Eloise. I am Sun. I like your shirt. We are all *netizens*."

"Yes, so is my friend. His name is Fangyu. Do you know him?"

Now all of the students were crowded around Harper. They were assessing her, studying her face and her body language. Two of them spoke to her in Chinese, but she truthfully shrugged, indicating her inability to understand them.

The young woman was about to answer when one of the male students at the back of the group spoke up in English.

"Is this you?" he asked, pointing at the bulletin board.

Harper towered over the students so she was able to view the post the young man was referring to. Next to the posting about Fangyu was a photograph of Harper at the airport with her mask on. Harper reached to pull her mask up and thought better of it. Out of nowhere, Kwon appeared by her side.

He studied the posts and he tensed up. "Please, you must help us. Fangyu and his family are in grave danger. The MSS and Security Police are trying to locate them because Dr. Zeng spoke out against the Party."

He was taking a great risk exposing the purpose of their inquiry to the students. However, he trusted these young people to keep quiet more than any other strangers he might encounter.

Before anyone could answer, the glass doors to the dormitory burst open. The same dorm administrator who'd made the posting rushed into the opening. His cell phone was pressed to his ear as he spoke frantically to the party on the other end.

"Go! You must go!" said the young woman who'd responded to Harper. "They will be coming for you now."

Harper didn't give up. "Tell us where to look. We want to help them."

The young woman pulled them away from the bulletin board and the prying ears of the dorm administrator. She spoke under her breath. "Run through the woods. You can escape into the markets."

Sirens could be heard blaring in the background, growing louder and more numerous as they talked.

"Then what?" asked Harper.

"Stop! Now! Do not engage these people!" The administrator was shouting at the students while reporting Harper and Kwon's presence to the Security Police.

"Come on!" Kwon shouted as he grabbed Harper by the arm.

She resisted him to ask the student another question. "Where is he?"

"Under! He's under!"

Security Police cars were speeding into the administrative parking lot near the center of the campus. Students throughout the grassy areas had stopped to observe the activity.

"Where?" asked a confused Harper. Then Kwon grabbed her by the hand and forcibly dragged her away. Seconds later, they'd ducked into the woods in search of the trail that led off campus.

CHAPTER THIRTY-EIGHT

Urumqi, Xinjiang, China

Kwon fought his way through the underbrush, with Harper hot on his heels. The Security Police sirens continued to reverberate off the tall buildings surrounding the campus, and now they could hear voices shouting from the sidewalk connecting the dorm to the School of Journalism. They reached a chain-link fence and Kwon assisted Harper in scaling the eight-foot barrier. By the time they'd reached the other side, they could hear men approaching, shouting loudly to one another amid the crackle of two-way radios.

Harper and Kwon didn't bother to glance at their pursuers. They raced through a gravel parking area used by the students. They dodged cars seeking a parking space, resulting in one of the drivers honking their horn out of frustration.

"Which way?" asked Harper, who was beginning to breathe heavily. She was regretting her inability to stay in better physical shape due to her constant travelling.

They made their way to the cross street and Kwon pointed toward yet another police car closing on their position.

"Let's go up a block and then to the left. We've gotta make our way back to the safe house."

They darted through oncoming traffic along the one-way street, drawing the ire of those who had to brake to avoid hitting the jaywalkers. Once on the other side, they were able to make use of an alleyway between two office buildings to throw off any pursuers.

When they reached the end of the alley, they both stopped abruptly. Before them was a wet market, an open-air place of commerce that had become so well known to Westerners decades ago during the SARS outbreak and later with the spread of COVID-19.

Harper had grown up in a small community where local farmers would bring their produce into town on Saturday mornings for shoppers to make their purchases. At the farmers' market, prices might not necessarily be inexpensive and the produce might not be quite as eye appealing as the corporate-grown products bought into the grocery store, but people loved the thought of buying *farm-to-table*.

In China, the concept of a farmers' market was taken to another level. Not only could you purchase produce directly from the farmer, but butchers were there with plucked chickens and slaughtered cattle. They also brought wild animals, which were still alive.

It was not uncommon to see a customer purchase a porcupine or a deer, and then they'd wait while the butcher slaughtered it on a table before them. Whether the animals were used for food or medicinal purposes, the mess created by the blood and animal parts was one of the reasons diseases were frequently spread at the wet markets. The 2003 SARS epidemic had been linked to the sale of rare civet cats, animals related to the mongoose, at a wet market in Guangdong province.

These wet markets were unsanitary, and each of the vendors worked in very close proximity to one another. They were chaotic as the customers and vendors bartered and argued with one another. To Harper, it looked like a massive petri dish of bacteria and viruses.

She pulled the mask over her face and made sure it was affixed properly. She looked over to Kwon and advised him to do the same.

"This is perfect," he said. "We can get lost in here and make our way around the university complex back to the safe house."

"Just don't touch anything," warned Harper. "I have no words."

"I agree. This way."

They made their way through the aisles of vendors, trying to avoid contact with anyone and anything. The two of them were keenly aware of what was being sold and how close they'd come to the exposed meat of animals. Occasionally, they'd draw a glance from the locals, but mostly, everyone went about their business. As they reached the far end of the wet market, a parking area appeared, enclosed by a fence. Kwon stopped and assessed his options.

"Listen," said Harper. "I don't hear the sirens, do you?"

Kwon focused and glanced at his watch. "No. It's been twenty minutes since we jumped the fence. It's hard to believe they've given up already."

"Maybe we're not that important."

Kwon studied their surroundings. He didn't want to draw any more attention by scaling fences, but the most direct route to the safe house required them to travel along the edge of the university campus.

"Or they're sweeping the streets. It's going to take longer, but we need to avoid the university. Come on."

Harper walked briskly to keep up with Kwon's long strides. They were both wearing their masks and she continued to don the white Polo ball cap. They entered the main thoroughfare leading back in the direction of the hospital. They walked close to the buildings, using pedestrians on the sidewalk as a buffer between them and any unmarked Security Police vehicles driving by.

Suddenly, the high-pitched shrill from a whistle pierced their ears. Across the street, a city policeman was holding several flyers. Now he was waving them in the air as he continued to blow his whistle. Pointing toward Kwon and Harper, the officer ran toward the crosswalk and waited for the traffic to yield for him to cross.

"Kwon! Up ahead! They're coming toward us."

Kwon didn't respond. He ran forward in the direction of their pursuers and motioned for Harper to follow him down an alley. The alley must've connected back toward the wet market because it was full of vendors pushing carts or carrying crates full of dead animals or vegetables.

They were now the center of attention as their height and American appearance drew onlookers from on the street as well as from the windows in buildings around them.

He glanced over his shoulder and shouted to Harper, "Faster! They're on us!"

Harper led the way, pushing people down and racing in the direction of the wet market. Up ahead, she saw two uniformed police officers. They, too, were blowing whistles and forcing their way through the wet market vendors. She stopped and Kwon crashed into her.

Both of their heads were on a swivel as they frantically looked around the alley for options. They were sandwiched between two tall residential apartment buildings. For as far as the eye could see, the residents had their windows open and were poking their heads through the openings to watch the chase.

Just beyond an overflowing dumpster, Kwon saw a small alleyway. He wasn't sure if they could get there before the two uniformed officers who were moving briskly towards them, but it was all they had. He motioned for Harper to follow, urging her to walk in a crouch so their heads didn't protrude above the much shorter locals.

They'd just made it to the dumpster when the officers chasing them from behind began to catch up. They were closing in, blowing their whistles and screaming at the wet market vendors to move out of the way. The congestion helped Harper and Kwon escape down the alleyway in search of a way into the apartment buildings. They'd almost reached the last doorway when a group of men jumped from behind tall stacks of wooden crates.

They tackled Kwon first and then grabbed Harper around the waist. She tried to fight them off, but in a matter of seconds, they had pulled a grain sack over her head.

"Kwon! Kwon!" she tried to shout, but her voice was muffled. She fought to catch her breath. She tried to wiggle out of the grasp of the men who'd restrained her, to no avail.

They dragged her along the concrete across the metal threshold of a doorway. The air around her became suddenly cooler, but not like the feel of air-conditioning. It was a dark cold. Damp. And stale. She tried again to call out for Kwon. But he didn't answer. She suddenly felt very alone.

PART IV

HIDING IN THE SHADOWS

*True friends are those rare people who come to find you in dark places
and lead you back into the light.*

CHAPTER THIRTY-NINE

Urumqi, Xinjiang, China

Harper was battered. Her body ached all over from being manhandled and dragged for what seemed like hundreds of yards. She tried to focus on the external stimuli that entered her brain through her senses of hearing, smell, and touch. The grain sack over her head blocked her vision and constricted her smell, also leaving her gasping for air and searching for any form of light.

After her initial protestations, she chose not to say anything else. When Kwon didn't respond to her at first, she thought he'd evaded capture. She was certain, at this moment, he was most likely coming for her, so any efforts she made to call out to him might put him in danger.

At first, two powerful hands held her arms behind her back. After a few minutes, as she was dragged down an incline into a darker, colder space, her kidnappers stopped and restrained her with the ties. She twisted her wrists in an attempt to break free of the multiple zip ties used to bind her wrists.

Now she was lying on a cold, somewhat rough floor. The dampness was soaking into her clothes, but she tried to ignore the chill that was coming over her body. She summoned all her mental acuity to take in her surroundings. As she did, her mind raced to stories of prisoners in Russia, North Korea, and China being interrogated and tortured.

When Joe and Dr. Reitherman had tried to warn her off of this ludicrous idea, they told her anyone considered a threat to the Communist government simply disappeared. There would be no arrest. No trial. No prison cell. She would simply vanish.

They were right.

And it had happened so fast. One second, they were running from their pursuers, a combination of Security Police, local law enforcement, and most likely the MSS, whom Kwon seemed the most concerned with. Then it dawned on Harper. Neither she nor Kwon had seen evidence of the MSS agents chasing them. They were all uniformed officers. No, the MSS was involved, and Harper began to believe that was who snatched her off the street.

Great, she thought to herself. *At least I could've demanded a lawyer with the other guys.*

Or not.

Footsteps. Someone was coming. Without warning, two sets of hands brusquely pulled her upright and, in the same motion, untied the grain sack and pulled it off her head. Harper's vision was blurred and she tried to adjust to the minimal light available to her.

Before her stood a smallish woman, probably in her late sixties and modestly dressed. Next to her was a young man. College age. He had his arms crossed and stared down at Harper.

She continued to adjust her eyes to allow the faint light in the room to enter her retina. They adjusted and converted the light into signals to the brain. She began to make visual recognition. The young man resembled the photograph of Zeng Fangyu on the posting at the dormitory.

Harper coughed as she attempted to speak. A man reached around her and spun off the cap of a bottle of Nongfu Spring water. Harper opened her mouth and the man poured too much into it at first. Harper drank half, then choked slightly and allowed the rest to drip down onto her netizen tee shirt.

"Thank you," she said softly. "Please don't hurt me. I am trying to find someone."

"He found you," said the young man, speaking in third person. "Why do you seek him?"

Harper knew nothing about being held hostage and how she should act. However, she remembered her grandmother always saying, *kill 'em with kindness.* So she gave it a try.

She had to assume her captors, if they were the MSS or police related, which she doubted, knew of her identity. She told the truth because she was most likely going to die anyway.

"My name is Dr. Harper Randolph. I am an epidemiologist with the American CDC. I am looking for Fangyu. I believe he is the nephew of Dr. Zeng." Harper continued to keep Kwon's name to herself. She wasn't out of the woods yet and knew Kwon would come for her.

"Why do you seek Dr. Zeng?" the young man asked after he translated for the older woman.

"I need his help. We have a viral disease in America that we cannot identify. I believe Dr. Zeng can help me stop the spread. It has already killed and time is running out."

The young man translated. Then he turned to the two men standing behind Harper. He gave them instructions. Seconds later, her zip ties had been cut loose and she was being helped to her feet.

The woman stepped forward and studied Harper's face. She motioned for the young man to join her. She instructed him in Chinese to speak to Harper. She never took her eyes off Harper's face.

"I am Fangyu. I know you are sought by the Security Police. We have eyes and ears everywhere."

"Hello and thank you for taking this off my wrists," said Harper. She rubbed the deep indentations left by the hard-plastic zip ties. She took a chance, mainly because she was concerned Kwon might come for her with guns blazin', or at least fists.

"I have a friend. He is Dr. Li Kwon. He is here to assist me find you and search for the cause of this disease. He might be coming—"

Fangyu raised his hand and began speaking to the men who stood in the shadows behind Harper. They left the enclosed area where she was being held. Her eyes darted around and she glanced over her shoulder to see them leave.

"What's wrong? Did I do—?"

She heard a man coughing and then his voice. "Harper! Are you okay?"

It was Kwon. Her reaction was spontaneous and startled their captors. She ran into his arms. It was an emotional response. A natural showing of relief that she wasn't alone in this dark dungeon.

The usually stoic Kwon gently hugged her back, but his eyes remained focused on Fangyu. He spoke to the young man in a low, growling snarl that frightened Harper somewhat. She needed to speak fast before Kwon killed everyone associated with their abduction.

"Hey! Hey!" she began, standing in front of him so her body blocked his access to Fangyu. "It's okay. Actually, I think they saved us. Right?" she asked Fangyu directly by turning to face him.

"Yes, but there is not much time," he replied. "They will be coming for you. We must go to another place and seal off this aqueduct."

"Are we, um, *under*?" asked Harper.

"Yes. This is the Underground Great Wall. Now come with us, as we must leave."

Harper and Kwon whispered to one another as they were led through a series of tunnels, some partially filled with water and others completely dark, illuminated only by Fangyu's flashlight. After twenty minutes of wandering through the maze of openings and aqueducts, they arrived at the karez beneath First Affiliated Hospital.

"Wow!" exclaimed Harper, whose spirits had lifted considerably when she realized she wasn't going to die. "This is amazing. I always wondered what the Batcave looked like." She laughed as she made reference to the famous base of operations for the fictional character Batman.

Out of the shadows a smallish man appeared, wearing black slacks and a plain white shirt. He stood with his hands behind his back and his belly protruding somewhat. Fangyu rushed to his side and explained in a hushed voice. As he spoke, the man nodded his head repeatedly. Then he approached Harper and Kwon.

"I am Dr. Zeng Qi. I am the man you seek."

Harper stepped forward and the large men who'd manhandled her earlier moved quickly to guard Dr. Zeng. Kwon, in turn, did the same, leading to a standoff between the potential adversaries.

Dr. Zeng ensured there wouldn't be any need for violence by walking forward to meet Harper face-to-face. He smiled as he spoke. "My nephew tells me you are with the American CDC."

"Yes, Dr. Harper Randolph. This is my associate, Dr. Li Kwon."

Dr. Zeng glanced at Kwon. "If there were not two of you, I would declare you to be insane. Perhaps both of you have lost your minds."

Harper laughed. "Actually, as the Chinese proverb goes, insanity is doing the same thing in the same way and expecting a different outcome. I do not believe anyone would be so stupid as I am to try this."

The English-speaking citizen journalists, along with Dr. Zeng and Fangyu, burst out laughing. "This is very true, Dr. Randolph. Perhaps I should have used a different word."

"Unwise?" suggested Harper.

"Yes, much better. Unwise is appropriate. Come, there is much to discuss." He motioned for them to follow as he made his way to the office space created for him by the citizen journalists.

For the next hour, the two Americans and Dr. Zeng immediately got down to business. Using his makeshift blackboards, they compared notes and began to create a revised case definition based upon the timetable in China. It was clear the four Chinese soldiers who'd succumbed to the novel virus in Las Vegas had brought it with them. Now they had to determine where they had contracted it.

Dr. Zeng relayed to the two visitors the information found in the most recent cryptic posts from Lhasa. Dr. Zeng repeated the conclusion he'd reached the day before.

"The answers are not here, Dr. Randolph. The body of the helicopter pilot is in Lhasa. That is where we must go."

"You don't know where it is, do you?"

"I do not. However, I do know where to begin looking."

Fangyu had entered the space and overheard the last part of the conversation. He was holding his cell phone for them to see the screen. A video was cued up.

"You cannot fly to Lhasa, Uncle. Look."

He pushed play. The video, taken by Fangyu's fellow citizen journalists, showed the military descending upon the airport and bus stations. They had the train terminal surrounded. Everyone coming and going was required to show their documentation. American travelers, mainly tourists, were being pulled into a special holding area for further questioning.

"They are looking for us," commented Kwon.

"All of us," added Fangyu. "It is no longer safe here, Uncle. We must leave. If the destination is Lhasa, we must go as soon as possible before roadblocks leading out of Urumqi are established."

"We have a car," said Kwon. "And we have weapons."

Dr. Zeng and Fangyu glanced at one another. "They are forbidden."

"Kidnapping and persecution by the Communist Party should be forbidden, too," countered Harper. "We will take the guns."

Dr. Zeng patted his nephew on the back. "It is necessary. Time to go."

CHAPTER FORTY

China National Highway 109
Xinjiang, China

While Kwon and Fangyu used the tunnels of the Underground Great Wall to emerge in a location closest to the location of the CIA safe house, Dr. Zeng and his wife said their emotional goodbyes. Harper, with the aid of the citizen journalists, was brought up to speed on the news reports out of the U.S. concerning the virus.

The governor of Nevada had relaxed the lockdown requirements after a heated exchange with Mrs. Mayor and an emergency court hearing in front of the Nevada Supreme Court. There were more cases reported in Los Angeles and Phoenix, Arizona. Contact tracing reported by the CDC indicated there were ties between the Phoenix patients and the Gold Palace. Reporting also indicated those individuals had been participants in the poker tournament.

Meanwhile, the Chinese state media continued to downplay the new illness as related to yak meat. Harper read about the European epidemiologists who'd traveled to the northeastern part of China in search of clues. She shook her head in dismay as she realized the

Europeans were being used as pawns to advance Beijing's cover-up. It was no wonder Beijing needed her captured and silenced.

Two young men appeared in the karez and announced that Kwon and Fangyu were ready for them. Dr. Zeng said goodbye to the mostly college-age students, and Harper thanked them for their efforts. She also encouraged them to keep up the good fight. She even taught them two words in English. They were words used by her family since she was a young child to express love for their country.

Choose Freedom.

They were quietly chanting the rallying cry as she and Dr. Zeng left. It warmed her heart that these brave young people were willing to risk their lives to battle the oppressive government led by the Communist Party. Now she would do her part to help save their countrymen.

The four passengers piled into the Volkswagen C-Trek. During the process of loading their luggage into the hatchback opening of the wagon, Kwon discovered what the third magnetic keycard was used for. Under the rear carpet, where the spare tire was supposed to be located, was another compartment. He used the third keycard to unlock it, revealing a voluminous empty space to hide the laptop, their guns, money, and any documents they wanted to keep from prying eyes.

They agreed to swap driving duties, as the entire trip would take nearly thirty hours through a mountainous desert. Fangyu had made the trip before and cautioned they'd have to stop for gasoline at every opportunity. Purchasing gas would be tricky, as the driver must scan his identification to pump fuel. The Chinese authorities tracked the movements of their citizens as much as possible.

Fangyu, like many of his compatriots, had multiple false IDs to use for this purpose. Their network of citizen journalists spread the word as people died in local hospitals. It took up to seven days before the government surveillance apparatus updated their computers and deleted the deceased's information. Fangyu was constantly altering the app's contact information and updating it with a new dead person's biographical data.

There were many different tracking apps in China. One was the *virus app* that was required to enter many public buildings, restaurants and malls in China. It was similar to the one proposed in the U.S. during the height of the COVID-19 pandemic. The app enabled the citizen to show their health status to the *gatekeepers*, as they were known, in order to gain access to these types of public buildings.

To enter, you provided your phone to the gatekeeper. A green light let you in anywhere. A yellow light could send you into home confinement. The dreaded red light resulted in a strict two-week stay in a jail holding cell or a quarantine facility. The Chinese people praised the app. To them, within the context of a potential epidemic, divulging their movements and health status was a way to save lives.

When it was proposed in 2021 by the U.S. Congress, most Americans rebelled against the invasion of privacy and the restriction upon their freedom of movement. The two societies viewed the app from two wholly different perspectives, a natural result of living in a free country versus a Communist state.

After the virus app was conceived, the government came up with other ways to track its citizens, including the TownGas app. Designed to be used in China's new smart gas stations, it was part of an overall effort to transform the nation into a cashless society. As time passed, currency was replaced with plastic. Then plastic was replaced with applications on smartphones. Each transaction was recorded by the issuing banks, and that information was shared with the centralized government. Incredibly, despite the potential for privacy abuses, the cashless system instituted in China was looked upon as a model for the rest of the world's economies, including the U.S.

Harper enjoyed exchanging information with Fangyu about the American way of life compared to the only thing he'd ever experienced—Communist rule. Throughout the conversations she had with Dr. Zeng and his nephew, she managed to take in the sights.

The overland trip from Urumqi to Lhasa was extremely challenging, yet interestingly alluring. After they passed through Turpan, the last major city before they turned south on Chinese National Highway 109, the group enjoyed a serene and mesmeric view of the sun setting over the mountainous desert. The sky was crystal clear except for a few clouds. There were no buildings. No electricity-generated lights. They also had the road to themselves.

"No-man's-land," commented Kwon as he took his turn behind the wheel. "I have never seen a place so remote."

"Mind-boggling, right?" said Harper inquisitively.

"It is very beautiful," said Fangyu. "If my calculations are correct, when we approach the Tibetan border, we will see the sunrise illuminate the east face of Mount Everest. Its snow will glisten like diamonds."

"Snow?" asked Harper.

"Yes, year-round. Also, just today, there was an unusual snowstorm along the northern foot of the Himalayas. The scenery is far more pleasant once we enter Tibet. The dark is the best time to travel through the desert of Xinjiang."

Kwon glanced at Harper in the rearview mirror. "I would like to pull over and retrieve our weapons prior to the gasoline stop. They won't do us any good in the trunk."

"Agreed," said Harper.

Fangyu looked down at his watch. "At this speed, we should be ready for gasoline in approximately three hours. At midnight, retrieve the weapons and let me drive until the next fuel stop. Then, as the sun rises, Uncle can drive if I am tired. He is most awake in the morning."

Fangyu smiled and pointed at his uncle, who sat behind the driver's seat. He was asleep with his mouth wide open. The group shared a laugh at his expense. It would be their last lighthearted moment for a while.

CHAPTER FORTY-ONE

China National Highway 109
Xinjiang, China

The long, boring drive during the evening had been uneventful. They swapped drivers and Fangyu topped off their fuel tank. Kwon, following their progress on the GPS app installed on his Blackberry, had instructed Fangyu to pull over a couple of miles before the Tibetan border.

Although the provinces and autonomous regions of China were part of one large country, Tibet and Xinjiang, the autonomous regions, were governed differently. In an effort to reinforce to travelers they were entering a separate and distinctly governed region of China, checkpoints were commonplace at most roads that led into Tibet.

A number of government-issued documents were required. There was the Tibet Travel Permit as well as the Alien's Travel Permit. Depending upon your destination within Tibet, visitors would obtain a Restricted Areas Permit to visit religious grounds, and a Frontier Pass if they planned on traveling to Mount Everest.

Fangyu pulled off the remote highway onto a dirt road leading to a rock formation overlooking the massive Lake Manasarovar with the snow-capped Mount Kailash glowing from the early morning sun in the distance. The high-altitude freshwater lake was fed by the Kailash Glaciers. When they parked, Dr. Zeng informed them the lake was revered as a sacred place for Buddhists and Hindus.

While Kwon retrieved their weapons from the hiding space in the back of the wagon, Harper stretched her legs and spoke with the native of Xinjiang. "Doctor, this part of the world is incredibly beautiful. Unspoiled. Sadly, its people are ruled by oppression."

"Honestly, it is all we know. We are mentally conditioned to accept the loss of freedom in exchange for the government providing for us. For the most part, Chinese from all parts of this country are hard-working and family oriented. Rural people toil in the fields or tend to their livestock. City-dwellers work their mundane jobs without questioning authority or seeking advancement. There is no opportunity to grab the brass ring, as you Americans say."

"Fangyu and his friends seem to disagree."

Dr. Zeng laughed. "They are young and idealistic. I was once, especially after my schooling in California. If it was not for the love and appreciation of my parents, I would have remained there. Over time, you come to accept your fate."

"I know very little about you, Dr. Zeng, but it appears to me that you are also idealistic."

He looked down to the ground and kicked at a few small rocks. "At one time, my simple goal in life was to enter private practice. I no longer wanted to answer to the administrators of the hospital, who knew nothing about practicing medicine. I did not realize how much the COVID-19 pandemic affected me. I vowed to do my part, as a physician, to warn others of future outbreaks. Here we are." He waved his arms in front of him and then shoved his hands in his pockets.

"All set," announced Kwon, who cradled the two weapons in his arm together with a wool blanket.

Harper patted the melancholy doctor on the back. "What you are doing is far more important than grabbing the brass ring. You are helping save thousands, or potentially hundreds of thousands of lives. You should be very proud of the risks you have taken."

A vehicle was approaching, so they stopped their conversation and returned to the car. Kwon was prepared to give instructions.

"Dr. Zeng, please sit in the front seat next to your nephew. Harper, I need you sitting behind the doctor. I'll take the seat behind Fangyu."

"Okay," said Harper. Kwon handed her the blanket and the MPX carbine. He'd already attached the suppressor. She held it with her finger away from the trigger and the barrel pointed at the ground.

"I know I gave you a crash course the other night, but are you good?" asked Kwon.

Harper nodded. "You know what helped the most? The dry-fire training. In that fifteen-minute timespan, I got comfortable with this. Honestly, I like it a lot better than the Glock pistol I have at home."

"Good. Now let's pray we don't have to use them. Just follow my instructions." Kwon hesitated for a moment and then added one more thought. "Harper, if I tell you to shoot, you cannot hesitate. They're a target. A trained adversary who understands that in a gunfight, it's kill or be killed. You have to accept that mentally."

"I'm there, Kwon. Believe that."

Everybody took their positions in the car, and Fangyu looked around the vehicle to confirm the group was all set. He fired the engine, and minutes later, he rolled up to the well-lit checkpoint as the only vehicle to be inspected.

"This is not good," he muttered as he slowed. "They will have no sense of urgency. I will leave the car quickly so they focus their attention on me."

The moment he pulled to a stop, Fangyu caught a break. The officers inside the guard buildings were drinking coffee and talking. The steel barriers were blocking any traveler's progress, so the arrogant officers could take their time in addressing them.

Fangyu exited the car with his phone and identification in hand. He'd already pulled up his state-certified travel app, and he held paper versions of other documentation ordinarily carried by Chinese citizens. The checkpoint required too many forms of ID for him to pretend to be someone else. Full of apprehension, he approached the booth, and the soldiers slid open a window near the door rather than coming out to greet him.

Fangyu did not try to engage in a jovial conversation with the soldiers. They were trained to look for nervous behavior. Anyone making an attempt to *get on their good side*, as Americans' put it, would be seen as using a ploy to hide something. Therefore, he was all business as he filled out his paperwork.

However, with his back to the vehicle, he was unaware that a guard from the other side of the checkpoint had wandered out of his building to inspect the car.

Harper pretended to be sleeping in the back seat under the wool blanket. Her ball cap was pulled over her forehead, but her eyes were open just enough to observe the guard's every move. He wandered around the vehicle, looking inside the windows and studying the passengers. Then he shouted to another guard, who immediately emerged from the building with a helper.

A Kunming emerged by the guard's side on a leash. The wolflike dog was a descendant of German shepherds introduced into China in the 1950s. They'd been trained to act as drug- and bomb-sniffing animals over the years. Now, like wolves circling their prey, the guards, with the Kunming, inspected the undercarriage and wheel wells of the Volkswagen.

"Stay calm," whispered Kwon.

Harper impressed Kwon. "How many guards have you counted? I think there are only two from this side. I haven't seen any more movement inside their shack."

Kwon responded, speaking in a whispered tone through his teeth, "Good. I count two over here as well. Each side of the road has a single vehicle. VW Santanas, I think. Not big enough for more than a couple of officers and their dogs."

Dr. Zeng was getting nervous as he stared at Fangyu. "Hurry up, nephew."

"Take a deep breath, Doctor," suggested Kwon. "They haven't asked us to—"

Suddenly, one of the guards tapped on Kwon's window. The other guard continued to wander around the car with the Kunming. Kwon couldn't lower the window because the vehicle had been turned off. With his right hand, he made the motion of starting the car and then shrugged.

"I have my permits," announced Fangyu as he walked briskly back to the car. "Would you like to see them?"

The guard turned away from Kwon and stepped toward Fangyu. The other guard approached him with the drug-sniffing shepherd.

I hope he doesn't smoke weed, Harper thought to herself before questioning whether they have marijuana in China. She'd have to remember to ask.

The Kunming circled Fangyu, and he raised his arms in the air as if he were being frisked. The dog showed no interest in him, and as a result, the two guards lost interest in this stop as well. The other guards activated the steel gates blocking their car, so Fangyu hurriedly slid into the driver's seat. Within seconds, they were pulling away and around a curve.

"Everybody can breathe now," said Fangyu. "But we do have a problem."

CHAPTER FORTY-TWO

Lhasa, Tibet, China

Fangyu continued to drive as he relayed what he'd seen on the bulletin board located within the guard building. A flyer, similar to the ones described by Harper seen in at the dormitory, was posted along with a dozen others. It was for his uncle. He'd strained to see inside the room, but he was certain he didn't see a picture of himself or Harper on the wall.

"Do we need to mask his appearance when we are in Lhasa?" asked Harper.

"We will do the best we can to hide all of our faces. There is a new Miniso store in Lhasa that I read about online. The Tibetans resisted it for decades, but finally gave in."

Miniso was a Chinese low-cost retailer and variety store chain that specialized in everything from clothing to household appliances. Their store style was akin to a much smaller version of a Target, but they marketed themselves as selling consumer products made in China to look Japanese. Today, they operated two thousand stores around the world with revenues approaching two billion dollars.

"Why?" asked Harper.

Dr. Zeng responded, "They are traditionalists and have attempted to avoid the lures of Western-style living trends. Tibetan culture is distinct to any other in China. It is heavily influenced by the religions of India, Nepal and the Himalayan regions. Because it is remote and inaccessible due to the geographic features, the Tibetans have been able to avoid outside influences. Allowing Miniso to open a store in Lhasa was met with great resistance."

The rising sun illuminated the city as they approached, but it also revealed a cold front moving in from the west. In addition to the approaching rain clouds, the skies were filled with black smoke.

"Do you think there was a fire?" asked Harper.

Nobody responded as Fangyu approached some of the outlying residential areas of Lhasa. He pulled over to the side of the road before they entered the city.

"We should contact the person we interacted with on WeChat. Give me just a moment."

Fangyu sent a message and waited. When the local physician didn't respond immediately, he frowned and continued driving into the city. The momentary delay allowed the cloud cover to increase. He leaned forward in his seat and observed the skies. "Rain is coming."

"It will be a welcome distraction to evade police detection," commented Kwon, who was a student of human nature. At the end of the day, police were people and sought to do their jobs in the most comfortable environment available. Rainstorms were an aggravation. During his Navy SEAL training, he'd endured a variety of adverse conditions and learned to endure them all while undertaking an operation.

Kwon searched for the location of the Miniso store and set his GPS to create turn-by-turn instructions. He activated the voice command feature of the app and set his phone on the armrest between the front-seat passengers.

Fangyu drove closer to the Miniso store and made an

observation. "The streets are very quiet. No pedestrians. Very few cars."

"They are self-quarantining," observed Harper.

Dr. Zeng shook his head and grimaced. "Yes. We have learned our lessons from the pandemic. Nobody is willing to wait for the Party to tell us it isn't safe. We don't want to die as a result of their propaganda."

Without speaking, they made their way into the downtown shopping district, when it started to sprinkle. Harper was the first to notice that something was wrong.

"It's black. Seriously, black rain?" she said inquisitively.

"Oh no," Dr. Zeng replied with a sigh.

"What is it?" asked Kwon.

"It is Wuhan again."

"The rain is filled with soot," said Kwon just as Fangyu activated the windshield wipers.

"Nephew! Stop!" shouted Dr. Zeng. He was suddenly animated, waving and pointing to the right. "Please take this street. We must see something."

Fangyu stopped the car in the middle of the street without concern of being hit by another motorist. They were virtually alone on the normally busy street entering the city of Lhasa. He crossed over the right lane and pulled down a side street toward a large open parking area. Only, there were no cars parked in it.

"What are those?" asked Harper. The sprinkle turned to a driving rain, and the amount of black soot mixed with the moisture dissipated due to the volume of water.

"Another repeat of Wuhan," replied Dr. Zeng. "Those are incinerators. In the early days of the COVID-19 pandemic, we learned the Japanese reported mysterious black rain falling on the northern parts of the country. The meteorologists traced the weather pattern back to Hubei province and then directly to Wuhan."

As he spoke, dark blobs of rainwater collected on the hood of their car. It had a greasy appearance like oil mixed with water.

Fangyu parked the vehicle so they could study the flatbed trucks lined up in rows with unmarked silver boxes affixed to the back.

Harper recalled the investigation. "This is just like Wuhan. The Chinese government was doing everything they could to hide the real death toll from the world. They had a problem—disposing of the bodies. Their morgues and funeral homes could not keep up with the number of corpses."

"Yes," interrupted Dr. Zeng. "They incinerated the bodies. We believe it was sixty thousand per month during December, January, and through the end of March as the outbreak spread."

"Hundreds of thousands," added Kwon. "During its early investigation, our intelligence agencies studied satellite images showing funeral homes overwhelmed. They were working twenty-four hours a day. If I recall correctly, the trucks looked just like these."

The rain started to lighten up, making visibility better. Dr. Zeng tapped the windshield and pointed. "There! Do you see them? The urns."

Under temporary tents spread throughout the parking area were hundreds of ash urns either awaiting pickup by loved ones or waiting to be filled with the remains of the cremated. The lack of activity around the site other than security personnel led Dr. Zeng to a conclusion.

"They are using these incinerators, but not as much as Wuhan yet. There must be more, as those are not generating the black smoke. My guess is they are in a more remote area west of here. Perhaps closer to the airport."

"We have a response from our new friend," interrupted Fangyu. "He wants to meet in a busy public place."

Harper looked around. "Not many of those around here today."

"The store," suggested Kwon. He leaned forward to glance at the GPS app on his phone. "We're not that far from Miniso. We can make contact without being out of place. Harper will stand out here, but it wouldn't seem unusual for her to be shopping."

She shot him a glance and decided not to defend her penchant for shopping.

Fangyu apparently agreed because he immediately sent their mysterious contact a message.

Seconds later, it was confirmed. They were about to take an important step in finding patient zero.

CHAPTER FORTY-THREE

Lhasa, Tibet, China

Fangyu parked a block away from the Miniso store. They separated into pairs, with Dr. Zeng and his nephew leading the way. Harper and Kwon remained back about a hundred feet so they could react to any threat created by facial recognition of Fangyu. Kwon didn't like it, but he left their weapons in the car. They couldn't take the risk of metal detectors, which might be installed at the store entrance.

"Another sign that we've come to the right place," commented Harper as they passed the storefronts. Signs had been printed and affixed to the plate-glass doors of the businesses. They read in a variety of languages, including English, NO MASK SOLD OUT.

"This could be a trick, you know," said Kwon. He was always in a threat-assessment mindset.

"I've thought of that, too. One of the military men my father admired most was General Mattis."

"Mad dog," interjected Kwon.

"The one and only. Dad had a tee shirt that read *be polite, be professional, but have a plan to kill everybody you meet.*"

"It became a motto that others like myself adopted at DARPA. *Trust no one* is shorter, but in our business, killing is commonplace."

Harper glanced over at her companion. She'd come to respect the man, who was the epitome of the strong silent type. She could only imagine what he'd seen and experienced firsthand. Now was not the time, but at some point, she intended to ask Kwon how many people he'd killed. It was one of those things she just had to know.

She pushed those thoughts out of her mind and got back in the game. She leaned in to Kwon and whispered, "Look, Fangyu has come back out of the store. He just nodded."

Kwon saw the gesture as well. "Eyes open, Harper. Assume nothing. Once inside, please separate from me and keep a watch on the entrance. If something goes wrong, you get out and back to the car. Keys are under the mat."

"But—" she began before he cut her off.

"Do not wait for me. I'll be fine. Just get out at the first sign of trouble."

Harper nodded and they continued their casual walk toward the store. Once inside, Harper immediately noticed a circular rack with a large variety of graphic tee shirts near the bank of cash registers. She made her way to them, but her eyes darted around the interior in search of Dr. Zeng and Fangyu. As she flipped through the designs, she found the two men in other parts of the store. They'd successfully lent the appearance of shoppers. With the four of them spread apart, they could observe the entire interior as well as the entrance.

After several minutes, she moved on from the tee shirts and went to the perfume counter. She didn't ordinarily wear perfume, although when she was out with Joe, 1111 by Lake & Skye was her favorite.

She was surprised at the low prices of major brand-name perfumes. Her first thought was that they were counterfeit. She sprayed a Chanel perfume on a card and sniffed it. She desperately wanted to immerse herself in the scent, but she didn't know what the rest of their investigation might bring, and she didn't want to bring attention to herself.

The others saw the new customer enter the store before she did. Both Kwon and Fangyu swung their heads around to observe the man enter alone. His gait was unusually stiff and slow. He didn't swing his arms as he walked, which was a natural human trait. His face, wrinkled and formed into a perpetual frown, appeared still with little or no expression.

Nobody moved, but their eyes followed the newcomer as he walked directly toward the health care section of the store, where, ironically, Dr. Zeng had migrated towards. They stood next to one another for a moment without saying a word. Then they engaged in idle conversation. They appeared to be comparing brands of acetaminophen. That was when Harper knew he was their contact in Tibet.

She locked eyes with Kwon and provided him an imperceptible

nod, which he acknowledged in a similar fashion. He began to walk toward Fangyu, who was thumbing through a comic book titled *Cloud and Wind* featuring martial-arts-themed characters.

Kwon whispered to Fangyu as he picked up a copy of *Duzhe*, a magazine similar to *Time*. Fangyu took his instructions, made his way to the register, and purchased the comic book to lend realism to any surveillance cameras monitoring his activity. He would be bringing the car closer to the entrance in case this was a trap.

Kwon looked back to Harper and nodded his head toward the door. Her job was to join Fangyu in the car and have her weapon ready in case they had to shoot their way out of the city. As she began to leave, she noticed Kwon approach Dr. Zeng. The weary doctor had managed a smile. They'd made contact and everything appeared safe.

Five minutes later, Kwon joined Harper and Fangyu in the car while Dr. Zeng and his companion walked down the sidewalk toward another vehicle. Kwon took the front seat and explained.

"Okay, we've found the right guy," began Kwon as he reached under Fangyu's seat to retrieve his weapon. He carefully slid the suppressed Sig Sauer 9 millimeter onto the seat next to him before covering it with a blanket. "His name is Dr. Basnet Dema. He supervises the infirmary at the military base located at the airport complex."

"That complicates things if we have to go there," said Fangyu. "There is usually heavy security around the installations."

"We're going to have the opportunity to ask him about that," added Kwon. He pointed ahead to get Fangyu to focus on following Dr. Basnet. "He's taking us to his home, which he assures us is safe. Let's hear what he has to say before we take the next step."

Fangyu pulled out onto the street and crept up on the back of Dr. Basnet's vehicle. They drove south out of town on a winding road that led through a valley cut into the mountains by the Lhasa River. Kwon studied the GPS and the accompanying map. He was feeling uneasy.

"I don't see many residential areas between here and the airport. My understanding was we were going to his home."

The doctor turned on his blinker and slowed as a gravel road appeared on their right. He turned up the slight incline and sped up the hill between several rocky outcroppings. As they crested the rise, the road leveled off and a modest, rectangular home came into view. Its exterior was a sand-colored stucco and it was surrounded by rocks and dirt. A two-car carport was supported by two heavy wood beams.

The doctor parked first and exited his car. He motioned for Fangyu, who'd rolled down his window, to pull under the carport as well. He spoke to them for the first time. Harper immediately noticed the speech impediment. After recalling his mannerisms in the store, she determined he might be afflicted with Parkinson's disease.

After everyone had exited their cars, they gathered by the entry door and made their introductions. Dr. Basnet's misgivings about their weapons gave way to his intrigue with Harper. Most of the Americans he'd dealt with in his medical career were men, and the women he'd met were never as remarkable as Harper.

"Please come in," he said in English. "I hope you don't mind if I practice my English on you, Dr. Randolph. At times, I may have to switch to my native tongue, but you seem to have a very capable translator." He nodded toward Kwon.

"Yes, Dr. Basnet, that would be appreciated," said Harper. She glanced around the open living space once they were all inside. The interior was paneled with wood and contained exquisitely ornate cabinetwork. She was immediately drawn to it. "Dr. Basnet, these cabinets are incredible."

"Thank you. They were a hobby for me before ..." His voice trailed off.

"Parkinson's?" she asked.

"Yes, you are very observant. I have early stages. The disease has prevented me from doing many of the things I love."

Kwon sat quietly while Harper exchanged pleasant conversation with Dr. Basnet. It was the proper thing to do and expected by a Tibetan who'd invited you into their home for the first time. However, he was understandably concerned with their exposure to the surveillance cameras located within the Miniso store. In his mind, they needed to gather their information as quickly as possible and move on to the next lead.

He spoke in Chinese. "Dr. Basnet, please forgive my sense of urgency, but we must move quickly for two reasons. One, the disease is spreading rapidly, from what we can see in Lhasa. Secondly, we believe there has been a bulletin disseminated by the MSS and the Security Police to locate Dr. Zeng, his nephew, and possibly Dr. Randolph."

The old Tibetan doctor nodded his agreement and replied in English, "I am aware of the postings in the governmental buildings concerning Dr. Zeng. I was sent one to post as well at the base, and inadvertently deleted the email." A smile came over his face as he made eye contact with Harper. The older gentleman was clearly smitten with her.

She asked, "Doctor, have you been in contact with a patient who has contracted this mysterious disease? Perhaps at the local hospital?"

"No, not recently. My experience occurred early on. At my medical facility located at the Lhasa Gonggar Airport, I am the administrator of the infirmary and pathology lab for the 85th Air Defense Brigade. I am not a soldier, nor am I loyal to the PLA. I am my own man." He sat a little taller in his chair, his pride swelled in his chest.

Harper continued. "I was told you had treated a helicopter pilot. Did you perform an autopsy?"

"No. The young man had no family, and his commanding officers forgot about him. His body is still kept in a refrigerated cadaver locker."

"For how long?" she asked.

"Eight days."

Harper winced. After twenty-four hours, a body would need

some level of embalming. After a week, it begins to decompose despite the embalming fluid and the refrigeration. However, it was something.

"Dr. Basnet, I have to ask. Are you capable of performing an autopsy?"

He winked and smiled. "Fortunately, my hands have received only limited effects of the Parkinson's." He held them up, palms down for a moment. They didn't shake, much. "I can no longer operate on live patients. The autopsy would not be a concern."

"I can assist, of course," said Harper.

Dr. Basnet sighed. "Naturally, I would have no objection. However, base security would not approve. We must smuggle you into the infirmary."

"Do you have a suggestion?" asked Kwon.

"I do. It will require the assistance of a friend, but he can be trusted." He turned to Fangyu. "He is the young man who put me in touch with you. He comes from a family of sherpas and is a true Himalayan—not Chinese and certainly not a Communist."

"How will we do this?" asked Kwon.

"It will require the use of an ambulance and two body bags. If they are available."

Harper scooted forward on her chair to get Dr. Basnet's attention. "The ambulance?"

"No," he replied. "The body bags. Most are occupied at the moment."

CHAPTER FORTY-FOUR

Near Lhasa Gonggar Airport
Lhasa, Tibet, China

A light snow was falling when their ride arrived. The all-white Toyota van with a raised roofline pulled to a stop outside Dr. Basnet's home. A young man in his late twenties emerged, wearing the navy-blue uniform of the Tibet Ambulance Service, and greeted the group. He'd procured two body bags from the hospital where he borrowed the ambulance with the help of his girlfriend, an assistant in the hospital's transportation department. They would have use of the ambulance for a few hours, but because Dr. Basnet only lived three miles from the airport, their task was easily achieved in that time span.

The talkative young man, who identified himself as Yeshi, was proud of the fact he was able to locate two body bags. He, like so many others, seemed to enjoy the opportunity to speak English with an American. He and Harper hit it off immediately, so she took a moment to joke with him before they left.

"About these body bags, um, they're not used, are they?"

"Used?" he asked.

"You know. Recycled. Previously occupied. Rinsed out for our benefit."

The young man began to laugh. "No, lady. They are brand new. I do have to return them, however."

"Well, I will try not to die in it," said Harper. She turned to wave to Dr. Zeng and Fangyu, not considering she might not see them again. They wished her luck and she climbed into the rear of the ambulance to join Kwon.

Dr. Basnet had already left for the infirmary to confirm there wasn't any extraordinary security. He would call the driver, Yeshi, and warn him to return to the house if it wasn't safe. Before they pulled away, Harper and Kwon slid into the body bags and sat upright on the gurneys. During the five-minute ride, Yeshi explained who he was.

"I have been employed by the hospital in the past as a driver. This is why my credentials are still active. In the spring months, I assist my family as a sherpa. We Himalayans know Everest and the surrounding mountains better than any other. During the months when the climbing is forbidden, I make extra money for the hospital. Really, my favorite job pays nothing, but it is very rewarding."

"Are you also a citizen journalist?" asked Kwon.

"I am, proudly."

"You have a lot of friends," Kwon added as he contemplated the vast network of citizen journalists. "Aren't you concerned about getting caught by the Security Police?"

"Yes, of course. That's the excitement of it. I grew up a mountain climber. I can scale the jagged cliffs of Everest as well as anybody. To some, the threat of death provides a thrill. Not for me. The possibility of capture by the Party sets my heart racing more than the sight of a beautiful woman." He glanced at Harper through his rearview mirror, causing her to blush.

"We saw incinerators in the city," said Harper. "Are there more?"

"Oh, yes. *Convenience police posts*, too."

"What are those?" asked Kwon.

"The Communist Party believes Tibetans are inferior, yet they are obsessed with our sense of independence. Last year, they announced a *stability maintenance* campaign to be initiated in Lhasa."

"Let me guess," began Kwon. "They're still obsessed with followers of the Dalai Lama."

"Very good, sir! You are correct. The first stability maintenance campaign took place fifteen years ago in the time of the 14th Dalai Lama. After his death during the pandemic, the 15th Dalai Lama, his reincarnated self, was revealed. The Party claimed the right to choose him. Foolish atheists. Their time will come in the afterlife."

"Is the increased Security Police presence a result of this campaign to, I assume, reprogram Tibetans?" asked Harper.

"Yes, that is exactly what it is. They are arresting many for political offenses and forcing them through a trial for treason or giving them the option to be reprogrammed, as you call it. The convenience police posts are operated by the MSS and the Security Police dispatched from Beijing. They don't even trust their own minions in Lhasa. The only thing convenient about these new locations is the numerous built-in holding cells and the ability to make people disappear."

"Wow," said Harper.

Yeshi laughed at Harper's response. "Yes, wow. Do you see why this is far more exhilarating than climbing a tired old mountain?"

"I suppose," she replied, although Harper had dreamed of climbing Mount Everest as a child. The closest she got to her dream was climbing Mount LeConte in the Great Smoky Mountains during a family trip to Gatlinburg, Tennessee, as a young girl.

Yeshi continued to enlighten his passengers. "There is a growing outrage in Tibet over the stability maintenance campaign and the deaths from this new mysterious disease. They are angered because the People's Government, led by a puppet of the Party, refuses to disclose the nature of the disease and how widespread it is. Instead, they deliver incinerators and burn up the evidence."

Harper was amazed at the local knowledge this young man

possessed. "Are the other citizen journalists assisting in spreading information?"

"Yes. There are images circulating on WeChat and other social media sites of medical personnel carrying out bloodied clothing in rubbish bags at all hours of the night. Dead bodies have been left on gurneys outside the entrances to hospitals because everyone is afraid to handle them. My girlfriend cries at night out of frustration and exhaustion."

"Why don't they speak out?"

"Because of Wuhan," he replied bluntly. "The Security Police have taken control of the hospital administrator duties. Each facility has a full-time arbitrator who removes staff who speak of the mysterious disease. They rule through fear."

Kwon and Harper exchanged glances. They were surrounded by vipers and had been fortunate to avoid being caught up in the massive Orwellian surveillance network imposed on China's citizens in every major city. Harper recalled the conversation she'd had with Kwon about luck. One statement left unsaid was that luck can run out.

Yeshi glanced back at them and let them know he was approaching the military base.

"Okay, I must insist you bag-up. I don't expect the guards to look in the back. Everyone is afraid of this new disease, and when I tell them the bodies are going to the quarantine cooler, they will wave us through."

Harper and Kwon quickly got into position. They pulled the body bag zippers closed from the inside and then gently rested their hands on their guns. They were headed into the den of the lions and might need an assist to get out.

PART V

FOLLOW YOUR NOSE

You do not have to know where you are going to be headed in the right direction.
~ Pei Wei Fortune Cookie

CHAPTER FORTY-FIVE

Military Quarantine Facility
85th Air Defense Brigade
Lhasa Gonggar Airport
Lhasa, Tibet, China

After Yeshi cleared security and backed the ambulance to the intake doors at the infirmary, Dr. Basnet welcomed Kwon and Harper before leading them into his office. At this late hour, the infirmary was empty. He took a seat at his desk and quickly reviewed his WeChat account regarding news reports of unexplained outbreaks in Europe. The spread of the virus was slow but certain, if the cases developing worldwide were connected.

Harper and Kwon were quiet and respectful as the elderly doctor concentrated on the messages. Under the circumstances, it wasn't easy to read a post. The text was filled with emojis, symbols, unnecessary words and inconsequential references. It hearkened back to the days of World War II in which the Nazis and Allied intelligence played a high-stakes game of *Spy vs Spy*.

Yeshi had taken a moment to stow away their body bags just in case a base patrol insisted upon inspecting the ambulance. He appeared in the doorway and leaned against the jamb with his arms crossed, awaiting instructions.

"Tell me what you know about this patient," said Harper after Dr. Basnet finished relaying the news reports to the group.

Dr. Basnet opened a file folder and leaned back in his chair with it cradled in his lap. He pulled his glasses out of a drawer and rested them on the tip of his nose. He alternated between reading and making eye contact with the Americans.

"He is a local man. Enlisted in the military eight years ago and quickly became one of their top search and rescue pilots."

"Did he live on the base?" asked Kwon.

"No, many of the soldiers do not. There is very little room at the Gonggar Airport due to the air cargo requirements. The overnight personnel are primarily base security and fighter pilots who patrol the Nepal and Indian borders to our south."

"I know a few of his relatives," interjected Yeshi. "He is, um, was, Himalayan. No wife or kids. He was alone except for cousins."

"Is there any record of his deployments over the past several weeks?"

While Dr. Basnet thumbed through the files, Yeshi answered, "I know a few things. He rarely worked except in the spring and summer of the year. He ferried soldiers into the mountains for training and occasionally had to assist in the rescue of a new recruit who was unable to complete the course."

Dr. Basnet tapped on the file with his fingers. "I have not reviewed the details of this man's file, but I see something familiar, a possible connection."

"What is it?" asked Harper.

"There was a mission undertaken two weeks ago. A climbing accident resulted in the Chinese military making a rare rescue trip to Mount Everest. One of the injured was being transported back to Lhasa."

"Did he survive?" asked Harper.

"I know about this," replied Yeshi. "The man's body was brought to my girlfriend's hospital. He was already dead."

"Would she know if the body was still there?" asked Harper.

"I know it is not," Dr. Basnet quickly responded. "The man had no identification. Because of the odd circumstances surrounding his death, the hospital contacted me and asked that I secure him in our quarantine lockers."

"Odd circumstances?" asked Harper before adding, "What was the cause of death?"

"Not the fall," replied Dr. Basnet. "It was deemed to be some kind of internal injuries other than trauma."

Harper's face contorted as she considered the possibilities. She sat up on the edge of her seat. "Is it still here? Can we examine the remains?"

"No. Upon the corpse's arrival, I was instructed to prepare it for travel. I assumed it was being sent to the family. He was a white male of unknown nationality."

"Where was it sent?" asked Kwon.

"Military transport took it to Urumqi," the doctor replied.

Harper and Kwon exchanged glances. "Whadya think?" she asked.

Kwon shrugged. "It might be the same one. Tell me again about this rescue mission. Helicopters have a very difficult time at high altitude, much less Mount Everest. Do you know the circumstances behind his death?"

Yeshi stepped into the room so he could stand next to Dr. Basnet. "I heard through a friend that after he returned from the mountain with the body and the special forces soldiers, he later got sick."

"Wait," interrupted Harper.

"Special forces?" asked Kwon. Both of their voices revealed their inner excitement.

"Here," explained Dr. Basnet. He handed the file folder to Kwon.

Kwon scanned the report buried at the back of the folder. It was a brief assignment notification that had made its way into the man's medical file. He shook his head in disbelief and then turned to Harper.

"He was part of a mission to rescue hikers on Mount Everest. Apparently, the group was near the top when one or more of them became ill and brought many in the group down with them. The deployment was made because some kind of a ladder, I believe, was damaged, cutting off those on top of the mountain from returning to the base camps. Some of the bodies fell over the cliff and are still there. The families didn't have the forty thousand dollars required to retrieve them. They brought the one back."

"Yes, that is correct," interjected Yeshi. "It was a contentious topic among the sherpas. We are the most capable of rescuing stranded hikers. This time, because of the Chinese Ladder being damaged, they used the military and their Siberian Tigers."

Harper sprang out of her chair. Her eyes lowered and she leaned on Dr. Basnet's desk to bring her face closer to Yeshi. It frightened the young man.

"What did you say?"

"Siberian Tigers. They are—"

"I know who they are," Harper interrupted. She turned to Kwon. "Do you see any confirmation of this in the file?"

"Looking."

Harper was back to Yeshi and Dr. Basnet. "Are you absolutely certain of this?"

"Yes," replied the young man. "Why?"

"This is very important. Do you know how many of these Siberian Tigers were on board the helicopter flight with the pilot in there?" She pointed toward the plate-glass door leading to the quarantine unit's morgue.

He hesitated before replying, "I believe they said four." And then after a moment, he confirmed his belief. "I am sure. There were four soldiers plus the pilot."

"Kwon?" asked Harper as she spun around to stare at her partner.

"I hear you."

Harper walked away from the desk. She wandered Dr. Basnet's office and rubbed her temples with both hands. She tried to settle down. It had been a long journey and she didn't want to see something that wasn't there. However, it was a lead that couldn't be disregarded and was perhaps the most important step yet to finding patient zero.

"There's nothing else in here," said Kwon as he handed the folder back to Dr. Basnet. "What do you want to do?"

Harper turned and approached the men. "We have to conduct the autopsy and let me preserve blood and tissue samples the best I can. It's not a perfect scenario, but it's a start."

Kwon stood and pulled Harper aside. In a barely audible whisper, he said, "This may be the connection to the Chinese military the agency was looking for."

She nodded. Turning to Dr. Basnet, she said, "Let's get started."

During those intense moments when the group of four made this startling connection, a guard from the base security patrol wandered into the infirmary and down the hallway leading to Dr. Basnet's office. He stopped at the office's window unnoticed for a moment before casually strolling away.

CHAPTER FORTY-SIX

Military Quarantine Facility
85th Air Defense Brigade
Lhasa Gonggar Airport
Lhasa, Tibet, China

Dr. Basnet led Harper and Kwon down a hallway to an inconspicuous door marked quarantine morgue in Chinese script. The first space was designed to suit up. Harper immediately noticed the lack of sufficient PPE considering they were about to examine a corpse that likely belonged in a BSL-4. Before Yeshi took a position to watch the front of the building, he was sent to the ambulance to retrieve several rolls of duct tape used by the ambulance personnel to confine uncontrollable patients.

The dressing area contained both all-white cotton scrubs and yellow biohazard suits. Kwon and Harper chose to wear the biohazard suits over their clothing. Dr. Basnet, despite Harper's admonitions to the contrary, chose the scrubs. He commented that he was an old man and had no time to concern himself with diseases. Harper thought maybe he had a death wish.

They geared up and entered the morgue. Dr. Basnet, with the assistance of Kwon, retrieved the partially decomposed body of the helicopter pilot from the cadaver locker. At first sight, Harper shook her head in dismay. She'd gather as many samples as she could, but they might not stand up to the rigid scrutiny applied by the CDC.

The biggest drawback of this autopsy was that Dr. Basnet did not have the usual vials and secured containers Harper was used to working with. This small facility had none of the basics found at the CDC, or even Dr. Boychuck's examination room in Las Vegas. She'd asked to bring a UTM kit with her on the flight, but the CIA had issued a firm *not gonna happen*. It would've been a sure sign Harper was much more than an English tutor.

Instead of using the UTM kit's screw-cap plastic tubes, Harper was pleased that Dr. Basnet had a variety of glass tube vials and accompanying labels. Her samples of the body's organs couldn't be that large, but they were something. Also, Kwon could carry everything in the cargo pockets of his khaki pants.

They got to work and talked as they moved quickly but methodically through the process. Harper tried to put their next step out of her mind so she didn't overlook anything. However, she couldn't stop talking about the pursuit of patient zero.

Dr. Basnet understood the importance of her mission and relayed what he recalled from the pandemic of a decade prior.

"The Party stalled and covered up the truth for a very long time. By the time the rest of the world understood the threat in mid-March of 2020, our country had experienced infections and deaths dating back to the middle of November in Wuhan. You see, doctors were aware of the problem when a man of fifty-five years contracted the coronavirus in the Huanan Seafood Market located in Wuhan. The government hid this from World Health until December. Many warnings were issued by fellow physicians, but they were stifled."

Harper took samples as Dr. Basnet performed the autopsy,

which was anything but. It was more of a tissue-harvesting expedition, but none of the three doctors seemed to be concerned about the ethics of their actions at the moment.

"The seafood market was located near the Wuhan Institute of Virology, where they conducted testing on highly infectious diseases," said Harper as she worked. She used a scalpel to gather her samples, and then she provided the vials to Kwon for labeling. "It was determined that a lab worker had accidentally infected himself and then came in contact with the man you mentioned. He was patient zero, and the novel coronavirus strain originally came from a bat, as they often do."

"I must ask," Dr. Basnet began. "Bats are the most likely culprit in situations like these. Why is it so important for you to risk your lives to look for a different answer?"

Kwon looked to Harper to provide the response. It was a question he'd asked her on the flight to Hawaii from Fort Belvoir.

"The genetic markers don't add up. Our analysis indicates this novel virus carries the genetic traits of SARS-like viruses from horseshoe bats, which enables it to use angiotensin-converting enzymes to gain entry into human cells. More specifically, ACE2."

"You're saying these markers are not precise?" asked Dr. Basnet.

"Close, but there is something else involved. It doesn't give us sufficient accuracy to create a vaccine. Without a vaccine, we cannot stem the spread without a repeat of the lockdown measures of 2020. As my fellow Americans proved during the flu season of 2020 into 2021, we had no appetite for a lockdown as the second wave of COVID-19 hit us."

"We did not have a second wave," commented Dr. Basnet.

"The Chinese are more compliant," said Kwon in a low voice. "The Party sees to that."

Dr. Basnet shrugged and finished exposing the patient's vital organs to Harper so she could collect the last of the samples. Just as she stepped away from the table, Yeshi began slapping the glass windows in the hallway looking into the dressing area. He was waving his arms and pointing toward the door. Harper and Kwon swung around just as Yeshi darted away.

"We have to go!" exclaimed Harper.

"There is no time," countered Dr. Basnet. "Allow me to stall them while you prepare."

"Prepare for what?" she asked, her voice rising a few octaves. "Our guns are in the dressing area and we're covered in the blood of a diseased corpse."

"Lure them into the dressing area," instructed Kwon. "We'll be ready."

"With what?" asked Harper.

He ignored her question and turned to Dr. Basnet. "Go!" The man afflicted with Parkinson's steadied his nerves and exited the room. He positioned himself by the door, his bloody hands held stiffly by his sides.

"Do we have to fight?" asked Harper. "Maybe we can—?"

Kwon rummaged through the autopsy room's tool cabinet. He retrieved a bone saw and a twelve-inch knife that resembled a kitchen butcher knife. He handed the knife to Harper so she held it in a reverse grip in her right hand. Then he placed the bone saw in her left hand.

"We'll know based upon the way he's treated," replied Kwon. He took charge and issued his instructions. "Listen to me. Hide behind the door. When they enter, I will act nonchalant, but I will have something for them. When the last of them enters the room, I will say *last*. I want you to punch hard at the last soldier with your right hand. The knife blade will slash into the guard. Then slash backwards with the bone saw. Make as many cuts as you can to force him to drop his weapon. Watch."

Kwon punched the air with his right hand and then drew his left arm across his chest before slashing outward toward the imaginary assailant. Harper emulated his actions.

"I'm ready," said Harper with obvious determination in her voice.

Kwon motioned for her to get ready, and he turned back to the mutilated corpse with a handful of scalpels in his hand. With Harper's back pressed against the wall behind the door, Kwon stood over the pilot's body. He positioned himself so he could observe what was happening in the dressing room through a mirror affixed to the far wall. With a deep breath, Kwon prepared for battle, as they were about to have company.

CHAPTER FORTY-SEVEN

Military Quarantine Facility
85th Air Defense Brigade
Lhasa Gonggar Airport
Lhasa, Tibet, China

Kwon made quick work of gathering his weapons, continuously monitoring the mirror to observe who interacted with Dr. Basnet. The guards came into view, and he verbally announced the tally to Harper. Four men, all armed with rifles. They forced their way into the dressing area, and shouting could easily be heard through the glass window that separated the two rooms. Dr. Basnet tried to assure the soldiers that there was no need for alarm. Their response caused Kwon to grip his first weapon out of anger. The interrogating soldier swung his rifle around and, using the butt-end of the weapon, slammed it into the chest of the old doctor, knocking him backwards onto the floor.

Kwon gritted his teeth and snarled, "Be ready!"

His body tensed as the soldiers moved toward the autopsy room with their weapons at low ready. They assumed Kwon, who continued to simulate working on the corpse, was unaware of their presence. They were wrong.

One of them slammed their fist on the plate-glass window in an attempt to get his attention. Without looking up, Kwon raised a bloody glove partially in the air as if to acknowledge that someone wanted to enter the autopsy room.

They beat on the window a second time. Kwon kept his eyes on the mirror to watch them. He hoped they didn't open fire out of frustration. If they were going to do that, he assumed, the first gunshot victim would've been Dr. Basnet.

The guards' chatter was barely discernible through the door and the plate-glass window. The men seemed to be debating what to do next.

Good. Uncertainty.

Kwon set his jaw as he readied himself. Then the moment came in which they breached the space. He watched as they entered, one by one, until the last had cleared the door, allowing it to close behind him.

"Last!" he shouted as he simultaneously shoveled blood-soaked organs out of the cadaver's body cavity.

Heart. Spleen. Slices of the lung, liver and stomach peppered the guards.

As instructed, Harper struck. She let out a guttural, primal scream as she ripped the knife into the bicep of the last guard to enter, followed by a slash across his midsection with the bone saw.

Before the other three could recover from the onslaught of blood and gore, Kwon had spun around. His left hand held half a dozen #10 blade scalpels, the large curved cutting edge used for large incisions in soft tissue. He flung them like he would a knife, the delicately balanced surgical instruments striking the other three guards like they were pincushions.

The guards tried to fight off the attack but only crashed into one another before losing their footing on the blood-soaked tile floor. Neither Kwon nor Harper hesitated. Kwon threw three more of the triangular-bladed instruments. All of them were precision strikes reaching their victims about the face and neck.

With the last assailant still standing, he grabbed his last tool, a Virchow Skull Breaker, a chisel-like tool with a three-inch-long handle. He gripped it between his bloody-gloved fingers and rushed the last guard. With an upward motion, he drove the chiseled blade into the man's esophagus, leaving him gripping his throat before dying.

He confirmed the soldiers were all dead, and then he turned his attention to Harper. She was shaking. He grasped her by both arms and firmly squeezed her.

"Harper, I need you to keep it together, do you understand? This is not over!"

Her eyes were wide as she glanced down at the carnage. "Okay."

He intentionally used her name to remind her of who she was. "Look at me, not them. Harper, we have to go."

She nodded and then looked around the room. "Where are the samples?"

Kwon patted a yellow, fanny-pack-style pouch tucked against his left hip. "Got it. Come on."

He took the knife from Harper and slowly opened the door. Dr. Basnet was doubled over on the floor, gasping for breath.

"My god!" she exclaimed. She was about to kneel down by his side when the Tibetan doctor raised his hand to stop her. His body was shaking.

"I'll be fine. You must go!"

"Doctor, where does it—?"

He cut off her question. "Go, now! There will be more."

"Harper, listen to him. Carefully get out of your suit." Kwon had already removed the biohazard suit and was in the process of retrieving their weapons from a locker when he heard voices. "Hurry!"

His sense of urgency snapped Harper back into the present. She moved away from the plate-glass window overlooking the hallway and hid behind a wall. She quickly, but delicately, removed the biohazard suit and gingerly stepped away from the blood splatter on the floor. She grabbed some nitrile gloves off a utility shelf and put them on. She found a red biohazard bag and crammed the fanny pack full of vials into it before sealing it.

Kwon nodded to her and handed her the carbine. "Don't shoot me, please."

Harper frowned and then nodded. She pulled the rear charging handle on the Sig MPX and stood behind the wall. Kwon assisted Dr. Basnet to crawl under a wooden bench near the lockers. Kwon then dropped to a low crouch in the far corner of the dressing area and trained his weapon on the door.

Two more soldiers rushed down the hallway, glanced into the dressing area, and charged in with their weapons ready to fire. The staccato burst of hollow-point rounds from Kwon's weapon tore through their bodies and killed them instantly.

"Let's go!" he shouted, stepping over the bodies into the hallway, his head on a swivel, looking for his next target.

Harper paused and spoke to Dr. Basnet. "Thank you, Doctor. You have saved many lives."

"*Thug je che.*" A simple thank you and a slight wave of the hand. But it was his smile that spoke volumes. He was a courageous man prepared to deal with the aftermath of the slaughter.

"Harper!"

"Coming!"

She raced into the hallway and joined Kwon at the front entrance of the infirmary. "Yeshi is still here somewhere. I hear sirens, so more on the way. Let's roll."

"Lead the way," said Harper. As they exited the building, Yeshi's head poked out of the driver's window.

"Back! Get in the back!"

He started the ambulance and revved the engine to get their ride ready. He turned on the sirens and lights before speeding toward the gated exit.

CHAPTER FORTY-EIGHT

Military Quarantine Facility
85th Air Defense Brigade
Lhasa Gonggar Airport
Lhasa, Tibet, China

"They're closing the gap!" shouted Kwon. He moved into the passenger seat to view their options. As Yeshi sped closer to the guarded exit, Kwon realized they couldn't shoot their way through it. Two security patrol vehicles were blocking the way. "Bear right!"

"But the exit is there!" shouted Yeshi in response.

"We're going to make our own exit. Where the security wall began near the cargo warehouses along the road, a chain-link fence cut across the perimeter, separating the civilian area from the base."

"Yes." Yeshi nodded.

"Guys, they're closing on us!" shouted Harper.

Both men turned to confirm.

Kwon patted Yeshi on the right shoulder. "Drive through it."

"Then what?" He studied the cars closing on his bumper through the driver's side mirror. "They're almost here."

"Just do it and we'll figure it out."

Kwon made his way to the back of the ambulance. He looked around through the cabinets until he found what he was looking for. He motioned to Harper. "Stay down!"

She slid against the side of the vehicle and lowered to one knee. Kwon took a portable oxygen tank and began to beat the two rear windows inset into the doors. They soon shattered and the glass fell onto the street behind them and onto the ambulance floor. He tossed the container out the back, startling the driver of the nearest pursuer. He unnecessarily swerved, but the distraction was all Kwon needed.

He rose and began firing his weapon at their pursuers. His magazine emptied and he efficiently dropped it to the floor of the ambulance and retrieved another from his cargo pocket. The Security Police vehicle sped forward, closing the gap. The passenger began firing at the ambulance.

After pulling the rear charging handle, Kwon returned fire.

"Bull's-eye!" he exclaimed.

The bullets pierced the windshield, striking the driver in the head and killing him instantly. The passenger's efforts to gain control of the car were in vain as the nose swerved to the right and T-boned the block retaining wall, throwing both men through the windshield.

The second car continued its pursuit. They fired upon the ambulance, riddling the rear doors with bullets, but none of them pierced the steel outer panel and frame.

Kwon returned fire, the hollow-point bullets tearing through the grille of the sedan and penetrating the radiator. The vehicle suddenly seized, causing the men to be thrown forward in their seats. With the vehicle disabled, Kwon conserved his ammo and turned his attention forward.

"Hold on!" shouted Yeshi.

The young man never slowed as he drove from the paved surface onto the rocky perimeter and crashed into the chain-link fence. The galvanized fencing ripped apart and tore at the sides of the ambulance. The steel top rail of the fence row shattered the windshield and then broke the plastic housing of the bar-mounted emergency lights on the roof.

Yeshi slammed on the brakes to avoid crashing into a metal storage building directly on the other side of the fence. Harper and Kwon were thrown backwards when he hit the fence and then forwards as he brought the vehicle to a sliding stop just within feet of the building.

Kwon found his footing first. He glanced at Harper, whose head was bleeding, but he kept his attention on possible pursuers.

"Keep going! Hurry!" He patted Yeshi on the back again and the young man responded with determination.

He pressed down hard on the gas pedal and the ambulance spun in the grass before lurching forward. He navigated through a few random boulders and then drove directly for the parking lot of the building.

Kwon turned his attention to Harper. "You all right?" He knelt down by her side. Her hand was pressed to her forehead, blood dripping between her fingers.

"Just peachy," she replied with a smile.

Yeshi turned onto the road leading back to the main highway, fishtailing on the wet pavement. The light snow continued to fall, but it wasn't sticking at the lower elevation. His maneuver threw Harper and Kwon back and forth, bouncing them against the cabinets affixed to the back of the ambulance. They regained their balance after Yeshi steadied the vehicle.

"Let me see." Kwon slowly removed her hand and examined the cut. It wasn't deep. "It appears worse than it is. There's plenty of supplies in here to bandage you up."

Harper nodded. "I'm sure I can—"

The sound of gunfire blocked out the rest of her sentence.

Bullets sailed through the rear windows and embedded in the ceiling of the ambulance. They were close.

"Where did they come from?" Kwon yelled his question.

Yeshi's voice revealed his excitement. "Out of the side street. I see another one up ahead."

Kwon reached for a handful of gauze that had fallen out of a cabinet onto the floor. He shoved it into Harper's hand. "Here, keep pressure on it."

He stood and fired off a couple of rounds through the window before ducking back down.

"There are more ahead of us!" shouted Yeshi.

"Dammit!" exclaimed Kwon. "We can't outrun their radios."

"I can help," said Harper as she pulled bloody strands of hair away from her face. That, combined with the streaks of blood pouring out of the wound, made Harper resemble Sissy Spacek on the vintage *Carrie* movie poster.

More bullets ricocheted off the back of the ambulance.

Yeshi's voice was panicked. "Kwon! They are coming toward us!"

Kwon took the gauze from Harper and carefully wiped some of the blood off her face so her vision wasn't impaired. He spoke to her in a soft, calm voice. "Okay, stay crouched down below the windows. Shoot at them Iraqi style."

Harper smiled. She understood.

She slid on her knees to the back of the ambulance, disregarding the small pieces of safety glass from the windows. She sat up as tall as she could on her knees and fired a three-round burst through the window. The sound of screeching brakes and the bullets bouncing off the hood told her she'd found her mark.

Kwon settled in the passenger seat next to Yeshi. He rolled down the window and readied his weapon. Then he assessed the situation.

"Do not stop. I will move them out of the way."

"You are the boss." Yeshi gripped the steering wheel until his knuckles were white. He leaned forward and furrowed his brow as if he was prepared to drive into them head-on.

As the two security vehicles approached from the front, Harper kept their pursuers at bay. Her periodic spurts of gunfire caused them to back off, allowing Kwon to focus on the vehicles that blocked their escape.

He fired.

The first four rounds ripped into the left side tires of the lead vehicle. They exploded instantly, causing the car to lurch toward the left and then flip. It rolled over and over in front of the ambulance and barely missed their right front fender.

The trailing security vehicle slowed, making it an easier target for Kwon. He fired again, this time aiming for the windshield. The bullets shredded the glass. Both front seat passengers instinctively raised their arms to avoid the flying shards of glass, but their flesh was no match for Kwon's bullets. Their bodies exploded in crimson before the vehicle careened off the shoulder head-on into a lamp post.

Harper fired again, reminding Kwon there was still work to be done. He pushed his way through the seats and charged toward the rear of the ambulance. Harper was about to rise on her knees again to fire when Kwon shouted, "I've got this!"

He stood defiantly at the windows and took aim. Like the last vehicle, he obliterated the windshield and the two men behind it.

But was it over?

CHAPTER FORTY-NINE

Lhasa, Tibet, China

Yeshi sped up to the intersection and the highway that would return them to Dr. Basnet's home. He began to make the right-hand turn when Kwon grabbed his right arm to stop him.

"Not that way," he said unemotionally. "We can't go back."

"What about your friends?" asked Yeshi.

Harper approached the front of the ambulance. She was dabbing the gash on her forehead to stem the bleeding. "Kwon, we can't just leave them. We have to warn them or get them out of there."

"No, Harper, we can't." He pointed to the left. "Go that way."

"They'll have no idea what's about to happen," she pleaded with Kwon.

"Go, Yeshi!" he ordered. His voice was stern as he ignored Harper's request. He turned his body to her as Yeshi pulled out onto the highway. More sirens could be heard off in the distance.

"Kwon!"

He furrowed his brow as he spoke. "You are my only priority. For all we know, Dr. Basnet broke under pressure and they've sent the Security Police to his home already. Plus, our work isn't done yet, and what we have ahead of us doesn't involve them. You know that."

Harper sat back onto the metal gurney and continued to dab at her forehead. The scowl that came across her face caused the wound to seep again. She was not happy. "Dr. Zeng and Fangyu got us this far. It's not fair that we've left them to the wolves."

Kwon continued to be emotionless. "It isn't fair. I can't disagree. But what we have ahead of us is bigger than Dr. Zeng and his nephew. They knew the risks and they've done their part. With a little luck, they heard the melee caused by the sirens and the gunfire. Hopefully, they took our car and left. There was a reason I left them the keys."

"You did?" she asked.

"Yes." He sighed and looked at the bits of glass that had fallen from their broken windshield. A gap was allowing the snow to slip through into the front seat. "Harper, I had to plan for all contingencies. If we didn't make it out, they needed to be able to escape."

Harper shook her head as Yeshi continued to drive west toward the Himalayan Mountains. "They would never have left us."

"You're probably right, but that is beside the point. We would never have taken them with us now, either. The thing is, we both know what needs to be done. I'm not sure how we'll do it, but we need to get clear of the brawl we left behind. We have to trust in Dr. Basnet to protect all of us, and Fangyu to protect his uncle."

Harper looked to Yeshi. "Do you know how to message them on WeChat?"

"Yes."

"Pull over! Do it now!"

"Harper," Kwon began to protest.

"Swap drivers, please."

Kwon relented and Yeshi slid off to the side of the road. In less than a minute, Kwon was driving away and Yeshi was composing an urgent message to Dr. Zeng to get out of the Basnet home.

"Thank you," said Harper sincerely. "So I assume we're going to Everest."

Kwon checked his mirrors to determine if they were being followed. The road was clear. "Yes, but we need another vehicle. Yeshi, will you help us?"

"Of course. Do you think I would miss out on this excitement?"

Kwon looked around at the deserted countryside. He presumed to know the answers to his questions, but he asked anyway. "What about another vehicle? Is it possible to rent one?"

"No rentals, but I do have friends here. They are also sherpas."

Kwon continued. "Can you and your friends help us get to Mount Everest?"

"I can ask. They are thrill-seekers like me. Our lives have no action. Not like yours, anyway."

Harper rolled her eyes and then glanced through the broken windows of the back door. "This was a lot of action. No doubt about it. We can arrange for payment."

"That is not necessary," he said. "I promise, we will enjoy this despite its danger. Please understand. Bodies that fall over the edge are usually left there for a reason. It is very dangerous to retrieve them."

Harper didn't want to risk any more lives. She wasn't sure she needed the entire body. If she could simply retrieve more tissue samples, she'd be able to connect the cases together. It was a morbid form of contact tracing but was required to locate patient zero.

She sighed. "We can make do with samples of blood and tissue, but we'll need to find some means to extract the samples while also preserving the specimens."

Kwon pointed toward the red biohazard bag. "I thought about this while we were in the autopsy room with Dr. Basnet. I placed half a dozen sterile vials and two scalpels in the pack. It's not ideal, but if we can obtain a long hunting knife, I think we can harvest a portion of the organs."

"The lungs and heart are most important, but they'll be protected by the thoracic cage," said Harper.

Kwon grimaced. "Will the kidneys or even a section of the carotid artery help?"

"I'll take what I can get," she replied. "The way this disease attaches to the body, most of the abdominal organs will be compromised. The carotid will help with blood analysis."

"Slow down up here and turn left at the stacked stone columns. He lives in a hut with several others. They are what you Americans might call *free birds*."

Harper chuckled at the reference to the 1970s hippies who grew up without a care in the world but with an abundant supply of marijuana at their disposal. She wondered if that was what Yeshi was referring to.

Kwon drove up the hill until the gravel road made a series of winding turns. The snow was accumulating now, and the tires of the ambulance began to spin. At the top, several Tibetan retreat huts were lined up overlooking a vast valley. The retreat huts, often used by the locals to separate themselves from the secular world, had no electricity or running water. They were made out of stacked stone using mud as mortar. The roofs were similar to a cedar shake system but couldn't possibly prevent leaks as several gaps were readily apparent. Each of the structures had a stone chimney with smoke wafting into the sky.

Kwon parked the ambulance and the three occupants exited simultaneously. Harper was the first to notice the pungent smell of marijuana.

"Whoa! And to think a *Rocky Mountain High* used to be the ultimate state of mind of hippies. They've got nothing on these guys." She pulled her shirt up over her nose.

Kwon shook his head in dismay. "Yeshi, I am not sure I can count on these guys with what we have in mind."

"Yes, you can. They are the best. Please trust me on this."

Two completely bald young men exited the first hut and waved. They wore a smock-style outfit with no shoes. They slowly approached Yeshi, undeterred by the rock soil beneath the thin layer of snow.

"Tashi delek, Yeshi-la!" One of the men used the traditional Tibetan greeting to friends. It was meant to convey wishes of blessing, good health, and luck. It was common to add *-la* after a friend's name to show respect.

"Tashi delek, Kunga-la!" Yeshi shouted back.

He then proceeded to explain his new friends' presence in his native tongue. After several minutes in which Harper and Kwon stood there listening to the back-and-forth conversation, Yeshi turned to them and interpreted, "They will help, but they do not want money."

"Great," said Harper.

"There is a concern," continued Yeshi. "They will not be allowed to ascend to the summit through the north face base camp. The route is still closed because of the accident."

"Can we get there another way?" asked Kwon.

"Yes, by snowmobile and rock climbing. It is dangerous but possible."

Harper looked at Kwon before asking, "Where do we get snowmobiles?"

"There is a military outpost at Gangga in Tingri County."

Kwon shook his head. "Do you think they will give us snowmobiles?"

"No. You must take them."

Kwon had no choice but to go along with the plan. "How long will it take us to get there?"

"Two days, normally. Twenty-four hours in my friends' cars. Let me show you."

Yeshi led them past the first two huts and down a slight incline toward a lean-to barn. When they crested the hill, Kwon stopped in his tracks.

"Really? This is what they drive?"

Inside the barn were five different colored street racers. All the popular motor brands were represented, including Mazda, Toyota, Mitsubishi, Subaru, and Honda.

"They purchase the cars and parts with the money they make as sherpas. They race along the highway from Lhasa to the Tibetan Plateau in the west. This is their life."

"As free birds," quipped Harper.

"And we can trust them?" asked Kwon.

"With your lives."

The conclusion to the Virus Hunters Trilogy.

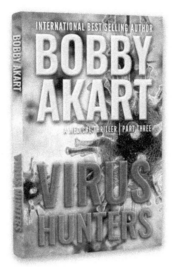

As Harper closes in on finding the origin of the deadly
Las Vegas virus, she learns the hunt
may be more challenging than the virus itself.

AVAILABLE ON AMAZON

NOW AVAILABLE ON AMAZON: *VIRUS HUNTERS PART 3*, the
final installment in the Virus Hunters trilogy. You can purchase it
by following this link to Amazon: *VIRUS HUNTERS PART 3*

A NOTE FROM THE AUTHOR

First, let me take a moment to thank you for reading my first novel featuring Dr. Harper Randolph and the Virus Hunters! These characters and their story have been planned for three years since the success of my Pandemic series published in May 2017. During the course of my research, I became thoroughly convinced that our world was wholly unprepared for a global pandemic. Here's why.

In the mid-twentieth century, a new weapon, the atomic bomb, shocked the world with its ability to destroy the enemy.

For centuries, another weapon has existed…

One that attacks without conscience or remorse…

Its only job is to kill.

They are the most merciless enemy we've ever faced…

And they're one-billionth our size.

Be prepared to become very, very paranoid.

WELCOME TO THE NEXT GLOBAL WAR.

Over the past half century, the number of new diseases per decade has increased fourfold. Since 1980, the outbreaks have more than tripled. With those statistics in mind, one had to consider the consequences of a major pandemic and now we're living the nightmare.

Death has come to millions of humans throughout the millennia from the spread of infectious diseases, but none was worse than the Black Death, a pandemic so devastating that uttering the words the plague will immediately pull it to the front of your mind. From 1347 to 1351, the Black Death reshaped Europe and much of the world.

In a time when the global population was an estimated four hundred fifty million, some estimates of the death toll reached as high as two hundred million, nearly half of the world's human beings.

This plague's name came from the black skin spots on the sailors who travelled the Silk Road, the ancient network of trade routes that traversed the Asian continent, connecting East and West. The Black Death was in fact a form of the bubonic plague, not nearly as contagious and deadly as its sister, the pneumonic plague.

Fast-forward five centuries to 1918, an especially dangerous form of influenza began to appear around the world. First discovered in Kansas in March 1918, by the time the H1N1 pandemic, commonly known as the Spanish flu, burned out in 1919, it took the lives of as many as fifty million people worldwide.

A hundred years later, in 2020, the COVID-19 pandemic swept the planet destroying lives and the global economy. As of this writing, the death toll is still climbing as a treatment protocol hasn't been established; there is no vaccine, and testing is in short supply.

Why does the history of these deadly pandemics matter?

Because it has happened before and it will happen again and again—despite the world's advanced technology, or because of it. People no longer stay in one place; neither do diseases. Unlike the habits of humans during the Black Death and the Spanish flu, an infection in all but the most remote corner of the world can make its way to a major city in a few days. COVID-19 has proven that.

Terrible new outbreaks of infectious disease make headlines, but not at the start. Every pandemic begins small. Early indicators can be subtle and ambiguous. When the next global pandemic begins, it will spread across oceans and continents like the sweep of nightfall, causing illness and fear, killing thousands or maybe millions of people. The next pandemic will be signaled first by quiet, puzzling reports from faraway places—reports to which disease scientists and public health officials, but few of the rest of us, pay close attention.

The purpose of the Virus Hunters series is not to scare the wits out of you, but rather, to scare the wits into you. As one reader said to me after reading the Pandemic series in 2017, "I now realize that humans can become extinct." Not a comforting thought.

This series is also designed to give you hope. You see, the stories depicted in the Virus Hunters novels are fictional. The events, however, are based upon historical fact. Know this, there are those on the front line of this global war. The burden lies on the CDC and their counterparts around the world who work tirelessly to protect us. This series is dedicated to the Virus Hunters—the disease detectives and shoe-leather epidemiologists of the CDC's Epidemic Intelligence Service who work tirelessly to keep these deadly infectious diseases from killing us all.

If you enjoyed this Virus Hunters novel, I'd be grateful if you'd take a moment to write a short review (just a few words are needed) and post it on Amazon. Amazon uses complicated algorithms to determine what books are recommended to readers. Sales are, of course, a factor, but so are the quantities of reviews my books get. By taking a few seconds to leave a review, you help me out and also help new readers learn about my work.

And before you go ...

SIGN UP for my mailing list at BobbyAkart.com to receive a copy of my monthly newsletter, *The Epigraph*. You'll also learn about special offers, bonus content, and you'll be the first to receive news about new releases in the Virus Hunters series.

VISIT my feature page at Amazon.com/BobbyAkart for more information on the Virus Hunters or any of my other bestselling survival thrillers listed below which includes over forty Amazon #1 Bestsellers in forty-plus fiction and nonfiction genres.

Lastly, for many years, I have lived by the following premise:

Because you never know when the day before is the day before, prepare for tomorrow.

My friends, I study and write about the threats we face, not only to both entertain and inform you, but because I am constantly learning how to prepare for the benefit of my family as well. There is nothing more important on this planet than my darling wife Dani and our two princesses, Bullie and Boom. I've always said, one day the apocalypse will be upon us. Well, sometimes I hate it when I'm right.

Thank you for supporting my work and I hope you enjoy the next installment in the Virus Hunters series.